God's Email Address

Tim Koop

Copyright © 2019 Tim Koop

All rights reserved.

PRAISE FOR TIM KOOP'S WRITING

"Interesting"
      - almost everyone

"Good writing. Good action and suspense."
      - Cynthia A. Robison

"Well paced... the technical aspects were accurate... the story was interesting... I want to read the next one."
      - Thomas Sewell, editor

"It was very interesting and held my attention. You did a nice job of developing the characters and making them believable. The plot developed quite well also."
      - Jenn Haslam

"It's great!"
      - 17 year old young man, after staying up till 4:30am to finish the book

"I just finished reading this book and I love it! First, it is a great story that kept me involved from beginning to end. The contemporary themes were totally relatable. The story arch is very well done and the characters were well-developed and recognizable."
      - Patti Virkler

"This could be the best book I've ever read in my life."
      - Tim Koop

This book is dedicated to Dr. Mark Virkler, who had the audacity, nerve, and chutzpah to say that if you followed his four steps, he would guarantee the result. I took him up on his guarantee, and sure enough, it worked.

PROLOGUE

At 9:07 PM on a Wednesday evening, an unfeeling, unemotional security camera captured video of two men meeting in a dimly-lit, multistorey parking garage.

Looking down from the ceiling of the first floor, it saw mostly empty spots, but there was one carbon black BMW 7 Series still waiting for its driver.

One of the men, the one on the left, was already into his sixties and wearing an Armani suit. He approached the driver's door of this vehicle.

When he did, the camera clearly picked up the other man on the right. He entered the scene from where he had been standing in the shadows for some time. He was not yet fifty, but also wore a dark suit. His tie, however, was bright green.

If this security camera was listening, which it was not, it would have heard the man on the right say, "Mr. Thompson."

Thompson, on the left, turned toward him. "You are?" he asked.

"I am someone who can help you."

Thompson paused, while looking at the man, then said, "I don't do deals after hours. Make an appointment." He opened the car door with the soft click of BMW luxury.

"Trust me, sir. You and your company will be very interested in what I have." The man smiled like only a salesman could.

"And why should I listen to you, since it's probably illegal?" He glanced up briefly at the security camera, which continued to stare down, emotionless, at the two men talking.

"Oh, the legality of it is a matter for the lawyers. We are men of business. We buy and sell. You buy what you need to, to give your company a competitive edge, and I have something to sell that will give you exactly that."

Thompson crossed his arms. "And what exactly do you want to sell me?"

"Imagine you are planning your budget, and you need to know how much to put into advertising or research. If you knew what your competitors were up to, you would know how to respond appropriately. You don't want to get caught unaware when they launch a large ad campaign. You don't want to be left behind when they come up with better technology, do you?"

"What are you saying?" Thompson asked.

"I'm saying it would be worth a lot of money to know what your competition is up to, wouldn't it?"

Thompson paused, as if to consider the idea, then snorted. "That's not information you would have."

"What if I did?"

"I don't believe you." Thompson placed one foot into his car.

The man in the green tie took a step closer. "Sir, this is a great opportunity for you. Don't walk away from the greatest thing that has ever happened to you."

Thompson rested his arms on the car door and roof. "OK, if you have insider information, tell me something I don't know."

"It will cost you," the man said.

"No. I get the first one for free. The deal is you tell me something I don't know, or I walk away." Thompson held up the car key in his hand.

The man's smile faded, but then he recovered. "Of course. I'll prove that my information is accurate. But when I do, you have to agree to purchase the rest of it."

"No promises."

"At least consider it."

"Fine, sure, I'll consider becoming a loyal customer."

"OK, this is your freebie. Glad Mobile is going to begin a large advertising campaign with the slogan 'We're everything you need'."

Thompson sneered. "That's all? That's nothing."

"It might be nothing, but what if you preempted them and ran some ads saying 'Adams is all you need'? That way every time their customers hear 'We're everything you need', they will think Adams, not Glad. An investment for you, and a large return. Just think of the jump on your competition I just gave you. It's worth millions. And there is more where that came from."

"They probably trademarked the slogan."

"They didn't. At least not yet. I checked. I'm here to help you, Mr. Thompson. I can give you a lot more information like this, for the right price of course."

Thompson looked up at the security camera again, then said to the man. "All right. If Glad really does launch this campaign like you say, you have a deal. How can I contact you?"

The man on the right smiled approvingly. "I'll be in touch, sir," he said and turned and walked away.

Thompson watched him leave, then got in his car and drove off.

The building was left empty except for the security camera that recorded the whole scene in full colour, including the bright green tie. The video was compressed and saved it to a hard drive on the computer that controlled the security of the building. Twenty-four hours later, since nobody requested the video, it was unemotionally deleted to make room for the next day's recording.

CHAPTER 1

Tuesday, 8:05 AM

I got God's email address and the call from the hacker on the same day.

I was late for work that morning, so when I jerked my car to a halt in the parking lot and threw it into park, I jumped out and ran.

I darted through the crowded parking lot, toward the payment machine, and fed it my credit card. My fingers smacked the buttons like they had every morning for a few years. It rewarded me with a ticket.

I rushed back to my car and slapped the ticket on the dash. I grabbed my bag and glanced at the car's clock. I frowned.

Three minutes later I scrambled up the stairs in front of our building, the Johnston Terminal, breathing hard. I took the stairs up instead of the elevator, just to save time.

As I pushed the large glass doors open into our company's lobby, I couldn't help noticing that the regular receptionist wasn't there. Another woman sat at the desk. She held the phone against her ear, and looked worried.

Noticing me, she blurted out, "Do you work here?"

"Yes", I replied, trying to avoid a conversation, not just because I was late, but because I didn't enjoy talking with people all that much.

"Could you take a phone call?"

I took evasive action. "I have a meeting," I said.

"Yeah, I know. Everybody's in the meeting."

"Can't you take a message?" I inched my way slowly toward the hall, where I would be safely away from this conflict.

"I don't think so. It sounds important."

I didn't answer, but kept working my way toward the hall.

"What's your extension number?" the receptionist asked.

"125", I replied before I could think of a way out of it. I scowled to myself because of how quickly I lost that battle.

The woman went back to the phone, so I escaped toward my desk. I dropped my bag and glanced at the clock. I was late for the staff meeting, and I had no excuse. Then my black desk phone rang, and suddenly I found my excuse.

I took a deep breath and picked it up. "Hello. This is Jeff."

"Who are you?" came the voice. It was deep and angry.

"This is Jeff Davis. I'm a developer here at Omniscient Technologies."

"Are you responsible for Omniscient?"

"Well, I work on it, as do lots of other people." I didn't know where this was going, but I didn't like it.

"It has a bug in it, and with this bug I can hack into anyone's account I want to, and steal all their information."

Wow. That was bad, and I had no idea how to handle it. "If... if you want to report a bug, I can direct you to our bug tracking website..."

"Ha!", the caller scoffed. "I'm not going to just give this away for free! You'll have to pay for this one."

What?! Payment too? If I was lost before, I don't even have a map now. "I'm... not... sure... if we do that. Generally people just report bugs."

"Maybe the losers do, but I'm not a loser. You will pay me ten thousand dollars in Bitcoin, or I'm going to start hacking into Omniscient accounts. That won't be very good for your business, will it?"

"No." I didn't know what else there was to say.

"As far as your business goes, ten thousand dollars isn't much to stay safe, is it?"

"Well... ah... I guess not." If this guy was trying to steamroll me, it was working.

"Then send me the money, and I'll tell you the hack."

"Well, I'm not the guy to talk to about that. I'm just a developer."

"Then put your boss on the phone!" the caller screamed.

"He's in a meeting. I should be there too."

The caller cursed. "Listen! I'm going to tell you how to send the payment to me. Once I receive it, I will tell you the hack. You got it?"

"Yes."

I grabbed a pen and paper and started writing. The caller gave some website address that ended with ".onion".

"Tell your boss to send the money, ten thousand dollars in Bitcoin, or I will start hacking accounts. Maybe I'll start with yours."

Like a deer in the headlights, I didn't know what else to say, so I just said, "OK."

He disconnected.

I checked the time, and pondered what in the world to do now. On top of this hacker's phone call, there was a meeting in progress I should be in, and the only thing worse than talking on the phone is walking into a meeting late. Maybe I could pretend I was on this phone call the whole time. No. Maybe I needed to go to the bathroom. No. Maybe... No. There was only one thing to do. I would have to walk into the middle of the meeting.

8:12 AM

I advanced to the board room and stopped outside the closed door, my heart pounding. If I opened the door now, my boss Randal might stop and look at me. And everyone else would too. Even the big boss might be there. I tried not to think about that. There isn't much worse than a room full of people staring at you for arriving late.

I put my hand on the door handle and took a deep breath. I was no longer a child. I was a grown man, and I needed to act like it. But before I dove inside, I planned out where I would walk and sit down. There will probably be a free chair on the far side of the room. I would walk around the back with my head down, and slide into a chair and try not to move. Maybe people won't notice me.

I made my move.

Swinging the door open, I walked in. I chose a pace that was fast enough to make it look like I was running late, but not so fast to draw attention to myself. I glanced up and saw an open chair on the far side, just like I anticipated. Randal, my boss, was standing at the front of the room talking.

"Thanks for joining us, Jeff," he said mostly pleasantly.

I acknowledged the greeting with a small smile on my way to my chair. This was not a time for public speaking. Soon I would be at my seat and could peacefully observe the rest of the meeting.

But Randal wasn't done talking to me. "I trust everything is well?"

I sat down and felt a little better. "I'm fine," I said, but then remembered the phone call. That was not fine, and now I would have to mention it.

Randal continued. "Good to hear. Now I want to show you all something that we have just received."

Oh great! Now I have to interrupt my boss while he is

speaking in front of everybody. I might not be able to do that, but I'll try. As he continued talking, I looked for my opportunity, if there would be one.

Randal stood at the head of the large mahogany conference table and held up a normal-looking box. "It's a hologram," he continued. "The manufacturer, Classic Holograms, has sent it to us to see if we can integrate it into Omniscient."

My fellow geeks oohed and aahed, and someone said, "Can we see it working?".

"We only have the one, so we can't make calls to each other. But someone should look into it. Doug, will you?"

Doug, a middle aged man who always wore a shirt and tie, replied. "Yeah, I'll look into it." He didn't sound very excited, but Doug never did.

"Thanks Doug. In other news, how did the Adams upgrade go, Garth?"

Garth wore a Star Wars t-shirt that covered most of his stomach. I hope he wore something else when he visited Adams Corporation the other day to upgrade their Omniscient software.

"As good as can be expected. There were no large, glaring errors. And everything had the appearance of normality when the install was complete. They are now happily running Omniscient 4.0"

"Did you activate the god role?", Scott asked. Scott is my friend and fellow developer. At 38 he was only ten years older than me.

Garth said, "Yes. It is enabled by default, which is against my better judgment, but that decision has already been made."

"Did you ask them if they wanted it enabled?" Scott asked.
"I mentioned it to them, yes."
"And?"
"They don't question us. They take what they are given,

like so much sheep." Garth was not known for his diplomacy.

"I think we should at least discuss the feature with them," said Scott.

"When you, Scott Stark, install major software at a multi-billion dollar company, you can take as much of their very valuable time as you wish. As for me, I do what I'm there to do, and leave."

Randal took control again. "We've already discussed the god role a lot and decided to roll it out. It is in 4.0, and we can't take it out now."

"But we can disable it by default," said Scott.

Randal sighed.

I made my move. Mustering all the courage I could, I raised my hand. Randal took the bait. "Yes, Jeff?"

I cleared my throat. "Right before I came in, I got a phone call from someone who said there was a bug in Omniscient and said he wanted ten thousand dollars in Bitcoin or he would start hacking our accounts."

There was silence in the room for a moment, then the questions came.

"Did he say who he was?"

"No."

"Did he say how we can contact him?"

"He left a website on the dark web, but only how to pay him."

"Have you visited the site?"

"No."

"Do you believe him?"

"I don't know."

"Why did you take the call?"

"I was the only one not in this meeting."

Randal said, "OK, let's think about this clearly. Are there any bugs in the bug list that could let someone hack into an account?"

"No," said Scott.

"If we would have known about such a bug," said Garth, "we would never have released 4.0."

"Of course you're right, Garth," said Randal. "But maybe there is a bug we don't know about."

"There might be, but by definition, we don't know about it," Garth replied.

"OK, Jeff, you can be the point man for this hacker guy. If he calls back, you can talk to him."

"What would I say?" I asked.

Randal thought for a moment, then said, "I don't know. Try to get him to file a bug, I guess."

"I don't think he would. He didn't seem very friendly."

"Well, there's nothing else we can do, is there?" Randal said.

Doug spoke up. "Why don't we just pay him?"

"Ten thousand dollars?" Randal asked. "For an unsubstantiated bug? I don't think so."

Now Ronja commented. She was the system administrator. "I'd rather see ten thousand dollars go into our own server. With 4.1, we'll need extra hard drive space with all the video we'll be storing."

"Let's talk about 4.1 then," said Randal. "Ronja is going to upgrade our own system this evening to 4.1, which is still in beta. We will be beta testing it ourselves."

Ronja continued. "As we know, it supports video storage on the server, so we will need all the storage we can find."

"We could disable video storage until we get more room," said Scott.

"In order to properly beta test, we will need to test all the features," said Garth.

"We have enough hard drive space for now," said Randal. "If all goes well, we'll be using 4.1 beta tomorrow morning."

"OK, that's all for now." Randal looked at the time. "Have a good day. Oh, one more thing. We have a new customer service rep starting this morning. Veronica Stansin. Jeff, will you please show her around the office?"

Me? Talk to a girl?

8:46 AM

"Jeff, this is Veronica Stansin, the new customer service rep," said Randal. "Veronica, this is Jeff Davis. He's a developer. Jeff, please show her around." And with that Randal walked away, and I was left standing in Veronica's cubicle with her. It was a corner cubicle, down the hall from the corner room where I worked. Her walls were still free of decorations, presumably because this was her first day.

Veronica smiled and held out her hand. "Hi Jeff." She had straight black hair, and was about as tall as I was.

I shook her hand. "Hi".

"So, tell me about this place. We make software, right? I know that much, but I should know more, so start talking. What does Omniscient do?"

"Well, it's a full package communications software. It handles email, chat, voice, and also video, as of version 4.1."

"That sounds complicated. You can explain it to me while we get a coffee. This place does have coffee, doesn't it?"

"Yes," I said, as we left her cubicle.

"You'll have to show me where it is, because all these halls look the same. Blah. They need artwork or something."

I had never noticed any lack of artwork. I guess I'm not a visual person. "Well, we could call this hall the West hall." I pointed to the far wall. And that could be the South hall."

"Are you serious?" she asked.

"Well nobody actually uses those names, but everything

needs a good name, just like variables."

"What?"

"In programming, you need to give your variables meaningful variable names. It's important. I was just suggesting we could name our halls."

"Is that what you do here? Name variables?", she asked.

"No. Well, of course sometimes. But I specialize in email, mostly. You know, POP and SMTP and the web interface."

We turned the corner into the South hall and met Veronica's boss.

"Hi Kaleisha," Veronica said. "Jeff here was just showing me around."

The head of Customer Service looked me up and down but spoke to Veronica. "Honey, there's one thing I need to tell you about this place. Those computer geeks on that side of the building love to spew their knowledge of computers. POP this and SMTP that."

"Oh, I don't think that will be a problem," Veronica looked at me.

Kaleisha continued unhindered. "Some of it you should probably know, but all the rest... this is what I do when they spout their technobabble. I just put my head down like this and kind of stare at them over my glasses. Then I just say, Mmmm hmm. Just like that. It lets them know I can't be intimidated."

"I think I can handle it, thanks." Veronica smiled.

The thought of me intimidating anyone else was laughable. If that's what she would do to me, then what was I supposed to do when I felt intimidated by the head of Customer Service?

"Good girl," Kaleisha said then walked away.

We continued to amble toward the kitchen and Veronica asked more questions. "How much does the software cost?"

"It's open source."

"What does that mean? It's free?"

"It means it's free as in speech, not free as in beer."

She laughed. "Ha! Beer. What does that have to do with software?"

"I guess I could explain it…" But then Scott interrupted us.

8:51 AM

"Hi, I'm Scott," he said and stuck out his hand.

She took it. "Hi Scott. I'm Veronica."

"I see you've met Jeff here," he said.

"Yes, he was showing me around."

"Has he shown you where the coffee is? That's the most important part." Scott was very friendly, especially with the ladies.

"He was about to."

"Come on," Scott said. At the end of the South hall we found the kitchen, complete with the usual cupboards, fridge, table, and chairs. There was even a sofa at one end. "This is the coffee. These are cups," Scott said. He grabbed a cup and poured coffee for Veronica.

"Thanks, Scott," she said, accepting the mug. She took a sip and he poured one for himself as well.

They looked good together, even though they looked so different. Scott had short blond hair somewhat curly, and Veronica had long black hair, poker straight. They sat down at the table and I joined them. I had to pour my own coffee, but I didn't mind.

"So how do you, I mean we make money if we give away our stuff for free?" Veronica asked.

Scott explained. "We give away the software to make it popular, then we charge money for things like installation and custom features."

"Garth just did an upgrade at Adams Corporation a few

days ago," I interjected. "We probably got a good chunk of money for that."

"And what does that have to do with beer?" she asked.

I said, "With free beer, you get something for zero dollars and nothing else. With open source software, you get actual freedom."

"What kind of freedom?"

Scott said, "You get the source code the software was made from, and you get the freedom to modify it and redistribute it."

"Really? Wow. So we don't just give our product away for free, we also give away the source code, and let people do whatever they want with it?"

I said, "Mostly, yes."

"And things like support are enough to keep us going?"

"Actually, no," said Scott. "We're not profitable yet. We have investors who keep us going and growing. But hopefully soon we'll be profitable and won't need more investor money."

"And then it will be smooth sailing?"

Scott said, "Ha! If we can get there. And even then it's not easy. Just this morning Jeff got a call from a blackmailer threatening to hack our system, says he knows how."

"Really?" Veronica looked at me. "Can't you stop him?"

I said, "He says he knows a bug that will let him hack in, but we don't know of such a bug."

Scott said, "And Randal said Jeff should be the point man for this hacker. How do you feel about that, Jeff?"

How did I feel? I hated the thought of me trying to fix this problem. I felt completely incapable and overwhelmed just thinking about it. Who was I? I couldn't accomplish something this big. I was just a little programmer working in his little corner of a big world. But on the other hand, I wanted to see this guy come to justice. Wouldn't anybody? I was caught in the middle. To answer Scott, I shrugged.

"I think you can do it. You'll do a great job," said Scott.

"Thanks."

"Has Jeff shown you where we work?" Scott asked Veronica.

"No, but I would love to see it. Let me guess. It's just down the East hall?"

Scott said, "What?", and looked at me and Veronica as if we knew something he didn't.

Veronica laughed. "Never mind!"

We got up and strolled down the East hall to where some of us had our desks. There was a room in one corner of the building with multiple desks in it. Windows on both walls showed a view of downtown and the river. This is where I worked, with Scott, Garth, and Doug. We were the main developers.

The other two, Garth and Doug, were already there. Scott and I sat down on our swivel chairs, and I swivelled around in mine to see Veronica looking around the room. There wasn't much to look at. The walls were an empty expanse, except for a few Dilbert comics on the walls. Doug kept his spot tidy, but Garth's desk was littered with coffee mugs and Dr. Peppers.

Then Veronica took a step toward Garth's little white board hanging on the wall. "What's this?" she asked. It had "Joke of the Day" written on it.

Garth turned around from his computer to answer. "This is the Joke of the Day. It is a place where I post witticisms of the programming nature."

She read it out loud. "Why do computer programmers keep getting Halloween and Christmas confused? Because oct 31 = dec 25." She looked around at our smiling faces. "I don't get it."

Garth answered. "You are correct. You don't get it. That's because you are not a programmer. I keep this Joke of the Day here as a reminder to everyone that it is we who are the programmers. It is we who create things like gods. And it is you who are not. This small whiteboard of mine separates the gods from the mere mortals."

I looked at Garth, then back to Veronica. She wasn't smiling. She wasn't saying anything. She just glared at Garth, and Garth happily returned the glare.

She pointed a finger at his face. "You're a jerk."

Garth placed his hands over his heart in mock sorrow. "Oh, did I hurt the poor mortal's feelings? Listen, poor mortal, if you can't take this corner of the building, there are many other places where customer service reps can feel more comfortable. Perhaps you should seek them out."

Veronica turned and stormed off, and we four were left to ourselves.

"I think she likes you," Scott said to Garth.

"Pshaw!", Garth replied.

"More importantly, I think Garth likes her," Doug said without turning his chair.

"Oh, please!", Garth was aghast. "Please do not put me in bondage to any relationship with a girl, and a mortal at that!"

I chuckled. Yes, Garth was an interesting character. But then again, so was Veronica. She actually stood up to him. She had courage, and that was an admirable quality.

9:06 AM

I had just swung around in my swivel chair, to study my two large screen monitors, when my ears were suddenly and mercilessly assaulted by an abominable shrieking sound.

"That's the fire alarm," said Doug.

"Goodbye, everyone. I shall vacate the premises." And with that Garth grabbed his Dr. Pepper and left.

There was nothing unsaved on my computer so I stood up

to leave with everyone else. Some of us put our fingers in our ears and some of us tried squinting away the screech as we made our way down the halls toward the front door.

When I was right at the big glass door, the lights went out, too. It was still morning, so there was plenty of light in the building, so much that not everyone noticed the lights going out, but I did. I think the power had just gone off. I looked around for anything that still had power. I knew the desktop computers did, because they had UPSes, battery backups, but all the ceiling lights were dark.

I stopped walking and made my way back through the crowd. I paused at a light switch and toggled it on and off again. It did nothing. I continued to walk against the crowd, until the flow of people melted away. I went down the South hall and turned left. There in front of me was the server room.

The nondescript door to the server room was locked of course, with a keypad whose combination I didn't know. I looked around for anyone else. There was nobody else around, so I just stood there, with my fingers in my ears.

Then I saw a large figure coming down the hallway. It was Garth. I took my fingers out of my ears.

"Aren't we supposed to all leave the building?" he said. "It could be on fire and we'll all die a horrible death."

"I just thought that someone should watch the server room."

"And why's that? It's clearly locked."

"Well, the phone call this morning from the hacker."

"What about him?"

"Well, we received a threat to hack us, and now there is an alarm to clear the building. And the power is off... so..."

"So what?"

"So someone could break in easier."

"You watch too many movies, movie boy. The door is clearly locked. There are security cameras, and if somebody did break through this door, they still don't know any passwords to get into anything, do they?"

"I just thought we should be safe."

"It is not your job to keep us safe. You may run along. I will stand guard." He took a step to the side to let me pass.

I stood there sizing him up. It didn't take much. He was taller than I, and certainly heavier. And his words carried a lot of weight. I turned and scurried away down the hallway, around the corner, and out the doors. I took the stairs down to the main floor. The whole building was deserted.

I walked out the big glass doors and saw everyone outside. They stood around, huddled in small groups. And when I looked up, I noticed the sky was cloudy and threatening to rain.

I found Scott and the guys. "The power's off," I said to him.

"Stupid power!" he said. Then he looked up at our floor. "Maybe we should power down the servers." He went to find Randal. I tagged along.

"Jeff says the power went off," he told him. "Maybe we need to power down our servers."

Randal replied, "I think the UPSes tell the servers to automatically do that, but let's find Ronja."

As he looked around for her, I said, "Garth is there guarding the server room."

Randal looked confused. "Why?" he asked.

"Originally I was there, but he came and took my place. I thought the fire alarm and the power going off would make it easy for the hacker to break in." I waited for Randal to snort at my naiveté, but he didn't.

"I don't think anybody at all should be there. There's a fire alarm." He said.

"I don't smell any smoke," I said.

Randal went to talk to Ronja. Scott and I joined him.

"Ronja, Jeff says the power is off. How will the servers

handle it?"

She replied, "Our UPS is intelligent enough to know how many minutes of battery is left, and when it is ten minutes from the end, it tells the server to shut down."

"And how many minutes of battery should we have?"

"I would estimate about thirty."

"Jeff says Garth is guarding the server room."

Ronja looked worried. "He should not be there. There is a fire alarm going."

"But there's no smoke," I said.

Scott said, "I'll go get him," then turned to go.

Randal said, "Scott... I'm coming too."

"Me too," said Ronja.

As Randal advanced toward the door, he stopped, turned around, and addressed the crowd. "We're just going to check on something. Stay here."

9:17 AM

The four of us entered the building through the main doors and marched up the stairs. Apart from the cry of the smokeless fire alarm, everything was empty and silent.

I was glad to be in a group, because I had no desire to run into anyone by myself.

When we reached the third floor, we went through the large glass doors to the offices of Omniscient Technologies. I noticed it wasn't locked. It probably should have been.

Past reception, we turned right into the South hallway, then left into the East hallway. Garth was nowhere to be seen. When we reached the door to the server room, it was locked tight. Randal punched in the code and opened the door. It was dark inside. He turned his phone light on and went in. There was nobody else in there.

Scott said to me, "I don't see Garth anywhere."

"Yeah," I replied, a knot forming in my stomach.

Then he appeared, walking toward us from the kitchen, drinking his Dr. Pepper. "I see you came to join the fun," he said.

"What's been going on, Garth?" Scott asked.

"Nothing at all, Scott Stark. I was trying to scare off the bad guys, and it must have worked, because they didn't dare show their faces."

"Are you all right, Garth?" Ronja asked.

"Perfectly," he replied. "Are our servers all right, system administrator?"

"They are still running. Our internet is still up, so our Omniscient clients should still be connected happily. I will send a test message to be sure." She took out her phone and tapped a message.

Instantly Randal's phone chirped and he looked at it. "I got it just fine."

Ronja continued. "It looks like we're using battery faster than I thought. I will shut down the server in a few minutes, if we don't get power back soon."

"Who will lose connection?" Scott asked. "Our server only serves us, right? This office?"

"Correct," Ronja replied.

Randal explained. "All our other paying customers have accounts hosted on our cloud servers where they have generator power backup and redundant internet connections. It's a much better setup than we have here, but this is good for testing."

"One minute," Ronja said.

Then we heard fire engines approaching.

We stood around, watching Ronja log in to the console, and get ready to issue the command that would shut down the server. She typed in letters H A L T, and got ready to press Enter.

Then the lights blinked back on.

"Oh. Very nice," she said, cheerfully. "We get to keep our server up. For a few more hours anyway. That is, until I do the upgrade this evening."

And then the fire alarm stopped. Wow. That made my ears feel a lot better.

With the power came sounds of beeping and whirring as computers and electronic devices of all sorts powered up. Among the mix of noise came music. It was "I still haven't found what I'm looking for", by U2, which was the email alert on Scott's phone. That was an old song. I wondered how old Scott was when that song came out, if he was even born yet. He pulled it out and started reading.

"Oh-oh. This is not good."

"What?" I asked.

"Adams Corporation just made the news.", Scott addressed us all. "Their email just got hacked."

CHAPTER 2

9:40 AM

"What?!" we all exclaimed as we stood together in the server room.

"That's the title of this article," Scott continued. "Here, I'll send everyone a link."

"What does the article say?" Randal asked. "Does it mention us by name?"

We all looked up when we saw a firefighter dressed in full gear walk up to us. "It was a false alarm. You can get back to work," he said.

"What about the power failure?" asked Randal.

"I don't know. It might be related. We will be in touch with the building owners. You could talk to them for the details. Now if you'll excuse me, we are doing a once over, just to be sure." He left.

I went to my desk, checked my email, and clicked the link that Scott sent. It was an article by a local reporter, Donald Roberts, with a video at the top of the page. I clicked the video to watch it, and it showed a reporter standing in front of a tall, downtown building, holding a microphone.

This was his report.

> Sources who wish to remain anonymous have told CKGD news that the mobile phone mega-company, Adams Corporation, has had a breach in their email handling system. They said they have seen evidence that confidential, internal messages have been leaked

to the public. When this reporter contacted Adams, they refused to comment, but when pressed further, they did not deny that at least one electronic message intended to be kept private is no longer private.

CKGD News has also learned that Adams' email system has recently undergone an upgrade to the system. Was the upgrade the cause of this problem, or was it an attempt to fix it? It's too soon to tell, and Adams is not commenting.

This is rather bad timing for the corporation, considering that their annual shareholders' meeting takes place in only two weeks. We will see if they let the world know what is going on by then. If not, we will see what happens to their share price.

For CKGD News, I'm Donald Roberts.

I sat back, trying to comprehend it all. I rubbed my chin. I rested my head on my hands behind my head. Then, quite unexpectedly, a wave of anger flashed through me and I hit my desk with my clenched fist.

"What?" asked Scott, also at his computer.

"It's just not right to pry into someone else's email. It's stealing. It's burglary. It's like rape is what it is."

"Yup, you're right," he replied. "But what are you going to do about it?"

I fumed to myself. "What can you do about it? Nothing. That's the world we live in. Bad things happen to good people. End of story."

"Maybe the police will do something."

"Well somebody should. It's just not right."

Doug turned around. "Garth, you did the upgrade. Did you hear anything about this when you were there?"

"I did not," he said, without turning around.

"Did you notice anything unusual at all?" Scott asked.

"Nothing unusual. Or everything unusual."

"Such as?" Scott asked again.

Garth whirled his chair around. "I noticed that his password was somewhat short. I don't believe it was more than eight characters, which is simply asking to be hacked."

"His user password, or the root password?"

"His user password, but he was a sudoer, so he could gain root access."

I asked, "Do you think that's how they got hacked? His weak password?"

"I do not know how they got hacked. We do not even know if they got hacked. This reporter might be making it all up for the ratings."

"Reporters wouldn't do that," I said. "That wouldn't be right."

Garth huffed. "Welcome to the real world, Jeffery. Not everyone does what is right. Some people do things for the money. A lot of people I suspect. Money is a very motivating factor in life."

There was a slight pause in the conversation, then Scott finally asked. "Are you one of them?"

Garth turned his gaze to Scott. "I work many hours a day for money, Mr. Stark. And so do you. Why are you here now instead of out with your latest girlfriend-of-the-week? I'll tell you why. It's for the money. We are all here for the money. It is a very motivating factor."

"Just because I have a job doesn't mean... I'm a bad person"

"Do tell us, Scott. You've never done anything under-the-table? Never anything legally shady? You've never done anything that you want to remain hidden? Would it make you nervous at all for the police to have a record of everything you've ever done?"

Scott didn't answer.

Garth continued. "As I thought. So then don't preach at me about having pure motivations. We all live this thing called life." He swiveled back to his work. "But as to your accusations regarding Adams, they are groundless. I did nothing wrong."

10:02 AM

I was just getting back to work when my desk phone rang. It startled me. I didn't like talking on the phone, but at least it was a double ring, an internal call, not a solid ring, someone from the outside, so that made it easier. I already had one of those external calls today, and I didn't want another one. I took a deep breath and picked it up. "This is Jeff," I said.

"Jeff, this is Randal. Will you please come see me in my office when you have a minute?"

"OK," I said.

"Thanks, bye."

"Bye." I hung up and walked over there. Randal's office was only one door over from our rooms. We didn't even have a door; it was just a corner room off the main room of our floor, but Randal got his own office, because he was the VP of Development.

His door was open so I went in and sat down. His room had shelves that held miscellaneous books and papers. More papers and binders covered his desk, except that they looked pushed aside to give himself some space. He only had one monitor, unlike us developers who had two. Randal sat back in his chair.

He said, "I was just wondering if there is anything else you know or have learned about the hacker."

I shook my head. "No."

"I read the article Scott sent. This puts a lot of pressure on us. First the hacker, then Adams. We have to assume they are related. We have to assume the hacker has successfully found a way to hack Omniscient, and has successfully hacked Adams."

I nodded.

Randal looked off to the side. "I don't know what to do. I think our code is tight, but I guess it's not. And how can we fix it? How can we fix something if we can't find anything broken?"

"And how can we make our code available knowing that it has a security vulnerability?" I added.

Randal looked at me. "What are you suggesting? We take it down?"

"Or at least put up a disclaimer saying we suspect it has a vulnerability."

Randal paused. "That would not look good for us. That might be bad for the company. I wouldn't want to do that without Peter's consent." Peter Steele was our CEO, Randal's boss. "No, let's not do that yet. We'll do what we can. We'll find the bug."

"What if we can't find it?"

"We'll find it. We have to. We don't have a choice." Randal sounded stressed. He was definitely not having a good morning.

"Have you heard anything about the fire alarm or the power outage?" I asked.

"No I haven't, besides the fact that it was a false alarm." He pulled his hands through his hair. "I guess I'll do that and see what I can find out. Until then..." He was interrupted by his desk phone ringing. He picked it up.

"Hello," he said. Then he opened his eyes wide. "Umm... OK. Send him right in." He put the phone down, then explained to me. "Apparently I have a visitor."

The new receptionist appeared at the door, then motioned

for the visitor to come in.

In walked a man in a suit and tie, who held out his hand to Randal. Randal rose and shook it. "I'm Randal Hillroy, VP of Development," he said.

"I'm Samuel Smith, Adams Corporation VP of Technology. I would like to talk with you for a minute, if I may."

10:29 AM

"What can I do for you, Mr. Smith?" Randal asked.

Samuel glanced down at me.

"Oh, this is Jeff Davis," Randal continued. "He's the one who talked with the... ah... he is a developer here at Omniscient. He is our email specialist."

Samuel looked at me, then back to Randal. "He talked with whom?"

"Oh, never mind. I trust the upgrade went well last week?"

Samuel stayed standing. "You haven't been talking to that reporter, Donald Roberts, have you?" looking down at me.

"No," I stammered.

"Well," turning back to Randal, he continued. "That's what I'm here to talk to you about. Have you, perchance, seen his latest news report?"

"Yes, we just did," said Randal. "It doesn't look good. For us or for you."

"No, Mr. Hillroy. It doesn't look good. Not good at all. In fact, it looks bad. Very bad. I have been asked by our CEO himself to come talk with you. Your receptionist told me that your CEO, Peter Steele, is away right now. So I'll talk with you. As VP of Technology, it is up to me to make sure our technology is functioning properly."

"And is it?" Randal asked.

"No. It appears as though it is not. I have reason to believe some of our private emails have been leaked into the hands of our rivals."

"That's too bad."

"Too bad?! From your perspective of a multimillion-dollar open source company, it might look too bad, but Adams is a multibillion-dollar corporation. Our share price is already down almost 1% since Donald's report."

"That's not so bad." Randal ventured.

"That's over two hundred and thirty million dollars of market cap, Mr. Hillroy. I assure you, we are taking this very seriously."

"Of course, Samuel. It is very serious. From our perspective too. Please have a seat and tell us how we can help you."

Samuel's facial expression relaxed as he finally sat down, as did Randal. "We have not yet decided what we will say to the media. We might deny everything--it was just a rumour and we are fine. We might say it is a classic case of corporate espionage--someone has just been spying on us, but they didn't get anything important."

"But is that true?" I interrupted.

"What?" said Samuel.

"If you know someone is spying on you, you shouldn't say they are not. And if you did get hacked, you shouldn't say you didn't," I said, a little annoyed.

"Jeff," Randal began. "Maybe now's not the time..."

The man in the suit turned toward me. "Thank you for the PR advice, computer programmer, but let us handle this." Then back to Randal. "What we need is this. We need you to make sure your software works. If there is a bug in it, find it, fix it, and make sure it's fixed. Go over every line. Test everything. Hire security specialists if you have to. We will not tolerate faulty software. We cannot run a multibillion-dollar corporation on faulty software."

Randal looked pained. "That would be a lot of time and expense," he said.

"Oh trust me. You want to do this, because the other option we have is to tell the media we used Omniscient which is full of security holes, and we're transitioning as fast as we can to anything else. And if we say that, what will happen to your software? Nobody will use it anymore, and when nobody uses your software, you can say goodbye to your company. Am I right?"

Randal started breathing faster. "Probably."

"And not only that. Before I was VP of technology, I was a manager in the law department, so I read your Terms and Conditions quite carefully when installing Omniscient. You have left yourself wide open to a lawsuit. If we determine that your negligence has caused us material harm, I don't think you will survive."

The man stood up. "I trust you will do the right thing."

"Of course," said Randal, also standing.

The man walked out of the office to the right, toward the front door. Randal looked fairly shell shocked, but when he had recovered a little, he said to me, "I think I'll go for a walk." Then he left his office and turned left, toward the back door.

I also got up to leave, but bumped into Samuel again. "Jeff, right?" he said to me, with a tight smile on this face.

"Yes."

"Do you, perchance, have a back door to this place?"

"Yes."

"Could you show me out that way?"

"OK." We started down the hallway, expecting to see Randal again, but he was gone.

"I seem to have bumped into someone I know. Heh! I sued him a few years ago and beat the pants off of him. I'd rather not see him again. I think he has it in for us. Took it personally

I guess."

We reached the back door and I opened it for him. I was about to ask who it was, but he disappeared and was gone. When I turned around and looked down the hallway, I saw him myself. It was the reporter, Donald Roberts.

10:59 AM

As I walked back to my desk, I sized up Donald. He was a slightly large man, dressed formal enough to garner respect, but casual enough not to be intimidating. He wore an easy smile that made you like him, but had a stare that would scare away the thought of lying to him. He had no mic or camera with him to intimidate you with; the man himself was enough. I thought he was probably very good at his job.

He was sitting in Garth's chair, leaning back casually with his hands behind his head. I went and sat down at my desk. I felt nervous about this man being here. He might report something that shouldn't be reported. It might be very bad for us. My stomach knotted up just thinking about saying the wrong thing.

"Ah, who is this?" he asked, turning from Scott to me.

I turned around to face him. "I'm Jeff," I said. So far so good.

"And what do you do here?"

"I'm a developer. I specialize in email."

"Oh! Have you heard that Adams had an email leak?"

"Yes." Careful!

"Do you think it came from Omniscient?"

"Umm..." His question came fast. I had to slow them down to think. "What do you mean?"

"Do you think Omniscient got compromised? Hacked?"

"I... couldn't say."

"Do you know of any vulnerabilities it might have?"
"N-no," I hesitated.
"But it could have some?"
"Well..."

Doug turned around to save me. "All software has the potential to have vulnerabilities, but Omniscient doesn't have any as far as we know."

"As far as you know, but there could be someone out there who knows of some." Donald countered.

"That would be unlikely. It is open-source, which means the whole world can look for problems. This security model has been proven to be extremely safe."

Donald frowned. "It's open-source. You mean anyone at all can look through your code for back doors?"

Doug frowned back. "The best security model is not to hide your code from malicious hackers, but to let the whole world polish it up until it is completely airtight."

"Because you think the good guys are smarter than the bad guys?"

"Well, no..."

Doug was interrupted by someone who could really give this guy a run for his money.

"Somebody please tell me why there is a person in my chair." It was Garth.

Donald jumped up and offered to shake Garth's hand. "Sorry about that. Hi, I'm Donald Roberts from CKGD news. I'm doing some investigative reporting on the Adams email leak."

Garth didn't shake his hand. "If you want me to like you, you're off to a bad start by sitting in my chair."

"I'm terribly sorry. Here, please have a seat," Donald said, backing away.

"I will not. It is still warm. I can't stand the heat of another person's bottom warming my chair and thus warming mine. I will stand until this nuisance goes away."

"Do you know anything about the upgrade at Adams last week?"

At this question, we all looked at Garth to see how he would answer. Of course he knew about it. He did it.

Garth paused as if considering how to answer. "Of course I know about it. But I won't speak about it. It's confidential."

Donald smiled graciously. "Hey, of course I'm not asking you to divulge any secrets. But some people might suspect things." He looked around at us all. "If you want to keep this company's name in good standing, I'm your man. Adams might want to throw Omniscient under the bus as a scapegoat for their own problems. If you talk to me, I can stand up for you. You need someone in the media who can defend Omniscient. Right?"

It sounded good. He might be right. Nobody answered, and he probably took our silence for agreement. He reached into his pocket and pulled out some business cards. "I'm going to leave you all my card," he said as he passed them out. "If you need your voice heard, let me know. If you find out something I should know, tell me. If you're innocent, the truth needs to be told. I'll see you guys around."

With that, he turned and walked away.

"What if we're not innocent?" I asked. There was no answer.

11:34 AM

"Hey Jeff," said Scott without looking up from his computer.

"Yeah?" I answered also without looking up.

"Let's do lunch."

"OK."

"I got a hankering for some Sri Lanka curry."

"OK."

"We should invite the new girl. What's her name? Vanessa?"

"Veronica."

"Right. I have a bad memory. Wanna go ask her?" Scott smiled to himself, knowing that I would never in a million years ask out a girl.

I didn't answer.

"Come on, Jeff. Go ask her. Let's go for some curry."

I still didn't answer.

"I think she likes you."

I rolled my eyes. "I need to go find Randal," I said.

"What for?"

"I need to know if he wants the code for the individual-email-signatures-per-email-address feature on the main 4.2 branch, or split it out into its own branch."

"Fine, go ask him. But come back then we'll do some lunch. I'm hungry."

I got up and glanced into Randal's office, which was empty, so I went to the kitchen, hoping to find my boss there. He wasn't, but Veronica was.

"Hi Jeff!" she said.

"Hi. I was just looking for Randal."

"Not here, but I'm glad you are. What does a girl do for lunch around here? I didn't bring a lunch. I hope there's a good place to buy something."

I felt the back of my neck get warm. This was getting a bit too personal for me. "Yeah, when you go outside, that building just over there has lots of restaurants."

"Is there something you would recommend? What are you doing for lunch, Jeff?"

"I... well... Scott and I were thinking of going to the Sri

Lankan place."

"Oh! That sounds fun! You don't mind if I tag along, do you?"

"Sure."

"Great! When are we leaving?"

"I have to find Randal first."

"OK. Come find me then. I'll be around."

"OK."

I scurried around the perimeter of the floor, looking for my boss and not finding him. I decided to go downstairs in case he was standing around outside. As I waited for the elevator to go down to ground level, I marvelled at how it was possible to have so much nerve that you actually invite yourself to go along with other people for lunch. I tried to imagine me doing that. I couldn't. Some people just have certain strengths.

At ground level, I looked around and saw Randal coming in. He looked a little better, but still haggard. He was headed for the stairs, so I ran to catch up to him.

"Randal," I said when I had caught up.

"Oh, hi Jeff. What are you doing here?"

"I came to ask you a question."

Randal paused, on the landing halfway between the first floor and the second floor.

I said, "I'm working on the separate signatures for each email address. Do you want it checked in to the main 4.2 branch, or kept separate on its own branch?"

Randal took a deep breath and let it out. "Keep it on its own branch for now, and then we can bring it in when we need to."

"OK."

"Let's take it easy until this thing blows over."

"You mean until the bug is fixed."

"I was thinking of the bad press we're getting, and it might get worse yet."

"But if there is a vulnerability in our code, I think our first priority should be to find it and patch it. That's the responsible thing. That's what the community needs."

"The community needs a company that will continue to support its software without going under. There is a chance that might happen, Jeff. We're still not profitable. We still rely on investors. If word gets out that Omniscient is full of holes, there goes the business. There goes the whole company. There goes all our jobs." Randal stared at me.

"Then we should make sure it works right as soon as possible," I said.

"Jeff!" Randal exploded at me. "You don't get it! You... you think all you have to do is sit at your computer and code and the world will be better. It might be nice to be able to just sit in front of your screen and write code, and that's all there is to life. But It's not. It doesn't work that way. If there is no business behind you, there is no job, no reason to come in. The business is everything. Whether we have a good product or not, the business has to continue. That's the only thing that matters. If you want to come in tomorrow morning, that's the only thing that matters."

I had no response. Randal turned and marched up the stairs two at a time. When he did, I noticed a few other people who had stopped to watch, also turn and go on their way.

I went back down the stairs. At the bottom, near the doors, I pulled out my phone and sent a quick email.

> To: scotts@omniscient.software, veronicas@omniscient.software
>
> From: jeffd@omniscient.software
>
> Subject: Lunch
>
> Ready for lunch. I'm at the main doors downstairs.

CHAPTER 3

12:09 PM

"What are you getting, Jeff?" Scott asked me as we walked through the doors of the Forks Market.

"Chicken satay," I replied.

"You always get the chicken. Get something else. Be adventurous."

I shrugged. "I like chicken."

"Veronica, what grabs you?"

Veronica walked with us. "I don't know. I've never had Sri Lankan food before."

"Everything tastes good. Lots of curry. Try the Kottu roti."

"What is it?"

"It's basically a bit of everything chopped up. Chicken, soup broth, pasta type stuff, vegetables."

"With curry?" she asked with a wry smile.

"You got it."

"If that's what you recommend, Scott, I'll take it. What are you getting?"

"I'm getting a hot bowl of meat curry. Beef and chicken and curry."

We lined up at the order desk of *Taste of Sri Lanka*, one of the many restaurants at the Forks Market food court, ordered, got our food, then sat down at one of the tables in the middle of the room.

Veronica looked around the building. "I love this place. The brickwork and steel have so much character. I wonder what it used to be."

"Don't know," said Scott with a full mouth.

"Maybe a train station," I said.

"Then what was the Johnson Terminal, where our office is?"

"Don't know," said Scott again, clearly more interested in his curry than in the rich history of the area.

"Well, this whole place, where the Assiniboine meets the Red River, used to be the centre of commerce, even back when people in canoes traded furs. It was the gateway to the west."

"Wow," said Veronica.

"Apparently a hundred years ago, property on Main Street sold for more than property on Main Street in New York City."

"Really?" she said. "What happened?"

"The Panama canal," I replied, putting more chicken into my mouth. "People went around the continent instead of going through the country by rail and river."

"Well, you learn something new every day," she said.

"I learned something today," said Scott. "I learned we're in big trouble."

"What do you mean?" Veronica asked.

"Well, first a hacker calls Jeff here and demands that we pay him for a bug or he'll hack us."

"Really?" She looked at me. I raised my eyebrows in agreement.

"And then we hear that Adams Corporation got their email hacked."

"Were they using Omniscient?"

"Yes," I said.

"And then," Scott continued, "a reporter comes snooping along. If he publishes that Omniscient is buggy, we're toast. Nobody will use us anymore."

Veronica leaned forward. "Shouldn't we be concerned about this? I mean, our jobs are at stake, right?"

I examined my chicken, not liking that thought at all.

Scott sat back and picked his teeth with a toothpick. "Yes, of course we should. We have to do everything we can."

Veronica questioned Scott. "Well Jeff doesn't seem very concerned."

They both looked at me. Scott said, "Of course he's concerned, he's just not showing it. There is something you need to know about Jeff."

"What?"

"Well, first of all, he's a man, which means he doesn't have emotions."

"Really?" she asked.

"That's not true," I interrupted.

"And secondly, he's a programmer, which means he doesn't have feelings either." Scott smiled. So did Veronica.

"That's also not true," I said.

"It might be truer than you think," said Scott. "As a man, you are more prone to actions than emotions, and as a programmer you are more prone to thoughts than feelings. Don't you have a lot of deep thoughts about all that is going on right now?"

I squirmed a little. "Well, yes."

Veronica said, "OK, Jeff, what are your thoughts? We're listening."

I examined them both to see if they were serious or just playing with me. Concluding they actually wanted to know my thoughts, I said, "Garth did the install," I said. "Maybe he messed up."

Scott looked at me. "You mean unintentionally or intentionally?"

I shrugged. "I don't know. I think he could be bought."

Veronica laughed. "Everyone can be bought for the right price. Right Scott?"

Scott didn't answer. He finished off his curry.

"I couldn't," I said.

"You don't think so, Jeff?" Veronica leaned toward me. "Maybe not with money, but maybe there are other ways into a young man's heart." She stared directly into my eyes.

I had no words to respond to that. My head and my heart were both going too fast. I avoided her stare and sat there, quite uncomfortable, until I thought of something else to say. "A man from Adams came to visit."

This got Scott's attention. Both of theirs.

"The VP of Technology met with Randal. He used to be a lawyer, and he was making some threatening statements. It got Randal scared."

"What do they want us to do?" Scott asked.

"Fix Omniscient. Patch the hole."

"Stupid hole!" said Scott.

"Do you think you can do it?" Veronica looked concerned.

I shrugged. "It's hard to fix something if you can't find anything broken."

"You don't have anything to go on?" she asked.

"Well, the problem might be the god account."

She looked confused. "What's that?"

I continued. "It's like God Mode in a video game. The god account in Omniscient lets you see everybody's email, chat, texts, voice, video, everything. It gives the user unlimited ability to do anything he wants."

"So you could use this to spy on a large corporation like Adams?"

"Yes."

"So it's basically a back door to hack a company."

I frowned. "It's supposed to be secure. Not everyone can just get in."

"Who can get in, exactly?"

Scott answered. "Anyone who knows god's email address and password can simply log in and see everything."

"So if you can find that somehow..." she said.

"You can sell the information you find to the highest bidder." Scott continued. "Corporate espionage. There's lots of money in that business."

"You would know?" Veronica asked him.

Scott just looked into his empty bowl. "Wow, that was some good curry."

"I think you're hiding something, Scott." she said.

He looked up with an almost sad expression on his face. "Not everything needs to be talked about." He stood up.

We all did. As we made our way back to our office, I wondered what else could go wrong today.

12:54 PM

Back at my desk, I was about to start bug hunting when suddenly my phone rang. I almost jumped. It must be nerves. It was the third time that day that cursed phone rang. I wasn't in the mood to talk to people right now, but what could I do?

I took a deep breath and picked it up.

"This is Jeff."

"Jeff, I have a call from Peter Steele. Will you take it please?" It was the new receptionist. I still didn't know her name.

"Doesn't he want to talk to Randal?" I asked.

"Randal is not answering his phone."

"Then why did you pick me?"

"Because I know your extension number, and you answered a call last time."

"Right."

"I'm putting him on. Here he is." She was persistent.

I replied meekly, "OK", then I heard a click, so I said,

"Hello, this is Jeff Davis."

"Jeff, this is Peter."

"Hello, Mr. Steele."

"Peter is fine, Jeff. Listen, I missed my flight back, so I'm still here in Florida, and I have a meeting with a big investor at one. Ah... what's the time now?"

I glanced at my screen. "12:55" I said.

"That's five minutes. Jeff, can you please go to my office and set up a video call? Then when Dennis McKinney arrives, we can talk on my computer."

I considered the request. "OK. Right now?"

"Right now."

"OK. Umm... I will log in as me and I will call you on your computer in a minute."

"Thank you, Jeff. I'll talk to you soon. Goodbye."

"Bye". We both hung up.

I walked out of our room, past Randal's door, labelled "VP of Development", and found Peter's door labelled "CEO Omniscient Technologies". The door was locked. Great! I ran to find Ronja. Maybe the local system administrator had keys to people's rooms. I found her at her desk, one of the cubicles in the middle of the room.

"Ronja, do you have a key to Peter's office?"

"I do not. Why would I?"

"You're the... never mind." I ran to the receptionist.

I didn't know her name, so I just stood there until I got her attention, then said, "Do you, perchance, have a key to the CEO's office?"

She said, "Ooh, let's see. We do have a number of things around here. She started opening drawers and doors, looking under and behind things. I was almost shocked. If the key to the CEO's door is just lying around one of these drawers, we have more security issues than just software. Maybe that's how the hacker got in. He just grabbed the keys to the CEO's office, or the server room, and walked right in. No. That didn't happen. I started hoping she wouldn't find anything.

Just then the main glass doors opened and in walked a normal-looking man. He wasn't even wearing a suit. I couldn't tell by looking at him that he was a multi-millionaire and owned a fair chunk of this company I was employed at.

He smiled at the receptionist. "I'm Dennis McKinney. I'm here to see Peter Steele."

The receptionist turned to him and replied, "I'm sorry, but Peter Steele is..."

I knew I had to act. I bolstered up all the courage I could find and interrupted this unknown receptionist talking to a millionaire. I may have turned red. "Um... Ah... I was just talking to Mr. Steele, and he asked me to get a video call set up for... his meeting with... Dennis McKinney here."

The receptionist beamed at the success of this venture. Turning to the visitor, she said, "I guess you can go right on in."

"Thanks," he said.

"This way," I said and walked down the hall between the outside offices and the inside cubicles. I turned the corner, and as I passed Peter's office, I said, "Peter's door is locked, so I think we can meet in Randal's office. Randal is the VP of Development."

"Is he in?" the man asked.

I had no idea where Randal was. "Ah, he might be." I let it go at that.

I went in and sat in my boss's chair, logged in, opened up Omniscient, and logged into that with my email address, jeffd@omniscient.software, and my password. Then I found Peter in my group contacts. I initiated a video call with him. As the connecting sound played, I looked up to see Dennis sitting quietly in one of Randal's visitor's chairs.

The screen in front of me came alive with the face of my

boss's boss, Peter Steele. He wore grey hair, glasses, a colourful button shirt, and a tan. "Hello Mr. Steele," I said loudly. "Is this working?"

"I hear you, Jeff." I think he was on his phone, because the camera angle was very low. Too low. He had a big nose. "Before Dennis McKinney arrives, has anything interesting been happening there?"

Wow, was that a question! Everything interesting has been happening here. But I don't know if I should be discussing them here in front of the investor. I glanced at him, trying not to look worried. He met my gaze by raising one eyebrow, as if to ask *Yes... how are you going to answer that?* And I wondered if he already knew, and that's why he was here.

1:25 PM

I swallowed hard then answered Peter's question. "Dennis McKinney is here already, just on the other side of the screen. But yes, interesting things have been happening here. Maybe you want to talk about them with Randal."

"Is Randal in?" Peter asked.

"I don't know where he is, maybe still talking to the building owners about the... ah... or still out for lunch or something."

"Talking to the building owners about what, Jeff?" Dennis asked pleasantly but firmly.

Peter must have also heard the question, because he kept looking at me, waiting for an answer.

"Well, the fire alarm went off, so we all evacuated. Maybe Randal was talking to them about what the firemen said."

"Was there a fire?!" Peter asked.

"Oh. No. They said it was a false alarm. And the power

went out."

"You didn't lose any information?" Dennis asked.

"No. The UPSes handled everything."

"The Parcel Service handled the power out?!" Peter asked.

"No, the batteries, the Uninterruptible Power Supplies."

"It sounds like you've had a busy morning," said Dennis.

"Yeah! No kidding!" And then I caught myself. If I agree too much, he might think something else happened. It did, of course, but it might not be my place to tell him that.

"Did anything else happen this morning?" he asked.

I looked at Peter. He also wanted to know.

I sighed. I may as well tell them. "We got a phone call this morning from someone who demanded we pay him ten thousand dollars in exchange for a bug report, or he will start hacking us."

Dennis pinched his eyebrows in concern. "I heard that Adams got their email compromised. You're not saying it came from Omniscient and we have a security hole, are you?"

"Well, I don't exactly know what happened at Adams. I'm not sure anybody knows..."

"And you know of someone who can fix that hole for only a few thousand dollars?"

"Well, he said ten thousand dollars in Bitcoin."

Dennis walked over to our side of the screen. "Peter, you need to pay the money," he said to the screen. "This is important." Then he added. "And move your phone up. We're looking into your nose."

"Ah, Dennis," said Peter, as the video of him changed angle. "It's good to see you again. Yes, about this hacker business. This is the first time I've heard of it. I agree we should certainly do something. But instead of paying directly, why don't we let our boys first try to find it themselves? They are good at what they do, isn't that right, Jeff?"

"Well, I guess. I would like to think so." I said.

"Besides, money is tight right now. We're hoping to begin another funding round soon."

Dennis replied, "Investors will not be interested in investing in a company that has security issues with its product."

"Yes, except for you, Dennis. You know us. You've been with us from the beginning. This company is a great asset to you, and I know you won't let us down in our time of need. We are almost profitable. Soon we will be. We just need a little more to get there."

Suddenly I felt very uncomfortable. It was like I was in the middle of parents arguing over family finances. My parents split a long time ago, but still I could imagine it.

Dennis replied. "I think I am also one of those investors who is not interested in a company that has security issues with its product. I will give you money to pay the hacker, but after that, you need to get your house in order, Peter."

"Of course," Peter replied. "We will do everything we can."

"Good. Now this is what you need to do. First, try to make sure bad news doesn't spread. If that news reporter shows up, don't give him any ideas."

"Right," Peter agreed.

I got nervous again. Should I mention the fact that he was here already and even left his card? If I don't say it, they will probably find out anyway. And it's just the right thing to do. "Actually, he was here already."

They both turned to me.

"We didn't tell him anything, at least we tried not to."

Dennis rubbed his chin and his face. "Is there anything else, Jeff, we need to know?"

"Umm... a VP from Adams stopped by to talk to Randal."

"What did he say?" asked Dennis.

"He basically told us to fix everything and make sure it works, or he'll sue us into the ground."

"I think that's a very good idea," Dennis continued. "You need to make sure everything works." Turning to the screen, he said, "Peter, you need to come home right now and take control of this situation."

"My ticket is already booked. I'll be there tomorrow."

"Good. And try to keep a lid on bad news spreading. That includes the hacker, paying the hacker, the security vulnerability, Adams suing us, the bad press, and especially layoffs. If people start talking about that, morale goes way down. Trust me."

Out of the corner of my eye, I saw him glance my way, but I didn't return it. I kept looking at the screen.

"Of course. I will do that."

"Good." Dennis paused, to try to think of anything else. He couldn't. "Take care, Peter. Goodbye."

"It was good talking with you too, Dennis. Bye."

As he left the room, Dennis said to me, "Goodbye Jeff."

He was gone before I could reply.

I was about to say goodbye to the big boss, when he said something to me. "Jeff, I would like to talk with you a minute."

"OK" I replied.

"Jeff, this business with the hacker is a problem."

"Yes."

"And I need someone to fix this problem. Not just add it to their already full schedule, but remove their other responsibilities and focus squarely on this until it is fully addressed. I would like you to be this person."

I stammered. "What... what would that all involve?"

"You would focus on this security problem full time. You would investigate all the installations at other companies. You would be the point man for the media. And you would coordinate with the police."

My throat started tightening up. My breathing became more laboured. I could feel myself start sweating. I took evasive action. "Randal is much better at that than anyone."

"Randal is busy leading development. We can't just remove management from a company. You are much better, because your other duties can be absorbed by the other developers."

"Garth is good at going to other companies. He does it all the time when he does installations."

"Garth is too closely involved. We need someone a little removed from the installs, someone who could investigate the installs, and the installer. And besides, Garth lacks a tact that you could offer."

"There are still other guys here who would be better than me."

"I think you are the perfect person, Jeff. Someone needs to make right what is wrong. Someone needs to bring this person to justice. Will you do it, Jeff? Will you be the point man?"

My head started swimming. Yes, someone should definitely bring this person to justice. It's just not right for anyone to get away with this. I would like nothing more than to see that happen. Everyone else seems to be looking out for their own interests. What about the right thing to do? Hacking is just wrong, and the hacker should be dealt with under the law.

I looked at the big boss, then looked down and shook my head. "No, I can't do it. You'll have to find someone else. Maybe Scott."

"Well! I was hoping you would agree, Jeff. I can't choose Scott for other reasons, which I won't talk about now. If you change your mind, and I hope you do, please let me know."

I agreed, then we said goodbyes and disconnected.

As I left the office, I just didn't know what we were going to do. Everything was a big mess. I might not be able to be the point man, but maybe I could do my little part. I set out for my own office to do just that.

1:49 PM

When I got back to my desk, Scott was there at his computer too. "I saw you in Randal's office with the owner," he said. "What was that about?"

"He wanted to talk with Peter, so I set up a video call to him."

"So they talked?"

"Yup"

"About what is going on here?"

"Yup"

"What did they say?"

I considered the fact that Dennis said to not spread bad news, so I considered not answering my friend's direct question, but I didn't want to do that. I wanted to be on the same side as him, not to be hiding stuff from him. And besides, I didn't think I could take the weight of responsibility of keeping all those secrets. Dennis hadn't told me anything directly. He was having a conversation with Peter.

"Dennis McKinney said we shouldn't spread bad news."

"Like the hacker."

"Yes…"

"And Adams."

"Yes…"

"And the reporter."

"Yes…"

"And what? The power outage? The fire alarm? What else should we not talk about, Jeff?" He looked at me like the friend he is, just wanting to help carry a heavy load.

"He talked about not giving us any more money if this can't get solved. He mentioned the word layoffs."

Scott considered the news soberly.

"He said it's bad for morale." I added.

"He's right," Scott said. "It is. I feel it myself already." But he recovered quickly. "Well then if that's the case, let's keep it a secret. In fact, let's spread some cheer around here. We might all be out of a job next week, but for now, let's enjoy life."

Right then Garth and Doug walked in.

"Hey guys!" Scott beamed. "It's a great day to go bug hunting, isn't it? The sun is shining, we've got lots of coffee, and the boss is away. Let's put our feet up, enjoy life, and hunt down this security vulnerability of ours. If we hurry, maybe we can get it found and fixed by the end of the day. What do you say, guys?"

Doug replied calmly. "OK, I'll help you."

Garth said, "I find your effervescent attitude suspicious, Mr. Stark. Is there something you're trying to hide? What is it you're not telling us?"

Scott was not disheartened by our coworker. He continued cheerfully. "I'm just saying we need to get to work patching our security hole instead of thinking about how bad it is to have a security hole in our software."

Garth sat down. "Ah, you don't want us to dwell on our possible imminent unemployment. Very well, let's attempt to make sure that doesn't happen."

For all Garth's interesting character, he was actually pretty smart. Maybe too smart. Could he be the hacker himself, implant a bug into our own code, then pretend to find it? I'll bet he could.

But then again, any one of us could. I considered Doug. He was a smart guy. And adding one single line of code was all it took to gain access to something you shouldn't. And Scott? He might mess around a bit, but he's not a bad guy. I couldn't believe it.

I opened up our software tracking system and noticed that

Garth had just checked something in. I dug deeper. It was the code that takes a user's email address and password and logs them in. Garth had just changed it.

Should I be suspicious? Surely he wasn't covering anything up. It was just a small change. I tried to sound friendly. "Oh, Garth. I see you just checked something in already."

"The email address and password were not being sanitized as much as they could be," he said. "It's an added level of security."

I couldn't pursue it anymore. I went back to bug hunting.

But Scott did. "Maybe we should double-check each other's code changes," he suggested.

"For what purpose?" asked Garth.

"Well, this is a security matter. The more eyes the better."

Garth swung his chair around. "You don't trust me," he stated.

Scott met his gaze but tried to defuse. "I'm not accusing you of anything, Garth."

"I should hope not. I'm not the one with the checkered past."

"My past has nothing to do with… " Scott threw his hands in the air. "Garth, would you like to review all my check-ins? You can look at every line I change. I won't be able to do anything suspicious if you see everything I do."

Garth sat there, contemplating. "An interesting proposition, but I decline your offer. We don't have time for such. I am free to look in the code for any of your changes, and you are free to look in the code for any of mine. We can keep an eye on each other if we wish. Does that sound fair to you?"

Scott nodded. "Yes it does."

"And to you, Jeffery?" Garth asked me.

"OK," I said.

Doug had also turned around to listen in. "I agree too," he said.

"Then let's get back to work," said Garth, as he got back to work.

We all hunted bug for a while until I saw Veronica walk past, on her way to the kitchen. Suddenly I felt like getting myself a cup of coffee.

2:15 PM

I watched Veronica glide toward the kitchen like a tigress, both graceful and strong. I wondered what made her so interesting. Maybe it was the fact that she could stand up to Garth. She had actually called him a jerk. Wow. Never in my wildest dreams could I ever imagine doing that. But she did.

As she got a mug out of the cupboards for coffee, she glanced over at me and smiled, which gave me some strange feelings. I had never met anyone who treated me that way. "Oh, hi Jeff. Fancy meeting you here."

"Hi," I replied. I also reached up for a mug. Standing so close to her, I noticed our heights. She was almost as tall as me, maybe taller. I almost looked up to her.

She sat down at one of the tables, then motioned me over. "Come join me, Jeff."

I did.

"So, explain something to me," she said.

"What?"

"Explain how Christmas equals Halloween." She leaned forward toward me, which gave me more unusual feelings.

"Well, It's... ", I started, then added, "You see if...", but then I decided upon, "OK, I'll start at the beginning."

"A very good place to start," she chuckled. I must have made her laugh. I wasn't trying to. Maybe I'm a funny guy.

"How many fingers do you have?" I asked.

"What does this have to do with Christmas and Halloween?"

"I'm getting to it."

"OK, I'll play your game. I have ten fingers, and I hope you do too."

"Yes, I do. Everybody does. That's probably why our counting system is based on ten."

"You mean the metric system?"

"No. Our numbers. When you count, you count zero through nine, then flip over to one zero, one one, one two. After nine nine, you flip over to one zero zero."

"I think I learned this in grade one."

"Now imagine you only had eight fingers."

"Ooo, I'm not sure I would want to imagine that."

"Well, if everyone only had eight fingers, we might count zero through seven, and *then* flip over to one zero."

"We would flip over at eight instead of ten?" she asked.

"Exactly. And that's why Christmas is Halloween."

"you're a funny guy, Jeff," and she leaned over and slapped my shoulder playfully. I didn't mind that at all. I smiled too.

I continued. "Numbers where you flip at ten are called decimal numbers, abbreviated *dec*. When you flip at eight, those numbers are called octal, abbreviated *oct*." Then I waited to see if she would catch on, and I was not disappointed.

She thought for a minute, then talked out loud. "So 25 (dec) is not actually the twenty-fifth of December, but the number 25 in decimal."

"Yes."

"And 31 (oct) is not actually the thirty-first of October, but the number thirty-one in octal?"

"That's right."

"And they're the same number?"

"That's right."

"Wait. But is it really? How does that work? "

I was about to explain further, when she suddenly got up. "Never mind! I know all I need to know." And with that, she marched down the hall toward our room. I ran after her, because I wouldn't miss this for the world.

When she got there, she sipped her coffee while reading Garth's little whiteboard. "So Garth, I'm reading this joke here."

"Don't hurt yourself too much, girly," he replied.

"You know it never occurred to me that twenty-five in decimal equals thirty-one in octal. That's quite a coincidence. Ha! That's funny. Good one Garth." She slapped his back and turned and walked away, leaving the large man speechless for probably the first time in his life. Wow. What a woman.

As I sat back down at my desk, the rest of us couldn't help but snicker.

CHAPTER 4

2:46 PM

My phone rang again, and I seriously considered running away. I had already taken three calls that day. One from a hacker threatening us, one from my boss, and the other from my boss's boss. Why can't people leave me alone?

It rang again. Maybe I should visit the washroom. No, the other guys were in the room and that would be too weird.

It kept on ringing. Maybe I should ask someone else to answer my phone. "Scott, want to answer my phone?"

"You answer it."

I took a deep breath and let it out, then I reached for the phone. "Hi, this is Jeff."

It was the new receptionist. I still didn't know her name. "Jeff, I have a police officer here for you."

"For me?"

"Well, maybe not you specifically, but someone needs to talk with him."

"Why did you pick me?"

"Because I called you last time."

"There are other people here."

"Peter Steele isn't in, and neither is Randal Hillroy."

Randal is still gone? I wondered where he went. Maybe something happened to him. Someone should call him or something. Or send him an email. That's easier. I should ask the receptionist to send me an email instead of calling me on the phone.

"What does he want?" I asked.

"He wants to talk to someone, but no managers are in. So I called you. Will you come to see him please?"

I tried to think of a way out of it, but couldn't. "OK," I said. Then, "Bye", and hung up.

I got up. "The police are here," I said.

"What could they possibly want?" asked Garth.

"I don't know," I answered. "Scott, let's go talk with the police."

"No, I don't want to. You go, Jeff."

So I made my way down the hall, around a corner, then down the other hall, to the receptionist. I saw a man dressed in a shirt and tie, dark pants with yellow stripes down the sides. He was wearing a police hat. As I approached, he scowled at me. His stare seemed to go straight through me, as if he were looking into my soul. If I ever had a choice, I would want to be on this guy's side, just because I wouldn't want to be his enemy.

The receptionist said to him, "This is Jeff Davis."

He extended his hand, and we shook. He said, "Detective Sergeant Joseph Wakefield. Criminal Investigation Bureau. I would like to talk to you about Omniscient Software."

"Sure", I said, and led him to the board room, near the main entrance.

He sat down at the big table, and I sat down on the other side, my hands in my lap.

He took off his hat and set it on the table. I tried not to stare at it. It was black, flat on top, with a yellow band all around it, and the police emblem in front.

"Is this where you make Omniscient?" he asked.

"Yes."

"Adams Corporation has reported to us that they suspect a breach in their security. They suspect theft of intellectual property, namely their private emails."

He paused, but I didn't answer, because he didn't ask me a question. So he continued.

"I am not accusing you or your company of any crime. I am just covering all my bases, and Adams was using Omniscient. They still are, as far as I know. So please tell me. Does Omniscient have any... way... that someone could break into it?"

I thought about his question, and answered truthfully. "Not as far as I know."

But he didn't let me off that easily. "But there could be?"

I thought some more. "If we knew of any, they would be patched already. You are asking me if something exists that I don't know about." I didn't mean to attach any attitude to that last remark; I was only trying to explain logically. He probably took my words as having attitude, a laughable thought, but he was professional enough to not give attitude back.

"Do you know of any reason to believe Omniscient *might* have a security hole?"

I looked away and fidgeted, which I'm sure he caught on to immediately, which means I would have to answer now or look like a liar.

"Someone called this morning, threatening to hack us all if we didn't pay him ten thousand dollars in bitcoin."

"Really?" His eyes drilled into me even more. "What do you know about this individual?"

"Nothing really. He called this morning, sometime after eight. He left a website where I could pay him."

"No name?"

"No."

"No other way to contact him?"

"Just the website. It ended with dot onion, so it's on the dark web. Untraceable."

"If he has a website, we can track him down."

I looked at the police officer, trying to determine if he was joking. No. He wasn't. That means he actually didn't know how it worked. Maybe I should explain. "The Tor network uses onion routers to hide where Internet requests come from and where they go. Each request is encrypted and layered inside other requests. Like an onion. It's untraceable."

Now he studied me. I could tell by his hard police features that he would probably not want to admit to a young punk like me that he didn't know how technology worked. I was right. He changed the subject.

"Has anyone else contacted you about this?" he asked.

"Someone from Adams was here."

"What did they say?"

"Nothing really. He just threatened to sue us if we didn't get our software working."

"Does he have reason to think something is wrong with it?"

"Oh, I don't think he actually mentioned anything specific. I think he was just scared, and when he's scared he starts making threats."

"It's not illegal to threaten to litigate. But if his threats turn real, let me know. Anyone else?"

"A reporter. Donald Roberts."

At the sound of the reporter's name, Detective Sergeant Joseph Wakefield took a deep breath and scratched the back of his head. I'll bet he knew this reporter, but I wasn't going to ask about it.

"Oh," I continued. "This morning there was a fire alarm and the power went out. I thought..."

"You thought what?"

"I thought maybe someone was going to break in. You know, like in the movies."

"Did anything happen?"

"No. Nothing at all."

"Thank you for your time, Jeff." He handed me his card. "I

will try to trace that phone call, but if this suspect is as smart as he seems, it will most likely be a dead end. I will probably be in touch. If anything else happens, please let me know."

The man turned to go and I was left holding a police officer's card. Didn't I tell Peter I didn't want to be the guy? When he gets in, I'm going to hand this card over to him, because I'm not going to be the guy. I can barely answer the phone, let alone talk to anyone in person. Yeah, I know the CEO asked me, and I do want to see justice happen here, but I just can't carry the weight of the responsibility. I can't.

3:18 PM

I checked my email.

> From: peters@omniscient.software
>
> To: randalh@omniscient.software, jeffd@omniscient.software
>
> Subject: Paying the hacker
>
> Dear Randal and Jeff;
>
> I am currently at the airport, about to board. I should be back in the office tomorrow morning.
>
> I heard that we received a phone call from someone claiming to be able to hack into our software, and that if we pay him ten thousand dollars, he will tell us how he does it. It is imperative that we not only keep Omniscient itself secure, but also that we maintain our good name as a company.
>
> While it may not seem like good press to be talking with hackers, it is something we must do. Randal and

Jeff, follow this man's instructions. Pay him the money. Do it immediately. Do not wait another minute. We cannot spare any time. We must deal with the situation before it gets out of control.

We are boarding now.

Goodbye.

--

Peter Steele

CEO Omniscient Technologies

As I sat at my desk and read this email from the big boss, it felt good that someone was taking charge and getting something done. Justice certainly needed to get done, and I'm glad Peter was doing something. I asked out loud, "Does anybody know where Randal is?"

Three people said they didn't. "Has anyone tried to contact him?" I asked.

"I sent him an email a while ago," said Scott. "I haven't heard anything."

"I just got an email from Peter," I said. "He says we should pay the hacker."

"Really?" said Scott.

"A bold move," said Garth.

"Immediately," I continued. "He says we shouldn't wait another minute."

"Then let's do it", said Scott happily.

"Randal should do it. He should be here," I said.

"Well he's not," said Scott. "So we'll have to do it ourselves."

"Maybe I should call Randal."

"Jeff is contemplating using the telephone," said Garth. "It must be serious."

As Scott started looking up how to buy and transfer Bitcoin, I considered the phone on my desk. I found Randal's cell phone number on my computer. I need to call him. We can't just go around spending thousands of dollars behind his back, without him knowing. Can we?

I picked up the phone and punched in the numbers. Then I took a deep breath, trying to steady my nerves. It rang. Then it rang again, and again. Finally his voicemail kicked in. I was relieved I didn't have to talk on the phone, but still troubled that Randal didn't know what we were doing. I left a quick message. "Hi Randal. This is Jeff. I just got the email from Peter Steele, where he says to pay the hacker, so we are going to do that now." I hung up.

"Hey!", exclaimed Scott. "I found a website that lets you buy Bitcoin with a credit card, and will let you transfer it to another Bitcoin wallet."

"A reputable company, I presume?" said Garth.

"Yes, a number of other people vouch for them."

"We still need money," continued Garth.

"Stupid money!" Scott interjected.

Garth continued. "And Susan might not be at her office." I got up and went down the hall to her office. The door, which read, "Susan Harth, VP of Finance and Accounting", was locked. She must have left early today. I looked around for her assistant. He was gone. Everybody was gone. I went back to our room and sat down.

"Everybody's gone," I said. "We can't pay him today. It will have to wait for tomorrow, I guess." I sat down.

"We could pay it!", said Scott excitedly.

"How?" I asked.

"We have credit cards, don't we?" he said. "We could all throw in two and a half thousand dollars, and we're good to go. The hacker gets his money, and we get our bug fix. Boom! Done! End of drama. Everybody wins."

At Scott's suggestion, Garth and Doug turned around to face him. We said nothing.

"Come on!", said Scott. "We'll just put it on credit card, and we'll get reimbursed tomorrow morning. No problem."

"It would be nice to have confirmation that we will actually get reimbursed," said Doug.

I said, "Well, Peter said so himself. In the email."

"Great," said Scott. "Jeff and I are in. What about you two?"

I'm not sure I was actually in. I would prefer to not be out that much money if things went south.

Garth answered. "Jeff, will you please forward Peter's email to me, so I can study it myself?"

I turned around and forwarded it to all three other guys in the room. Soon they were reading it for themselves.

"These instructions from Steely are very explicit," said Garth. "There is no room for ambiguity. I agree to it." He stood up so he could reach into his pocket better. We turned to Doug.

"If everyone else is doing it, I'll go along too," he also reached into his pocket.

"Great!" said Scott, as he turned to begin the transactions. "I'll get started. Feel free to look over my shoulder, if you want. It's your money too."

It took Scott a few minutes to work through the instructions of paying for Bitcoin online, but soon enough he had paid his share as well as Garth's and Doug's. He said, "Jeff, you're up. Your card?"

I guess I had no choice by then. If I had disagreed, I should have said something before, but it was too late now. I handed him my credit card. Pretty soon he handed it back and announced, "We now own ten thousand dollars of Bitcoin. Now what do we do with it?"

"His Bitcoin wallet address is shown on his onion website," I said, and found the piece of paper that I had written it down on. "Here it is."

"In order to see that website, we must go into the dark web," said Garth. "Luckily, I already have it installed on my computer. If you would hand me that slip of paper, Jeffery, we will see what lies therein."

"We're going dark, everybody," said Scott.

I handed him the paper, and Garth opened up the specially designed web browser that uses the Tor network to communicate. Each request on the dark web takes longer than normal, because the computer doesn't make a straight connection to the web server. It makes an encrypted connection to an onion routing server in the Tor network, which makes another encrypted connection to another onion routing server in the Tor network. After about three such hops, the original request exits the Tor network back into the real Internet. But this website had a top level domain of "onion", which means it lived in Tor, in the dark web. You can't get to it except using the dark web.

We all looked at Garth's screen, which showed a large QR code and a Bitcoin address which was 1GMB48qavpVK8krvuwJ5LCJJQhihsAUEon. Garth copied the address and pasted it into an email to Scott. Scott got the email and prepared a transaction from our Bitcoin wallet to this one.

While we waited for Scott to complete the trade, a terrifying thought came to me and I yelled, "Stop!"

Everyone else jumped and turned to me. I said, "How do we know this email from Peter is legit? If the hacker really has broken in, isn't this the exact kind of fake email he would send to get us to pay him?"

Scott's face went white. "But it's too late," he said. "I just clicked the button." He glanced at his screen. "The transaction just went through. He just got paid."

"Who got paid?" said a voice behind us. We whirled around to see the reporter, Donald Roberts smiling at us.

GOD'S EMAIL ADDRESS

4:04 PM

Our eyes were wide like a deer in the headlights, like we were caught with our hands in the cookie jar, as if we just admitted that we were guilty of some crime.

"We were just...", began Scott, "reimbursing someone...".

"For a bug report," I finished.

"Oh! The bug that caused Adam's email breach?" the man asked.

"Maybe," said Scott.

"No," said Garth.

"We're not even completely sure we have a bug," I said. But if Peter says he didn't send that email, that would be confirmation.

"But you're paying the guy for a bug report. Didn't he just report a bug?"

I hesitated.

"No? You're paying him first?"

Still no answer.

"So you're paying him, hoping that he *will* give you a bug report? This sounds like blackmail. Interesting. So, what do you all know about this alleged bug reporter? Do you have a name?" He pulled out a paper note pad, which seemed very old fashioned and cliche. I may have snickered to myself when I saw it, but he didn't seem to notice.

We looked at each other, not sure what to say.

"You don't have a name for him?" he asked again.

"No," I finally said.

Donald Robert cleared his throat. "OK, so to get this straight, an unknown person has said that he would give you a bug report in exchange for money, and you have just paid him.

63

Is that right?"

"This is not incriminating evidence," said Garth. "By tomorrow morning, the report may be in and our software fully patched."

Donald took this as good news. "Hey! Great! That would be wonderful for you. Once you've got your software fixed, just let me know. I'm sure you don't want the world to think Omniscient is broken, do you?"

"We're not sure it's broken right now," I said, trying to defend what might be the truth.

He looked at me. "But you just paid him a large amount of money for a bug report. That means you think it probably is."

"We don't have any proof it's broken," I said again. Not yet, anyway.

"Hey, no problem. When he gets back to you, let me know that you're working on the fix, and let me know when the fix is done. I'll tell the world Omniscient works again." He smiled. "I think you know how to contact me." Yeah, we still had his card from his last visit.

Now Garth said to him, "Just how did you get in here? An appointment should be mandatory."

"Oh, your receptionist just let me in. Nice girl." He turned and walked away.

When he was gone Scott said, "That man doesn't need to come back, in my opinion."

"I think he will have to," I said. "When we get the hacker's bug report, Donald Roberts will have to tell everyone that Omniscient is fixed."

"And what if we never get the report? What if we never hear back from the hacker again? Ever?"

I didn't want to think about that.

GOD'S EMAIL ADDRESS

4:40 PM

It had been a long day, and I was ready to go home. First I replied to Peter's email and told him that we paid. If it really wasn't from him, he would let us know.

Then I stopped by the kitchen for a cup of coffee.

While I was there, filling up my travel mug, I saw the plant lady watering the plants, pulling out the dead leaves, and generally making them feel loved. She had reddish-blond hair and a fair amount of good looks to her.

I've never spoken to her, of course. I don't generally talk to people if I can help it. I don't think she has ever talked with anyone here herself either, but I've seen her here every few days. She must be hired from some local company that takes care of plants.

As I stood there, filling my cup, she looked over at me and smiled. Boy, she had a pretty smile. Her face kind of glowed. Then she said, "Hi".

I wasn't in a people mood, so I said a quick, "Hi", and was about to turn to go, but she walked up to me.

"My name's Cheryl." She stuck out her hand.

"I'm Jeff," I said, shaking it.

Then her smiling face lost a little cheer and showed a bit of anxiety. I wasn't really interested in her social fears, so I said, "Well, have a good day," and turned to leave, but she stopped me.

"Umm…," she said, "Can I ask you a question?"

"Yup"

"No, it's not a question. Here, I have something for you." She reached into her pocket and pulled out a piece of paper and handed it to me.

I opened it up and looked at it. It said "god@heaven", then I looked back at her.

"It's God's email address," she said, a little nervously.

"For which server!? And how did you get it?" I was incredulous. God's email address and password should be strictly confidential. Did she work with plants at Adam's too? Was she a spy? Why was she giving this to me? Was this a confession? Maybe I should call the police.

She must have seen the concern on my face and shrank her posture a little. "I... don't know what you mean by server, and I got it from him."

"I mean is this God's email address for the Adams' god account?"

"N... no. It's for you... Jeff."

"It's for our local installation?" I gestured to our server room down the hall.

She looked really confused now. "No," she said, and took a deep breath. "It's for you. God told me to give you his email address."

Now I also felt confused. "For Omniscient?" I asked.

"God is omniscient, yes, of course," she said.

Then we stared at each other, both very perplexed for a while, not knowing what to say. I went next. "OK, let's start over. What is this, exactly?"

"It's God's email address, Jeff. You can send God an email if you want, and he will respond to you."

I didn't know how to respond, so I said, "God who?"

"Jeff, you know who God is. God. The creator of everything."

"You mean God God. Like actual God?"

"Yes!"

"And this is his email address?" I sounded out the last two words as if they were the strangest things in the world, even though I was an email specialist myself.

"Yes!"

"Ah, no it's not," I said.

"Yes, it is. You should try it."

"No, it's not. It's not a valid email address. It doesn't have a TLD, a Top Level Domain. It won't work."

"It will work, Jeff. You should try it. And I don't know what a Top Level Domain is."

"A TLD is like the dot com or dot net, or in our case, a dot software. This thing doesn't have one. The server is just 'heaven'. It might work on a local network where that name has a local DNS entry, but it won't work out there in the real Internet."

"I think you should try it," she persisted.

"I can tell you right now what will happen. First, the email client will not accept it as a valid email address. But even if it did, and tried to send it, the server would try to look up its MX record, which doesn't exist, because no Domain Registrar exists for it, because it doesn't have a TLD. That's what will happen."

"Please promise me you'll try it, Jeff."

How was I supposed to respond to that? I was too much of a nice guy to tell her she was crazy, and I didn't have the courage to tell her No to her face, so I just said, "OK", and walked away, adding a "Have a good day," just to be polite.

I put the paper in my pocket and didn't give it another thought.

5:01 PM

"So, are you going to ask out Victoria?" Scott asked me, looking both ways.

"Veronica," I corrected.

"Right. I forgot."

There was no traffic coming, so we walked. It might be nice to go on a date with her, but I don't know if I had it in me to ask, so I shrugged. "Are you?" I asked him back.

"Maybe I will. We could have something going. Sure, why not?"

The sun was out and it looked like the beginning of a warm evening. We walked toward the all-day parking lot, some distance from the Forks Marketplace and the Johnston Terminal, where Omniscient Technologies lived.

For some reason, the thought of Scott dating Veronica didn't sit well with me. "Maybe you shouldn't," I said.

He looked at me. "Hey Jeff, if you want her, you've got to make a move. If you make a move, I'll back off."

Great. Now I just got myself stuck. I just said Scott couldn't date her, and I don't know if I had the nerve to ask her out myself. Wonderful.

As we were walking out to my car where I had parked what seemed a very long time ago, I spied a very nice red sports car near us with a logo of a silver dancing horse in the black grill. "That's a nice car," I said.

"It sure is," Scott replied with a grin on his face. Then he pulled out his keys from his pocket, pressed a button, and the very nice red Ferrari roared to life.

My eyes went wide. "No way...", then, "No way... This is your car?!"

"Well, it's on loan from someone right now, but it might be, yes."

"And you're going to give me a ride?"

"Of course. Hop in." I hopped in, a large grin across my face too. The seat was extremely low. It felt like we were sitting on the ground, or almost lying down. The visibility wasn't that great, but the experience was amazing.

The engine revs danced in my ears as we pulled out of our spot, then forward. As we were almost out of the parking lot, another car pulled out in front of us. The driver naturally saw us as he was looking around. We saw him too.

It was Garth.

He stopped his car right where it was, blocking our way. He heaved himself out of his car and made his way toward us. He didn't look happy.

"What is this... vehicle... you are driving?" he demanded.

"It's a Ferrari 360 Modena. Do you like it?"

"And is it yours? Did you purchase it yourself?"

"I think my finances are my business, Garth."

"They most certainly are not. You will inform us right now how you came to be in possession of this vehicle."

"I don't think I need to. Now if you'll excuse me, I have to take Jeff for a little ride." Scott revved the engine to show his impatience.

Garth walked over to the back of the car and stood there, so Scott couldn't back up. His own car was in the way so Scott couldn't go forward either.

Scott opened his door, got out and stood up, facing his colleague. "What's your problem, Garth?" He seemed to have lost his smile.

"My problem, Mr. Stark, is that we just paid many thousands of dollars to an unknown hacker who appears to have inside knowledge into Omniscient, as you do."

"You're accusing me of being the hacker?"

"Or perhaps in partnership with him. I'm sure you cannot afford this sports car on your salary alone. And since I just added my two thousand five hundred dollars to the payout, that gives me the right to ask you where you got this car from. Now tell us."

Scott pointed at Garth. "I'm not the hacker," he said.

"Oh? You seemed very eager to pay him this afternoon. Do you have any bills coming due soon?"

"Garth!" Scott was mad. "I told you I'm not the hacker. I have nothing to do with these guys, and I'm bringing the car back today. It was just on loan. It's not mine." Then cooling down a bit, he added, "Now will you please get out of my way?"

Garth seemed to consider these words, then he said, "OK, I'll move out of your way," as he walked around my side on his way back to his own car. We watched him get in and drive away.

Scott got back in and drove around the parking lot once or twice, still steaming, the high-performance engine unable to lift his mood. Eventually he dropped me off at my car and I thanked him for the ride. He drove away, leaving me to process what had just happened.

Something was bothering me, but I couldn't put my finger on it.

In my own car, I turned onto Israel Asper Way, then onto Pioneer Avenue. As I waited at the lights to turn left onto Main Street, my brain relaxed just enough to let it bubble a thought to the surface. Scott had said, "these guys," referring to the hacker. Since when was the hacker plural? Was the hacker working with a group of people? Scott, what did you just let slip? Scott, what are you hiding?

CHAPTER 5

8:19 PM

After supper and some of my favourite shows, I decided to hit the shower.

I reached into my pockets to empty them onto the desk beside my bed. In my hands were my phone, my keys, and a small piece of paper that said, "god@heaven" on it. Then I remembered my conversation with the crazy plant lady. Too bad she was so good looking and seemed otherwise intelligent.

I took my shirt and pants off, then turned the shower on to let it warm up. I sighed. Since I did promise, I may as well type this non-email address into Omniscient to send a non-existent email, just to say I tried. What a waste of time.

> From: jeffd@omniscient.software
>
> To: god@heaven
>
> Subject: Hi
>
> Hi.

When I hit Send, it didn't complain about the bad syntax of the email address. It just appeared to send it, but I knew what would happen. In a few seconds, I would receive an email back from our server saying it was undeliverable. I made a mental note to file a bug to correctly detect proper email syntax before they get sent. I was surprised that wasn't working.

On my way back to the shower, I heard the email

notification sound coming from my phone on my nightstand. There it was, just like I called it. Silly plant lady. Silly me for even trying.

I scrubbed my body in the shower, trying to remove some stress of the day. It was the craziest day of my life.

I dried off and came back to bed, intending to browse some social media, not that I had a lot of friends, and not that any of my techy friends were on social media anyway.

I threw on pyjama pants and went to check that undeliverable email and found something else instead.

> From: god@heaven
>
> To: jeffd@omniscient.software
>
> Subject: Re: Hi
>
> Hi.

I was stunned. I didn't know what to think. My brain started analyzing what must have happened, and then found an answer. Somehow the email I had sent got mixed up on the server and my own email got returned back to me. That's it. Now I would really file a bug. This is a big problem. This could be evidence that Omniscient is already hacked. This could be the evidence we have been looking for. I sent another test email to confirm my theory.

> To: god@heaven
>
> From: jeffd@omniscient.software
>
> Subject: Another test
>
> Hello God, this is Jeff. Please respond.

I received this in reply:

> To: jeffd@omniscient.software
>
> From: god@heaven

GOD'S EMAIL ADDRESS

> Subject: Re: Another test
>
> Hi Jeff. This is God.

This shocked me so much, I instinctively put the phone down and moved away from it. This was not possible. What's going on here? I was almost about to consider that the impossible was happening when it occurred to me. Of course! Ronja was upgrading the server! She must be testing some AI plugin bot that responds using some artificial intelligence. Wow. Nice one. She almost had me there. I was about to be embarrassed tomorrow when she and everyone else would laugh at me. OK, I'll play along. I thought for a moment, then replied.

> From: jeffd@omniscient.software
>
> To: god@heaven
>
> Subject: Re: Another test
>
> So, if you're really God, what are the names of my parents?

I got this reply.

> To: jeffd@omniscient.software
>
> From: god@heaven
>
> Subject: Re: Another test
>
> Julie is your mom, and John is your dad. John is your earthly dad, and I AM your heavenly father.

Wow. That was a very good AI bot. Very good. My parents split years ago. Where could it be getting its information from? Wikipedia? Facebook? Personnel records? Some sort of genealogical database I don't know of? Maybe Ronja is replying manually in real-time, while she is sitting there. Nah, she's not the type. Someone else must be there with her, making this up. That must be it. I'll test that theory.

I was about to reply again when I had an even better idea. I went out to my laptop and searched for a company that could provide free email addresses. On the search results page, I clicked to go to the next page. Then the next page. Then the fourth page. On that page, I found a company I had never heard of that provided free email addresses online. I'm sure nobody else trying to trick me had heard of it either. I registered for an account and went to send an email online. I made sure the protocol was https, so nobody could listen in or interfere. I composed a new email.

> To: god@heaven
>
> Subject: Test
>
> Tell me something nobody else knows.

I waited on my screen for a reply. Nothing came. I was about to conclude it didn't work when I remembered I might need to hit refresh. I hit refresh. When I did, my reply was there.

> From: god@heaven
>
> Subject: Re: Test
>
> When you were young, you would sit in your sandbox and cry. Nobody saw you, but I did. I was there with you. I cried with you.

I moved my body away from the words on the screen, my heart beating loudly in my chest. My mind was trying and failing to comprehend what was going on. Something else in me, perhaps my heart, didn't even want to try. I stumbled away from my laptop, toward the door to my apartment. I put on a jacket and opened the door, expecting to go somewhere. Maybe to fill in gas in the car. That's it. I need to fill in gas.

Remembering my keys, I went back to my bedroom and spied the keys on my nightstand. I also saw my phone, which I tried not to look at. I left it there, grabbed my keys and left the building. I had to go somewhere, anywhere.

10:11 PM

I got into my car wearing nothing but pyjamas and a jacket. I was going to fill in gas in my car, because it needed gas. I looked at the gauge to confirm. Yes it did, it was less than half full. I needed gas. I needed to go get gas right away.

I drove out of my apartment's parking lot, down the back ally, and right onto Baylor Avenue, then left onto Killarney Avenue. There was a gas station right there. I used a self-serve station to fill in a few litres of gas. It didn't take long. Then I went inside to pay. I made sure my jacket was zipped up all the way to the top, since I wasn't wearing anything underneath.

After I paid, I got back in my car. What now? I started driving. I drove slowly down Killarney again, past my apartment building. My apartment was where those words were. That email stuff. The weird stuff. I couldn't understand it. I had no grid for it, either in my mind or in my heart. I didn't know what to do with it.

I considered talking with someone, but who? Nobody would believe me. And even if they did, I didn't want them to read those other words.

About the sandbox.

I tried not to think about that. I tried not to think about sitting in the sandbox as a boy. I thought about something else instead. When I was older, I worked odd jobs, and got student loans to go to University. Yes, it's better to think about that. I took classes in Programming, Data Structures, Analysis of

TIM KOOP

Algorithms, Nonimperative Programming Language Concepts. After that, just a few years ago, I managed to get work at Omniscient Technologies. I never moved; I still live here in this same apartment where I lived when attending University.

    Ah yes, my apartment, the place where someone claiming to be God wanted to talk with me. About memories that I had tried very hard to bury.

    What was I going to do? I looked at the time. It was getting late. Maybe I should just go home and go to bed. Yes, that is what I needed to do.

    I drove down the back alley, into our parking lot, and into my spot. I walked into the building, up the stairs, and into my small apartment. I took off my jacket, then crept over to my laptop and closed the lid. It would detect the lid closing and hibernate by itself.

    I went to my bedroom and saw my phone there. Maybe I should ask Ronja how the install was going or went. When I picked it up, I saw there was a message. I started to get nervous, but then saw that it was from Scott.

    It began like this:

> From: scotts@omniscient.software
>
> To: jeffd@omniscient.software
>
> Subject: Tonight
>
> Jeff, if you are receiving this message, it means I am dead.

11:05 PM

I read the whole thing immediately.

GOD'S EMAIL ADDRESS

From: scotts@omniscient.software

To: jeffd@omniscient.software

Subject: Tonight

Jeff, if you are receiving this message, it means I am dead.

And since I'm dead, I may as well tell you what's been happening.

I have been approached by a guy who represents an organization called The Information Underground. He goes by the name of Jade. He says there is a lot of money to be made in collecting and selling information. Corporations will pay a lot of money for competitors' emails. Famous people can be blackmailed if you have some incriminating or scandalous personal emails or pictures, and that sort of thing.

I made the mistake of going along with it for a while. I admit, the money was really tempting. The Ferrari you saw today was just a signing bonus. If I would have come on board with them, life would have been really good for me.

They wanted me to use my connections at Omniscient to harvest emails, of course. I don't know if I ever would have done it, but I went along with them too far.

This evening I'm going to meet with them one more time. I'm going to tell them I'm out. And I'll give the car back.

I don't know if they will let me out.

I have gotten the impression that they won't want me

to live knowing what I know already.

The meeting is scheduled for 6:00 PM tonight at the big statue of Louis Riel at the Legislative Building. I'm supposed to give them my final answer.

Jeff, I'm afraid that my answer won't make them happy. I'm going to say No.

So in case things go sideways, I'm scheduling this email to be sent at 11:00 PM this evening. If I come back successfully, in one piece, then I'm going to delete it and nobody will know what I've done. If you get it, that means I was unable to delete it before it got sent. I guess you'll have to drag the Assiniboine for my body. Ha ha.

Well, I've got to go.

I hope I'll see you tomorrow.

I read the email a second time, then a third, trying to comprehend it all. Then I quickly sent a reply.

From: jeffd@omniscient.software

To: scotts@omniscient.software

Subject: Re: Tonight

Scott, I just got this. Are you OK?

I got no reply, so I sent him a chat message that simply said, "Scott?". Then I called him on the phone. It rang once, twice, three times, four, five, then it went to voicemail. I said, "Scott, I just got your email. Call me", and hung up.

I looked at the time. 11:07. What should I do? Call the police? Ha! They would only laugh at me. Call Randal? Peter? Not at this hour. What else could I do? I had to do something. There was only one thing left. I had to drive to his place.

Tonight.

No. I already called him. First, I had to visit Louis Riel.

11:38 PM

I parked my Honda on the lot outside the Legislative Building, the place where laws were made and our lives were supposed to be made better. It was ironic that a good man lost his life here.

I sprinted down to the river, as if by my speed I could change the past. Halfway down to the Assiniboine stood a sixteen-foot high bronze statue of Louis Riel, a political leader who also led a rebellion and got himself hanged for it. Perhaps this was a fitting place for Scott to rebel against his own oppressors. It was hard to imagine Scott met with the same fate, but I had to believe it.

As I looked around, I didn't know what I was hoping to see, maybe my friend lying beat up and I could save him. But I saw nobody. I saw nothing except the tall lamps casting cold shadows on the ground. I walked around near the statue and heard nothing except for my footsteps and my own breathing. I looked out into the distance, and saw the river, black and silent. It didn't know what had just happened here. Or it didn't care.

I approached the bank and looked around for something. I didn't know what. Maybe signs of struggle, whatever that means, but I couldn't see a thing. It was just a riverfront. That was all. Empty and deserted. Full of nothing.

A light breeze picked up.

Suddenly I felt cold. Deep down inside. It was like the day I found out my dad had left us. It's the feeling you feel when the warmth of joy leaves you. You are alone.

Standing near the black river, with nobody else around, I was alone.

And cold.

Maybe Scott was right. Maybe I had no feelings. I should probably cry or something, but there was nothing there, just emptiness.

I checked my phone to make sure Scott hadn't replied to anything. He hadn't of course.

I made my way back to my car and started driving. I drove to Scott's house, went to the front door and rang the bell. Nothing. I rang it multiple times. I banged on the door. I shouted. I looked in all the windows. I sat down on the ground. It couldn't be true. It just couldn't be. Scott is going to come driving up to his house any minute now. But that's not going to happen.

I got back into my car and drove some more. I drove back home to Killarney Avenue and walked up the stairs, and into my bedroom. I was exhausted. I got ready for bed and lay there, completely spent.

With my eyes closed and my mind starting to relax, it occurred to me that finding the hacker, or hackers, suddenly became a lot more personal. To not get involved now would be a slap in the face to Scott. As scared as I was to get involved, it was unthinkable to do nothing about my friend, so I grabbed my phone and sent one last quick email.

>From: jeffd@omniscient.software
>
>To: peters@omniscient.software
>
>Subject: The Point Man
>
>OK, I'll do it. I'll be the point man.

GOD'S EMAIL ADDRESS

Wednesday, 8:20 AM

The next morning I slept through my alarm, but finally got up and made it in to work. The cheerful new receptionist smiled and said, "Good morning" to me. I tried to smile back at her, but the weight of yesterday still hung on me.

As I approached our room, I looked to see if Scott was there. He was not. "Has anyone seen Scott today?" I asked very weakly.

"Negative," said Garth.

"Nope", said Doug.

"I was beginning to wonder if we would see you today also," added Garth.

"I overslept," I said. I couldn't bring myself to say the words that needed to be said. But I could send an email. When I checked my email, there were a few waiting for me.

Ronja said the upgrade to Omniscient version 4.1 beta went well and to report any problems to her or submit a bug. I decided to not mention what happened to me yesterday evening with emailing that non-existent email address.

An email from my boss Randal said he got hit by a car while riding a bicycle yesterday. The only thing that got broken was his phone, but since he is still in pain, he might not be in this morning.

And there was an email from Peter Steele asking me to come see him as soon as I come in. I walked over to his office. He saw me through the glass wall and waved me inside.

"Come in Jeff. Have a seat."

I sat. Mr. Steele's office was as professional and tidy as Randal's was messy and cluttered. This was a real CEO.

He continued. "Right. First of all, I'm glad you've decided to be the point man. Very good. I want you to coordinate with the police and the media if necessary. Try to keep a good spin on things, you know. Also, go check out our latest installations.

Make sure nothing unfortunate happened there."

"Find out if the installer did something he shouldn't?" I asked.

"Yes, exactly. I don't want to raise too many eyebrows inside the company here, but these things must be looked into. You will do this."

"OK," I agreed.

"Also, I think you got the email that Randal had a small accident. This is too bad, but you won't be reporting to him while you're working on this. Report directly to me. Understood?"

"Yes."

"Good. Now, do you have any questions?"

I took a deep breath and let it out. "I... ah... Scott sent me an email... yesterday... he scheduled it to be sent."

"Yes?"

"In the email he said that he was... he had been talking with some people known as the Information Underground. They wanted him to work for them, but he refused, and in the email he said that he thought they might not let him live if he said no."

Peter frowned as he heard these words.

I continued. "He said he would delete the email as soon as he got back from the meeting. He said..." I took another faltering breath. "He said if I received the email from him, that means he..."

"He what?" Peter asked, deeply concerned.

"If I received the email, that means he was... dead." I said it.

"Oh my!" Peter put his hand up to his mouth and face. "Oh my. And have you seen or heard from him at all since then?"

I shook my head. "No. Nothing."

"Have you gone to the police?"

"No."

"Well, you have to go. Go right now. I will send a message to everyone telling them... " He paused. "I will tell everyone that Scott is missing and we think something may have happened to him, but we don't know what. Because we don't actually know what has happened to him, do we Jeff?"

I shrugged. "No, technically, I guess we don't."

"It's better that way. No need to alarm the troops if we don't have to."

"OK."

"Good. You go to the police, Jeff. Tell them everything. And keep looking for this hacker, or the Information Underground, or whatever they might be called."

"OK." I stood and left the room.

I didn't go back to my room. I went straight out the door and toward my car. I probably should have done this yesterday, but maybe I wasn't thinking straight then. The police officer that showed up yesterday is going to get a visit today.

8:32 AM

"Can you email that email to me?" he asked.

"Yes, I'll forward it to you," I replied. Joseph Wakefield, the police investigator, handed my phone back to me after he read Scott's email.

I forwarded it to him.

He reached back on his old, wooden swivel chair, into his filing cabinet, for a piece of paper. The chair squawked.

"What are you going to do?" I asked.

"I'm going to file a missing person's report for your friend Scott Stark," he replied.

"But... shouldn't you go after these guys?"

"What guys? The Information Underground?" he asked.

"Yes," I said, a little annoyed. "If they... did something to Scott, you need to go get them and bring them to justice."

Joseph leaned forward and the chair squawked again. "You tell me where they're hiding, I'll try to get a warrant and go pick them up," he said as he relaxed again. "Once I print out this email you're sending me, it will make good evidence to get an arrest warrant. But I can't make an arrest if I don't know who I'm arresting. And I can't bring someone in if I don't know where they are, can I?"

"I guess not."

"But tell me, Jeff. Do you have any other evidence of anything wrong anyone has done in this case?"

"Well... no."

Detective Wakefield leaned back in his chair, behind his desk, in his police department office that tried hard to not show its age. "If you want to help with this investigation, this is a step in the right direction. It's information. It's not hard evidence, It's not enough to convict anybody, but it's a step in the right direction. Now we know the name of the organization and an alias of one of the ring leaders. But we still need more information. We need to know who this Jade character is, and where to find him. We need evidence of what else they have done."

"What kind of evidence?" I asked.

"Accounting papers, photographs, video or voice recordings of a confession, or as close as we can get to one. Or someone in the know who is willing to testify."

I wilted. "How are we going to get that?" I asked.

"It's not easy," he said. "Especially since you don't know who these people are, or how to find them."

"So what can we do?"

"If I knew that, I would already be doing it."

"I just thought of something," I said.

"Yeah?"

"The hacker that we paid ten thousand dollars of Bitcoin to, he hasn't left a bug report yet, like he promised to do. Can you arrest him because of that?"

"If you have a written or verbal agreement with the guy, you can sue him for breach of contract."

I shook my head. "We don't have anything written. But we did talk on the phone."

"Did you record it?" he asked.

"No."

"You don't have much to go on. And you'll have a hard time tracking him down, too."

"Yeah, no kidding."

I sat there, dejected, not knowing what to do or even ask. "So what can I do?"

"If you want to do some digging, start at Adams. You guys installed your software there recently. Sniff around there and see if you can find anything unusual. Maybe not hard evidence, but a lead or information. Then let me know."

"OK, thank you." I stood. He didn't.

"Good luck," he said.

"Thanks," and I left.

CHAPTER 6

8:48 AM

I admit the thought of going to visit Adams to check things out scared me, but it had to be done. The question was, how was I going to do this? Call them on the phone? The thought terrified me, but at least I didn't know their number, so that made me feel better. Perhaps I could email them. That's a better idea. I drove back to the office to find their contact information.

As I walked into our room, I noticed Garth was not there. I was going to ask him for his contact at Adams, but maybe I'll email him instead. Doug wasn't there either. Nor was Scott, of course. As I sat down at my computer, I heard a voice behind me.

"Hey Jeff. Where have you been this morning?" It was Veronica.

I turned around. "At the police station."

She almost looked concerned, but then quickly regained her usual confidence. "Anything I need to know about?" she asked.

"I just talked to them about the hackers," I replied. "Hey, have you seen Garth today? I want to get his contact information for Adams."

"Yeah, I've seen him. He put up a new joke and really enjoyed laughing at it." She gestured to his little whiteboard by his desk, then read what it said. "A programmer's wife asked him to pick up milk from the store on his way home, and while he was there, get some eggs too. He never returned."

It took me half a second, but then I burst out laughing too. It kinda felt good. I hadn't laughed in a while.

"Not you too, Jeff!," Veronica complained, "or I'll never come visit you again."

"I'll explain it," I said while smiling. "In programming, there are a number of ways to control the flow of execution. One of them is a While loop. It repeats things until a condition is met."

"I don't get it," she said.

"OK, I'll show you." I turned to face my computer again, and typed in a few lines of code. "OK, come look at this." I pointed at my screen. She came over to me and leaned over my shoulder. Her long black hair touched my ear. I didn't mind.

```
function onHisWayHome() {
   atStore = true;
   pickUpMilk();

   while (atStore) {
      getEggs();
   }
}
```

I explained. "This function is called `onHisWayHome`. First, it sets a variable, then it calls a function to `pickUpMilk`. Then it enters the while loop. Everything in these squiggly braces gets executed as long as the variable in question, `atStore` is true.

"Yeah, so?" she asked.

"The point is that the variable `atStore` never changes, it never becomes false, so this poor programmer is going to `getEggs` until the end of time. The function will never return."

Veronica stood up and looked at me, in thought. "Obviously his wife didn't mean it that way."

"I know, but that's what makes it so funny."

She looked away, "I guess, if you're into that sort of thing."

Garth walked in and sat down in his chair, causing it to squeak and groan. "I hope you two don't mind if someone around here gets some actual work done."

Veronica plucked up her fighting spirit. "Of course not, Garth. Work away, and while you're at it, drink some Dr. Pepper. That way you'll never return to bother me." She walked off.

Garth turned to me. "I suspect you, Jeff, of talking to Veronica about my daily jokes," he said.

I quickly hid the window on my computer that contained the few lines of code I wrote. I shrugged. "If it comes up in conversation."

"Then how are we supposed to tell the mortals from the gods if you insist on blurring the lines?"

I shrugged again.

He turned back to his work.

I said, "Garth, can you send me your contact details for Adams Corporation?"

"Why would I do that?"

"Peter Steele wants me to go talk to them."

"For what purpose?"

"I'm supposed to investigate their email leak."

"To see if I messed up the install?"

I thought for a second. "I don't know, really. I'll look around for anything unusual."

"Fine. Their system administrator is a man named George Mannel. You'll want to talk with him. I'll send you his contact details. As for anything unusual in my install, you won't find anything. It was properly installed."

"OK, thanks."

GOD'S EMAIL ADDRESS

Soon my computer told me I received an email. It was George Mannel's contact details. This email is also accessible on my phone, since my computer and phone both run Omniscient. I thanked Garth, then sent an email to George asking if I can come over and investigate.

While I waited for George to get back to me, I checked to see if our hacker friend had left a bug report. He did not.

Then I went to see if Susan Harth was in, to ask her about getting reimbursed for the Bitcoin we bought yesterday. She was not in either. On my way back to my room I was notified of an email. It was my mom, asking if we could go for coffee at Moggle's in an hour. I replied and said yes. Then I received another one. It was George. He said to stop by any time.

I went straight to my car. This wasn't going to be fun, or easy, but it had to be done. I might even find something.

9:29 AM

"I'll tell you right now, you won't find anything wrong with my systems," said George, as he stuck out his hand for me to shake it.

I shook it. "Are you George Mannel?" I asked.

"Yes. And you're Jeff from Omniscient. Garth was in a few days ago and did the upgrade to version 4.0. I'll show you where he worked." He started walking away from the lobby where we met, presumably to their server room. I followed him. This George stood very straight and formal, like a military man. He seemed all business.

"Were there any hiccups during the upgrade?" I asked.

"None that I'm aware of. Your man said he had to install a library or two, because 4.0 now requires it."

"Yes." We walked down some stairs.

"Have there been any hiccups since the upgrade? Have users reported anything not working or unusual?" I asked.

"Nothing specific to version 4.0. You know users, they forget their passwords all the time, and don't know how to log in online, that sort of thing."

"Have you had any security breaches in the last while?" I asked.

George spun around and glared at me. "No. Absolutely none."

"That you know of?"

"I run a very tight ship, Jeff. Nobody has been able to break in on me yet."

"What about port scans?" We walked down a hallway.

"Ha!" he laughed. "People *try* to break in by scanning which ports are open on our server on a regular basis, but that doesn't mean that they can actually get in."

He unlocked the server room and we both entered. I was impressed by it. There were several racks of servers. In our office we only had one rack, and only a few servers on it. But I guess they had a bigger network--several networks actually. And every cable, of which there were hundreds, was plugged in neatly and positioned correctly, down to a fraction of an inch. And each network cable was colour coded.

"Wow!" I exclaimed. "Nice server room. You keep it very neat."

George lost some of his edge with that comment. He even smiled a little. "Thank you. Things can get out of hand quickly if you don't stay on top of it. That's why I always stay on top of things. Here, I'll show you what is what." He started pointing at different servers in his racks. "This is the firewall. We have two Internet providers coming in, and a microwave link to our other building. This is the firewall. Database server. This is the email server. Logging server. Those other racks are for internal stuff, like phones, domain controller, and Intranet."

"You have Omniscient on its own dedicated server?"
"Yes. It's much better for security that way."
"And its database is on a separate server?"
"Yes, but that database is also shared by other things."

I said, "So the email leak could be the result of either server being hacked?" It wasn't really a question, more of a statement, but it did not make George happy. He looked at me sternly. "Nothing got hacked."

"Then how do you explain the email leak?"

This made him think. He softened his features. "Well, it may have got hacked." He turned away from me.

"How often do you install security patches?" I asked.

He turned back. "We have scripts that automatically install security patches. Plus we monitor the lists that announce patches and new security versions every day. And some things that are most vulnerable, I compile myself by hand because the patches to the source code often come out before the precompiled executables."

"Wow," I said, with my mouth open. "You really do all that?"

"Of course. It's my job. Security is a major concern."

"It's hard to believe anyone could do anything malicious around here, with you here."

He turned away again, but I heard him say, "There are some bad people out there."

I was glad he had turned away from me, because I suddenly felt emotionally unstable. I felt my throat tighten and my breathing was difficult. He didn't have to tell me there were bad people out there. I knew it well.

Pulling myself together, I said, "Well, can I take a look at the Omniscient server? I want to see if all the software is right."

"Yes you can." On the desk in the room, he punched a button that connected the one keyboard, mouse, and screen to the correct server. A mostly black screen with a blinking cursor was shown. He logged in with a username and password, then he stood and motioned me into the chair. "We are not logged in as root, but if we need to be, I'll do it."

I sat down.

He sat down on a chair next to mine and watched me.

"OK, I'm going to download 4.0 and compare the files to the ones that are there now."

"Why?"

"To make sure that what's running is actually Omniscient 4.0, not a... customized version."

"You suspect Garth may have modified the code to give him access to something he shouldn't have access to?"

"I'm just making sure."

"You don't trust your own colleague?"

"In a minute we'll know."

I downloaded version 4.0 from our public repository, uncompressed the file, then ran a command to compare files recursively. I sat there, with my hands in my lap as the command ran. When it was done, it showed the two directories were identical.

"They are the same," George said.

"Yes."

"That means the upgrade was a perfect upgrade, and we can trust your colleague Garth."

"Yes."

I got up to leave and he escorted me out.

Back in the lobby, I asked him, "Oh, did you sit with Garth the whole time, like you sat with me?"

"Of course." Then he paused. "Come to think of it, I did leave him there for a minute while I... went to the washroom."

"And was he logged in as root?"

"Yes he was."

I looked at George while I wondered what, if anything, to

do about this. He stared back at me. He looked kind of nervous, and I didn't blame him. Then he said, "I'll go check it out and I'll let you know if I find anything." He turned and marched away.

I made my way back to the car and wondered if this little visit helped anything at all. Did Garth do a perfect job, or was there room for doubt?

10:09 AM

I drove away from Adams, and couldn't help but be impressed with George's system administration abilities. He sure seemed to know what he was doing, yet at the same time I smelled something fishy, but I couldn't say what it was.

I looked at the time on my car's dash. It was time to go for coffee with my mom, so I turned left and headed south onto Main Street.

In a few blocks, I turned right onto Ste. Mary Avenue. When I did that, a motorcycle behind me passed me and positioned himself right in front of me. I could see the rider wearing the typical leather jacket and pants. His full-face helmet was also black, so I couldn't see his face at all. Every minute or so he would look backwards. He was driving somewhat slowly, so I was forced to stay behind him.

In four blocks I turned left onto Garry Street, where the restaurant is. I could see the sign for the cafe up ahead, but the motorcycle in front of me had come to a complete stop.

Then a van pulled up beside me, to my right, and stopped. I couldn't go forward and I couldn't go right. To my left was a parked car. And behind me was another car, just sitting there.

I was beginning to think I was in a bad position. I wondered if I should be nervous about this. These cars around me weren't driving. They were just sitting around me, as if to box me in.

I tried to convince myself that we were just stuck in traffic, but my mind was unable to convince my heart. I checked to make sure my doors were all locked, and my windows were all up. They all were, except the passenger door was unlocked. Since I didn't have automatic locks, I quickly reached over to lock that door. I wasn't quick enough, because before I got to it, the sliding door on the van opened up, and a man stepped out, opened my passenger door, and sat in my car.

He was wearing all black, including a black balaclava on his head. I couldn't tell anything about him except that he appeared well muscled, and in his hand he carried a gun.

I panicked. And when I panic, I do nothing. I sat there, frozen in fear, sweating from every part of me, breathing erratically and staring wide-eyed at this unknown person who just violated my car with his presence and probably wouldn't hesitate to do something to me too.

Some words may have tumbled out of my mouth like, "Who are you?" or "What do you want?". I don't remember.

He pointed the gun at my head, so I was looking down the barrel. He spoke in a deep gravelly voice. "Jeff Davis. I have a message for you."

I don't think I replied.

He continued. "You are investigating the Information Underground. Stop it, if you know what's good for you. If you continue..." He pulled back the trigger and I heard a click sound.

There was no boom, no explosion, just a small click. The gun wasn't loaded. He sneered at my terror, then got out and back into the van.

Then the motorcycle, the van, and the car behind me, fled the scene, leaving me visibly shaking in my own sweat. I reached over and smashed down the passenger's door lock.

Hard.

By then some other traffic appeared behind me, so I slowly kept driving and parked in a vacant parking spot beside the road. Moggle's, the cafe where I was supposed to meet my mom, was right there. All I had to do was get out and go inside to meet her.

Before I left the car for the danger of the street, I called my mom on my phone and she answered.

"Hi Jeff," she said. "I'm here already, waiting for you."

"Hi Mom. Are you inside?"

"Yes dear. Where are you?"

"I'm outside in my car."

"Well, come in then. What are you waiting for?"

I looked around in all directions. There was nobody sinister around. I looked at the main entrance to Moggle's, then to the far corner of the building. Someone might be waiting behind that corner to get me. It's a risk I would have to take.

"Nothing. I'll be right in. Bye."

"Bye." I hung up.

Plucking up my courage, I unlocked the door, got out, locked it again, closed it, and looked around. All I could see was the front of the cafe, Gary Street, and a parking lot across the road. There were various cars, but nothing looked dangerous.

I walked toward the door, looking around me in all directions.

When I got to the door, I took a deep breath trying to steady my nerves. It didn't work. I went in anyway.

TIM KOOP

10:18 AM

"Jeff, you look pale. Are you all right?"

"Yeah, I'm OK."

"You're not sick, are you?"

"No, I'm not sick. Well, come to think of it, I don't feel that great. Something happened just now, outside, on the way here."

"What?"

I took a breath. "My car was… surrounded by some other vehicles. I was boxed in. Someone sat down in my car, pointed a gun in my face, and told me to stop investigating them." I sat back and looked around the restaurant, trying to get used to the fact that this just happened.

"My goodness! Jeff, are you OK? They didn't hurt you, did they?"

"No. No, not physically. But I'm… feeling… shaken."

"Well, sit right here, and let your mom take care of you." She motioned for a waitress to come over. "I would like a hot chocolate for my son here." The waitress agreed, smiled, and walked away.

"You ordered me a hot chocolate, Mom?" I said. "I'm a grown man. I drink coffee."

She looked me straight in the eyes. "I'm your mother, and inside of you is a little boy, just like inside every man. And I know that this little boy feels better drinking some hot chocolate. I would add some marshmallows if I could."

I relaxed a little. "Thanks mom."

"So tell me about this investigating you are doing. I thought you were a computer programmer."

"Yes, I still am. But there have been issues…" My hot chocolate arrived. "Hackers. Data breaches."

"You lost information?"

"No, Adams Corporation. They use Omniscient."

"Your software got broken into?" She asked.

"It seems like it. But we have no idea where or how to fix it."

"So what are you going to do?"

Before I could consider the fact that someone had just entered my car and threatened my life, a heat rose up at the back of my neck. And I felt something in my chest too. It turned out the Information Underground's threatening actions on me had the opposite effect of what they intended. Instead of scaring me into inaction, it made me angry.

With all the seriousness of a heart attack, I answered. "I'm going to stop them," I said.

"Well, you be careful, Jeff. These seem like bad people you are dealing with. I don't want you to get hurt. A mother always wants to protect her children."

Just as suddenly as the anger appeared, it was gone and fear took its place. "Yeah, I don't want to get hurt either."

"You should talk to the police."

"I have."

"And?"

"And they need hard evidence. I don't have hard evidence of anything."

"People just attacked you in your car. That's not evidence?"

"No. I didn't record it on video or anything like that." My mind slipped into thought. I sipped my hot chocolate. Mom sipped her latte.

Mom shuffled in her seat and got comfortable. Looking around she said, "The world has too many bad people in it."

"Yeah", I agreed.

"Your father was one of them."

I didn't answer. I didn't like to think about it. I tried not to.

"There is a lot of hurt and pain out there in the world, and in your life too."

"Do we have to talk about this?"

"No, we don't. Not right now. But you need to, Jeff. You need to talk to yourself about hurt and pain."

"OK, fine." Then changing the subject, I asked her. "And how are you doing, Mom?"

"Oh, I'm doing well. I go for walks. I'm still working at the library. It pays the bills. And there are good people there to work with. Good company."

"Good people who are single men, you mean?" I had seen my mom live a single life for a long time, and I wanted to see her happy, so I didn't mind asking.

She smiled and shrugged. "Aaa... I don't know... maybe. Maybe not. But what about you, Jeff? Any good women in your life?"

I smiled too. "Maybe. Maybe not."

We both laughed. "Well if something is going the right direction, bring her to see me. I want to meet this woman you have your eye on."

"OK, if something goes the right direction."

"Good. And what about friends? Do you have friends? People you work with? Do you get together with others? You need to get out, Jeff. You need to have friends. You shouldn't just sit at home every evening by yourself."

"I don't mind being by myself."

"You might not like being around other people, but you should. It's good for you. Now, tell me about your friends. Start with your best friend. What was his name? Rick?"

"Do you mean Scott?"

"Yes. Scott. How is he?"

I sat there, not saying anything, trying to keep the emotions inside from coming out. I shoved them all down, and sat on the lid. I looked away to distract myself.

"Is something wrong with Scott?" Mom was concerned.

My chin quivered.

"Honey, tell me what it is. Is he sick? What happened to him? Tell your mother." She got up and put her arm around me.

I stepped out of the way of the feelings inside of me. They made their way up to my eyes and spilled over. I scrunched up my face. I rested my head on my hands, elbows on the table, as my mom lovingly comforted her son. My throat got tight and my stomach muscles contracted.

"There, there, Jeff. It's OK. Have a good cry. Let it out." She kept her arms around me for a while, until I calmed down. Then she sat down again opposite me. "Do you want to talk about it? You should talk about it, Jeff. Tell me about Scott."

I wiped my cheeks with the back of my hand. "Yesterday evening, Scott sent me an email saying that if I got the email he was probably dead." My mom gasped. "He set it to send automatically, and he was going to delete it if he got back from a meeting. I haven't heard from him since.

"Oh my. Have you talked with the police?"

"Yes. They need hard evidence. But they filed a missing person's report."

"Do you know who Scott met with?"

"They call themselves the Information Underground. The same people who met me just now."

"Jeff, are you sure you should be dealing with these people? I mean..."

I interrupted her. "I have to, Mom. I have to. Yes, they are dangerous, but that is exactly the reason why I have to deal with them. Somebody has to stop them. And if nobody else will, then I will."

My mom considered my words for a while. "You were always a bit that way, Jeff. You always wanted the good guys to win and the bad guys to lose. Well I hope you win, Jeff." She checked her watch. "I have to go now, but I'm still your mother, and I'm still telling you to be careful. So be careful,

OK?"

I smiled. "I will, Mom."

She got up and left. I stayed. I wanted more answers to the problem of evil we had been talking about. Maybe God had an answer for me.

10:46 AM

I took out my phone and sent an email.

> From: jeffd@omniscient.software
>
> To: god@heaven
>
> Subject: The problem of evil
>
> God, I have noticed that there are lots of bad people in the world, and I don't like it. If you really are God, why don't you do something about this?

I tapped Send, and pretty soon I got this reply:

> From: god@heaven
>
> To: jeffd@omniscient.software
>
> Subject: Re: The Problem of evil
>
> Hello Jeff. It's good to talk to you again. I always enjoy talking with you, my son. You can always come to me with anything on your heart or mind.
>
> I love you, Jeff. Very much. I don't want bad things to happen to you, or to anyone else. I don't like evil and I want it to stop.
>
> I am doing something right now. I am preparing for myself someone who will stand up to evil, someone who will fight against the bad, and fight for justice.

GOD'S EMAIL ADDRESS

I thought to myself. There wasn't an election coming up, so maybe he was referring to a new police chief or something. I replied.

> From: jeffd@omniscient.software
>
> To: god@heaven
>
> Subject: Re: The Problem of evil
>
> Good, because bad things have happened, and are happening. My life was just threatened. Someone took Scott's life. And I don't want that to happen to my mom or Vanessa or anyone else. You need to do something, and fast. Who is this person? Maybe I should ask him to help us.

God replied.

> From: god@heaven
>
> To: jeff@omniscient.software
>
> subject: Re: The Problem of evil
>
> This person is you, Jeff Davis. I am calling you to be my hands and feet on the earth. Go out and accomplish the change that I am calling you to.

I put my phone down. I sat at the table, looking out the window. My heart had experienced a lot of emotions recently, fear, panic, sadness, but now I had no words to describe what I was feeling. God was calling me to something? What?! I had no grid for this in my mind. Yesterday I may have told you I believed God existed, but now I'm talking with him? And he's telling me I'm supposed to be this justice person? It made no sense in my head at all. But somehow, my heart felt... peace. My heart felt full, as if I had received something I had been waiting for my whole life. Somewhere inside of me I felt like someone had placed me, as a round peg, into a round hole. I

TIM KOOP

had never been here before, and it made no sense whatsoever, but oh it felt good.

CHAPTER 7

11:01 AM

I left the cafe and looked both ways. I also looked in front of me, and every other direction I could think of. I saw nothing suspicious. I made my way to my car, and looked into the back seat. There was nothing there. Good. I got in and locked the door, and all the other doors too.

I sat there, thinking what to do. Then I remembered what the police investigator said. I need hard evidence. It was too late to get evidence of my visit by the Underground a little while ago, but maybe I could get some for next time.

I pulled out my phone and did a search. I soon found what I needed and followed my GPS to 1053 Ste Mary's Road.

The door to the business had metal bars welded onto it. I noticed the display windows did too. I pulled open the door and looked around inside. The showroom had a lot of home entertainment equipment, car stereos, remote starters, and that sort of thing. Soon a woman came to ask me if she could help me. She looked too old to be a minimum wage young person, and she carried herself with the slow confidence of someone who has known what she was doing for a long time. She also lacked the spark or excitement that this new, fancy technology could provide. I guessed she was the proprietor trying to earn a living.

She asked what I was looking for, and I told her. I asked if they could provide it, and she said yes. I asked if they could install it right now. Thankfully she said yes to that too. I gave her the key to my car, and she went to the back with it. Presumably, someone would come, take the car behind the building and begin the install soon. In the meantime, I had nothing to do.

I found a small waiting room with some chairs and sat down and rested my head against the wall with my eyes closed.

I thought about the task in front of me. I needed to get hard evidence on the Information Underground. As I sat there, several ideas came to my mind on how to do this, but none of them were particularly good ideas. If I could get their remote IP address, the police could trace it back to a physical location. Then I thought about how to get their IP address, and logging, and the god account, and system administrators.

Then I gave up and opened my eyes. When I did, I spotted something across the street that got my attention. It was a convenience store that was advertising something interesting, lottery tickets.

And in my pocket I had access to someone claiming to be an all-knowing God.

It was time to test things out.

11:16 AM

I stood outside the convenience store, holding my phone. Instead of email, I decided to try some real-time chat. While customers came and went in and out, I stood on the sidewalk and fired up the Omniscient app. Soon I was chatting with god@heaven.

> Jeff: Hi God.
> God: Hi Jeff.
> Jeff: I'm at a place that sells lottery tickets.
> God: Yes you are.

GOD'S EMAIL ADDRESS

> Jeff: Can you please tell me the numbers on the ticket that will win?
> God: What for?
> Jeff: I want to win lots of money of course.
> God: Why do you want more money? I'm already taking care of you.

This idea got me thinking. God was taking care of me? Come to think of it, my sister and I grew up with a single mom. Then I got a university education, and now I'm a computer programmer making a lot more money than we ever had growing up. Maybe God was taking care of me. Maybe.

> Jeff: I would share lots with my mom.
> God: Let me take care of your mom, Jeff. Trust me with her.

This also got me thinking. Since Dad left, I was the man of the house. Had I been trying to take care of my mom myself? Maybe. But wasn't that a good thing? Everybody needs to love their mom. And now I'm supposed to give that up to God? This didn't make any sense.

> Jeff: So are you going to tell me some numbers or not?
> God: You are looking for security in lots of money. Look for security in me, Jeff. I am your security.
> Jeff: It's not just the security, it's also the happiness.
> God: Do I really need to tell you that money doesn't buy happiness?
> Jeff: I've heard that saying before, but I would like to try it out myself.
> God: You can trust me. Don't look to money to bring you joy. Look to me. All good things come from me.

I was about to give up, when I thought of one more strategy.

> Jeff: If you give me the numbers, I'll give half my winnings to poor people and charities.
> God: Would you really?

Hmmm... actually that was a good question. That might be a lot of money. I replied according to what I thought he wanted me to say, and since it was just a chat, I didn't have to try to keep a straight face.

> Jeff: Of course.
> God: I'm not calling you to support my work financially right now, I'm calling you to bring about justice with your actions. Focus on that and don't get distracted.

I shut off my phone and put it in my pocket. He may have won this round, but I was going to come back to this at some point.

I went inside to buy a coffee, then I walked up and down the street until I thought my car might be done. Soon it was time to pick it up and see what they had done to it.

11:42 AM

When I got back to the place, I went to the counter and talked to the woman.

"Is my car ready?" I asked.

"I'll check", she mumbled and disappeared into the back of the shop. Soon she returned. "It's all done," she said and told me the price. I handed over my credit card and she processed the transaction. Then she said, "Follow me, please", and led me behind the counter, to the back where they worked on the cars.

The floor was bare concrete, and the cabinets on the walls

didn't have doors on them. There were lots of tools and equipment, probably expensive equipment, laying around. There was room for two cars in this place, and both spots were full. My car was parked in front of us, but I didn't notice anything different with it. Once inside, however, I saw what I came here for.

I sat down in the driver's seat and the woman sat in the passenger seat.

"Your forward-facing dash cam is right here, of course," she said, pointing to a device on the dash. I saw the wire tucked neatly away behind it. "The rear one is at the back of course." I turned around and saw a tiny camera tucked away where it wasn't very distracting. "And your side mounting camera is right here," she pointed behind the rearview mirror. "It faces to the right, so you can see your passenger and everything outside the vehicle on that side."

Then she showed me how to transfer the video taken using a memory card or a cord.

As we went back inside to pay, she said, "People usually install these things after something bad happens to them. Are you one of these people? Or are you just expecting something bad to happen?"

I noticed she only asked this question after it was too late to change my mind.

"Already happened," I said.

She told me the price. "Well, if it happens again, you'll get a good clear shot of it. It must have been bad for you to install three cameras. Most people only get one."

"Most people don't have any," I said.

"Well, that's why we're here," then added without excitement, "Tell all your friends."

"Thanks." She got out and opened the big door. I backed out.

Just outside the building my phone rang. I looked at the

number. I didn't recognize it, so I didn't answer. I don't like talking on the phone.

But I noticed I had an email. It was from Randal.

> From: randalh@omniscient.software
>
> To: jeffd@omniscient.software
>
> Subject: Samuel Smith from Adams
>
> Jeff, Samuel Smith from Adams contacted us again. He is asking for our help this time, and I think he's serious. I gave him your number, since Peter says you are the contact person. He said he was going to call you.

"Great!" I said out loud. I had just missed his call. Now what? Wait for him to call back? I'd be a nervous wreck waiting for my phone to ring at any time. At least that's better than me calling him back. The very thought of calling up the VP of Technology at Adams Corporation terrified me.

I thought of Scott. I couldn't let his death go to waste. I had to find these guys, and if I went to help out Adams, I'd be more likely to find them.

I thought of the man with the gun in my car. It would be very tempting to run away and do nothing; I didn't have a death wish. But at the same time, those guys needed to be dealt with.

I thought of the email from God. He said he was calling me to fight for justice. For some strange reason I couldn't explain, that thought gave me strength deep down inside. I almost imagined I could do it.

I went to my call history, found the number, and considered pressing the Call button. Am I really going to do this? I might not. But would someone who was fighting for justice do this? Yes they would.

I took a deep breath and pressed it.

GOD'S EMAIL ADDRESS

12:01 PM

"Hi, this is Jeff Davis from Omniscient Technologies. Umm... I think Samuel Smith wanted to talk to me?" My heart was pounding, but I managed to distill my intentions into words, more or less.

"One moment please," the lady responded.

In a minute, a man says, "Sam Smith."

I respond. "Ah... um.. Mr. Smith. This is Jeff Davis from Omniscient Tech..."

"Jeff! Thanks for returning my call. I have a problem, and I would like you to help me solve it."

"What is it?"

"I don't want to discuss it on the phone." Good. That makes two of us. "Can you come see me?"

"Sure."

"Great. When?"

"Umm... right now? Ten or twenty minutes?"

"Sounds good. I'll see you soon, Jeff. Thanks."

"You're welcome."

"Bye"

"Bye"

For the second time that day I drove out to Adams.

And for the second time that day, I inquired at the information desk on the main floor about meeting someone. This time, however, I went up instead of down, because the receptionist directed me to the fifteenth floor. I rode the elevator, and on that floor I looked around. Everything from the reception desk to the art hanging on the walls to the carpet looked fancy, expensive, and intimidating. I was definitely out of my element.

But I plucked up my courage and talked with the receptionist behind the gold trimmed desk. She asked me to have a seat and made a phone call. Soon I saw the man who had visited our humble office on the third and top floor of the Johnston Terminal at the Forks. Now we were in his territory.

He smiled and shook my hand. After some polite greetings, he led me to his office. I took note of the "Vice President of Technology" on his door. His office was twice the size of Peter Steele's, and the view of the city was amazing. I tried not to stare.

We sat, and he swivelled one of his computer screens for me to see.

He said, "This is a diagram of what our new phone will look like, the A9, which is due to be announced in two months and come out in six months."

I looked at the diagram, then back at him.

"And this," he continued, showing me a different picture, "is the recently announced Magnus Metro 1"

I knew that Adams made phones, and I knew that Magnus also made phones. Magnus was a smaller company with a cheaper product, but still popular enough that I knew of them.

"They look the same," I said.

"Down to the tenth of a millimetre," Sam said. He leaned back in his chair with hands behind his head, staring at me.

"Coincidence?" I offered.

"Everything is the same. The screen, bevel, size and position of the camera lens. All the buttons. Everything. It is a complete rip off of our A9. Which we spent a lot of money designing, by the way."

I got the sense that he was waiting for me to catch on to something. "How did they get it?" I asked.

"Yes. How did they get it?" he repeated. "You tell me how they got it." He continued to look at me.

I squirmed a little. "Maybe they have a spy here."

"Could be. Could be. Maybe Magnus has an agent planted in our ranks. Or maybe someone here got paid a lot of money to betray their own company. Or maybe every last person here is innocent."

"Maybe your email server got hacked," I suggested. "It happens."

"Yes. Maybe it did. Or maybe your installer did something nefarious. Or maybe our own system administrator has done something wrong."

"So, what do you want me to do?" I asked.

He stood up and studied the cityscape, his hands behind his back. "The truth of the matter is that I don't know what the problem is. There most certainly is a problem, but I don't know what it is. That's why you are here." He turned to face me. "I want you to find it."

I was taken aback. "Don't you have your own people?" I asked.

He turned back to the window. "They might be compromised," he said. That didn't sound good.

"Or incompetent," he added. That didn't sound good either.

"There are lots of security experts out there. Why did you pick me?" I asked.

"Because you know Omniscient. If there is a bug in it, you can fix it. And..."

I waited for the And.

"And you said something at our meeting yesterday at your place. You said, 'If you know someone is spying on you, you shouldn't say they aren't. And if you got hacked, you shouldn't say you didn't get hacked.' You said something like that. At the time I dismissed your idea as bad PR. Well, it is bad PR. Terrible. But it is also something good."

"What?" I asked.

He turned to face me, and sat down on his chair again.

"Honest. You seem like an honest person, Jeff. Too honest in fact. I wouldn't want you anywhere near our PR department, or advertising. Or even the law department. But you are exactly the kind of person I need right now in IT. I need someone I can trust. Will you help me?"

"What do you want me to do?" I asked.

"I want to hire you. We can go through your company, that's fine. I want you to closely examine our email servers. I will give you full access to everything. If you can't find any problems, then add extra security. Log everything. Every transaction. Every email. Every connection, where it came from and where it's going. If anyone breathes on the email server, I want to know what their breath smelled like. What do you say? Will you do it, Jeff?"

I thought about it. If the Information Underground had stolen information from Adams and sold it to Magnus, then they must have got in somehow. And if they got in once, they will probably do it again. And the next time they do it, they must be caught. And if Adams can't catch them, then I will.

I said, "OK".

12:29 PM

We rode the elevator together down thirteen floors and found George in the server room, the same place I had been a few hours ago.

"George, this is Jeff Davis." Sam introduced me.

George looked at me and didn't look pleased. "I've met him before."

Sam continued. "I have hired him to do some work with our servers. Please give him everything he asks for."

"Everything?" George asked.

Sam considered, but only briefly. "Yes, everything. No matter the effort or cost."

"Really?" George asked again.

"Yes. It is important. Will you do this?" Sam easily asserted his superior rank.

"If you say so, I'll do it."

"Thanks George." As Sam left the room, he said to me, "I've given you a blank slate. Take advantage of it."

I turned to George, and he said to me, "So what is this all about?"

"Sam has hired me to add some logging to the email server."

"I am the best system administrator in the city. I can do it myself. I don't need to hire anyone."

"Well, Sam asked me to do it, and I already agreed."

"I'll tell you what, Jeff. I will add some logging, and I'll let you know what I'm doing and when it's done."

I didn't ask to step into this conflict. It wasn't my idea. I was happy to let George here do his system administrator thing. But now I agreed to this job and I'm here, on his turf, telling him what to do. This confrontation put knots in my stomach.

"Sam asked me to do it," I said.

"Fine, we'll do it together."

I took a deep breath. "I would like to do it myself."

George glared at me, then finally said, "No."

I had no reply.

George looked past me, at the door, to see or at least consider if he could catch up to Sam to convince him otherwise. He went for it. He rushed past me, muttering something about not touching anything.

I stood there alone.

In a few minutes he was back, and not happy.

"Very well. Do what you must. But I will stay right here."

"I need the root passwords for the Omniscient server, and the database server."

George stepped back as if I had just struck him a blow, but then silently recovered. He found a sticky note and wrote the passwords down. Handing the note to me, he said, "I'm going to change them as soon as you leave the room."

"That should be fine," I said. "I will also need command-line access to them."

He showed me to the chair, and showed me how to switch the KVM (Keyboard, Video, Mouse) to the Omniscient server or the database server. Then he found a chair and sat down on the far side of the room and watched me like a mother eagle watching a stranger in her nest. One wrong move and he would strike.

I tried not to notice him, but got to work. After a few minutes, he asked, "Will you be needing another server to log to?"

"No, I'm logging everything to the cloud."

At this, George got off his chair and threw up his hands, as if I had just posted directions to Facebook on how to gain illegal access to his network. But to his credit he didn't actually say anything.

It took me over an hour and a half. Every once in a while, when I didn't know exactly how to do something, I looked it up online. I used my phone because I didn't dare ask the eagle for a graphical web browser.

At last I stood up and said, "I think I'm done."

George stood up too. "Good," he said. "Will you be needing anything else?"

"I don't think so, at least not for now."

"And would you like to tell me what you did, or will I have to examine the systems myself after you leave?"

"I'm just logging everything."

"Everything?"

"Yes, as much as I can."

"And what exactly is everything?"

"Connections to Omniscient's website front end. POP and SMTP connections. All database queries."

"Including the god account?"

I looked at him incredulously. "Especially the god account." Then it occurred to me to ask him. "Do you actually use the god account?"

"Yes," he said. "Sometimes someone expects an urgent email that gets flagged as spam on the server. The user never gets it, so I have to look it up for them. And other things like that."

I nodded. "OK." Then I said, "Thanks for everything, George. Hopefully we will catch these guys soon, so we can stop logging everything."

At the mention of the bad guys, George looked distraught, and I don't blame him. "Yes, catch the bad guys." he said.

On my way out, I said, "Have a good day," because I'm always polite.

I looked at the time. Wow. No wonder I felt so hungry.

1:59 PM

I sat in my car in the visitor section of the large Adams parking lot and checked email. There was one from Veronica. She sent me a selfie of her holding her stomach, looking pained, but in a playful way.

> From: veronicas@omniscient.software
>
> To: jeffd@omniscient.software
>
> Subject: Hungry
>
> Jeff, I'm hungry. Let's go for lunch. :) :)

I decided to reply by chat.

> Jeff: I only got your email now, but I'm still available.
> Veronica: Great. How about the Sri Lankan place again?
> Jeff: OK
> Veronica: 5 minutes?
> Jeff: Make it 10
> Veronica: c u there
> Jeff: OK. Bye.

I didn't have a long history of chatting, so I might not have followed the correct social protocol. But at least it was better than talking on the phone.

I sent one more email before heading off.

> From: jeffd@omniscient.software
>
> To: god@heaven
>
> Subject: picture
>
> Why don't you send me a picture of yourself?

To my surprise, as soon as I hit Send, I received an immediate reply. I took a look at it.

> From: god@heaven
>
> To: jeffd@omniscient.software
>
> Subject: Re: picture
>
> I will show you a picture of me and you when you were young.

There was no attachment. No picture. I supposed it was still coming. I put my phone away and drove off to lunch.

I may have only been half serious about that picture from God. Come to think of it, I'm not sure I wanted to see a picture of me when I was young. I tried hard to forget about my childhood. Now God wants to bring it up? I didn't know if I wanted to go there. But part of me was curious.

CHAPTER 8

2:09 PM

Ten minutes later I pushed open the door into the Forks Market and Veronica was standing right there.

"Jeff! Finally! I'm starving," she said.

"I'm here."

On the way to Taste of Sri Lanka, she said, "You know, instead of Sri Lanka, since we're so hungry, why don't we just grab something from this Fish'n Chips place? It's right here and has almost no line."

"OK", I agreed.

We lined up behind one short old lady in a tall hat, and pretty soon we were ordering ourselves. She turned around to me. "How's the poutine here?" she asked.

"Good, I think, if you're into that sort of thing," I responded.

"Sure I am," she said, and ordered poutine.

I ordered my fries plain. I suppose she was more adventurous than I was. Not a bad quality actually. I could admire a woman who has the courage to order fries with gravy and cheese curds.

Soon we had our food and sat down at a small table built for two. If I didn't know better, it might have resembled a date.

"I heard about Scott," Veronica said between bites. "That's too bad. I hope he's OK."

"Yeah," I agreed. Then, "How's the poutine?", wanting to change the subject.

"Good. The fries are limp though."
"Maybe they're trying to be authentic British chips."
"Have you ever been to England, Jeff?" Veronica asked.
"Nope," I reply while munching a fry.
"Have you ever been anywhere?"
"Not really."
"Oh, I wish I could travel the world. England, France, Spain. Anywhere. I would love to get away from this place."
"Really? Why?"
"Why? Why?! Because getting away is wonderful. If you're on the other side of the earth, you leave all your cares and worries behind. You can kiss all your garbage goodbye. It's like starting fresh."
"Yeah," I agree. "Might be nice."
"Maybe you had it easy, Mr. University Diploma man, but not me."

I started into my fish.

"My mom never got married," Veronica continued. "She had an affair with some guy. There's where I come from. And then another with another, so I have a baby sister. My 'father' growing up was the man of the week."
"My dad left us when I was fifteen."
"At least you knew him."
"Yeah." I didn't mention that he wasn't necessarily a nice guy. And he didn't always treat us well.
"Were you sad when he left?", she asked.
"Yeah," I said. But I probably shouldn't have been. We were probably better off without him.
"Life is messed up." Veronica sucked on her drink straw. "Who needs dads anyway? All you need them for is to give you money when you're young. Then you get a job and you're on your own, you're fine."

I thought about my email conversations with God who claimed to be my father. Somehow they touched me in a way that my father never did. I think I respectfully disagreed with Veronica. I think there is more to a father than bringing the money. I think a father can impact you more deeply, somewhere deep inside. At least he should, even if mine never did.

"Maybe," I said.

"Hey, where have you been all day, Jeff? I haven't seen you around."

I wiped my hands and grabbed my drink. "I went to the police station, and visited Adams Corporation, twice, and some people surrounded me and threatened my life."

Veronica looked shocked. "What?! Who? Why?"

"It was the Information Underground. They surrounded my car, got in, and someone in a mask threatened me with a gun. He said I should stop investigating them."

"Jeff, you should stop," she urged.

I didn't answer. I shrugged.

"Jeff, if people are going to threaten your life, you need to seriously consider dropping what you're doing."

I shrugged again.

"I mean it. Do you really want to risk your life for this? Who cares? Let the bad guys be bad guys. You're not a cop, are you?"

"No."

"Then let the police do their job, and you just do your job. Keep on being a developer, and let someone else take care of it."

"Peter asked me to."

"Tell him No! Tell him, *Hey, thanks for thinking of me, and I agree that someone should probably look into this, but it won't be me, because I don't want to die.* That's a very good excuse if you ask me."

"Someone has to."

"It doesn't have to be you." She relaxed.

I felt like saying, *Yes it does*, but I had already made my point, so I said nothing.

"Well, I hope you do the right thing," she said as she stood up. "I have to be getting back to work. Will I see you later?"

"I think so."

"Great. See you later, Jeff." She touched me on the shoulder, then scampered away.

I watched her go, then checked my phone. I wanted to see if there was a picture of me in my inbox.

2:39 PM

I checked my phone for that email from God. Sure enough, there it was, and it had an attachment.

> To: jeffd@omniscient.software
>
> From: god@heaven
>
> Subject: Re: picture
>
> I love you Jeff, my Jeffery. You are my son whom I love. You are my joy and delight. It warms my heart to have a son like you.
>
> I am a proud papa. I am proud of you, son. Not because of anything you have done, but because of who you are. You are my child, and that is enough. My heart is forever always for you and with you.
>
> I have always loved you, Jeff Davis. I have always been with you. I have always been your father, looking out for you and watching over you.

There was more, but I stopped there. I felt something inside of me stirring. I didn't know what to call it, but it was stirring, or softening, or something. How was it possible for these few words on a screen to make me feel these feelings? I decided to get up and go somewhere else, in case I started crying.

As I walked outside I considered the idea of having a father who loved me. I wasn't familiar with the concept. My father was gone most of the time, and when he was home, he never ever displayed this kind of attitude to me. He put up with me if I was lucky. And here God is saying things to me that my own father never did. And these words seem to be doing something to me, as if they were alive.

"Hey Jeff." I looked up to see Doug walking into the building. He looked at me closer. "Are you OK?" he asked.

I raised my eyebrows and smiled. "Doing great!" I said, and kept on walking. So did he.

Pretty soon I was down by the river. I ambled along the bank until I found a bench to sit down on. Instead of admiring the dark river, two hundred feet wide in front of me, I pulled out my phone and looked at the pictures.

In the first one, a young boy was sitting in a tiny sandbox outside of an apartment. He was playing with a toy truck. Right next to him was a man smiling down on him. He had pure white hair, and white robes. He looked like the happiest man alive, and the source of his joy was the boy he was with. It wasn't that the boy was the actual source of his joy; the joy came from inside of himself, but being with the boy seemed to make him radiate it.

I recognized the apartment as the one I grew up in, and I was the boy of course. But the expression on his face, on my face, looked different than how I remembered it. I remembered going to play outside there by myself, all by myself, and feeling incredibly lonely. Now that this picture has jogged my memory, I remember thinking to myself as a child, *This is what life is all about. Life is about being alone.* And I believed it ever since.

I read the rest of the text from God.

> When you were a child, Jeff, I would sit with you in the sandbox. I would spend time with you. I enjoyed spending time with you, because I loved you dearly, and I still do. Life is about spending time with people you love. That's what life is about. Life is for enjoying each other.

Now I put my phone down and stared out at the river. I sat there for a long time, just thinking, processing, considering these words. I thought about me living apart from my single mom. Why aren't we sharing a place? I don't know. Maybe we should, if life is about spending time with people who love each other. I thought about a girlfriend which I have never had. Why not? Maybe I should pursue a relationship with someone. Veronica came to mind. Maybe I should get together with my friends from work more often. Huh, maybe I should.

I looked at the picture again. The boy didn't seem sad. He seemed happy. He seemed to enjoy doing his thing in the presence of his father who loved him. He was actually enjoying living life. And he seemed so healthy, so happy, so... peaceful. And that was me. I smiled to myself, feeling these peaceful feelings.

Eventually I pocketed my phone and started walking back to the office, somehow lighter. I noticed that the sun in the blue sky was very beautiful, and so were the trees beside the river. With a smile on my face, I walked up the stairs to the Johnson Terminal and took the elevator to the third floor.

When I opened the glass doors to enter the office of Omniscient Technologies, I saw the new receptionist. I decided to do things a little different. I said, "Hi, I'm Jeff."

She said, "I'm Luanna."

"Hi Luanna," I said, then made my way to my desk.

And life was good. What could go wrong?

3:04 PM

"Garth, has the hacker left a bug report yet?" I asked, back at my desk.

"Negative."

"I don't think he will either," I reply.

"What brings you to that conclusion?"

"Well, if the hacker is a part of the Information Underground, their whole business strategy is based on being able to exploit the bug. So there is no way they are going to tell us about it."

"That is an opinion."

"And on top of that, we just gave them thousands of dollars."

"It is expected that the company will pay us back for that, regardless of the actions or inactions of the party in question."

"Yeah. Have you heard anything about that yet?"

"Negative again."

I had a thought. "Maybe you could talk to someone about that. You might be more persuasive than me."

Garth looked at me and considered. "You might be right there. Very well, I shall see what I can discover." He hoisted himself off his chair and wandered off.

I decided to check the Adams logs. Maybe there was something suspicious. There was a lot of data, because they were a large company, but I eventually found exactly what I was looking for--activity on the god account. Bingo! Now we're talking! I checked the time of access. It happened at 2:09 PM today. Wow. That was only a few minutes after I finished setting up the log. I must have got them just in time. I quickly checked the IP address. It was 204.112.39.146.

I looked it up online to see what information I could find on it. I could see who owned the address block. It was owned by Tella, the most popular ISP in the city. No surprise there. But the exact physical address inside the city couldn't be determined. Maybe I could ask Tella to give me the address. I doubt they would, but maybe I should try anyway.

I quickly found their number. Then I took a minute to bolster up the courage to make the call, but I did it, and I called. Once I got through to someone who could tell me, they made it clear that due to privacy reasons they couldn't give that information out. I thanked them and hung up.

I might have other ways of getting them to cooperate.

I made one more call.

3:35 PM

I had never ridden in a police car before, so this was a new experience. Joseph Wakefield, the police officer in the driver's seat, however, appeared very comfortable with it. I wasn't used to having a barrier between the front seat and the back seat. And there were a lot more buttons, switches, and equipment added to the dashboard than I thought he needed.

"Remember, Jeff, we don't have a warrant," he said to me. "So we can't demand the location of this IP address."

"But we can ask," I said.

"We can ask. And I'll tell you what. To show up in a police car with the lights going and have a cop in full uniform come up to you and ask you for something, it gets your attention. It's amazing what you can get away with in uniform and some strength of character."

"Strength of character," I repeated. "I'll try that."

He looked over to me and chuckled. "You might be a smart computer guy, Jeff, but you'd make a lousy cop."

"Why?"

"No offence, but you're not very intimidating, if you know what I mean. Not that the police are supposed to intimidate. But you need strength of character to get stuff done, to get people to cooperate with you."

Yeah, he just called me weak, but I didn't care. Strength is overrated. If I need strength, I'll call the police.

Pretty soon we were parked outside Tella's building, not in the parking lot, but right outside their front door. We parked in a metered parking spot, but Joseph didn't put any money in. He was probably expecting the meter reader to "cooperate with us". I didn't say anything, but I did throw in a few coins myself. Hey, the right thing is still the right thing.

We walked into the building, me following behind the big man with the gun. As soon as we were inside, people started staring at us, and I don't blame them. As we stood around, Joseph explained to me that sometimes you don't need to stand in line. Sometimes a manager comes to you. He said the manager had probably already been called.

Sure enough, within two minutes, a man in a suit came to us and said, "May I help you?"

Joseph said, "We have some questions for someone in your tech department."

"Is there a problem, sir? We don't need a lawyer present, do we?"

"I'm not accusing you of anything. We just want some information."

He seemed to hesitate, but then he smiled and said, "Of course, right this way."

We followed him to the back of the building and down some stairs. Of course, the IT department is always in the basement.

As we were about to arrive at our destination, the man half turned and said, "I didn't catch your names."

"Detective Sergeant Joseph Wakefield", said the police officer. I didn't say anything.

We came to a woman behind a desk, and the man introduced us.

"We have an IP address we would like a location for," Joseph said.

"We don't usually give out that information," the woman said. "Privacy reasons, you understand."

"I'm an officer of the law conducting a criminal investigation."

"We would love to help, of course, but don't you need a warrant or something?"

"I could get a judge to force you to hand over the information, or you could do it yourself without a judge needing to get involved."

The woman looked uncertain. "Well, we do have this policy."

"Do you also have a policy of cooperating with the police?"

"Of course. Of course."

"I'm conducting a criminal investigation. You are on the right side of the law, aren't you?" I got the impression Joseph has done this before, because he seemed quite comfortable intimidating people. I felt uncomfortable just thinking about it.

"Of course we are, sir." She perked up as if she chose sides.

"We appreciate that." The detective gestured to me for the IP address. I handed over the piece of paper from my pocket.

She examined it. "This is certainly ours, a residential DSL line I believe." She sighed. "I'll go get you the address."

"Thank you ma'am."

She went and talked with another lower-level tech person and came back to us.

"63 Hargrave Street," she said.

"Have a good day," Joseph said, as he made his way back the way we came, and I followed closely behind.

"And that is how you conduct an investigation," he said as we were leaving the building and getting back into the car.

"So what happens now?"

"Now we call for back-up and go pay someone a visit," Joseph said and smiled.

4:03 PM

As we approached 63 Hargrave Street, I looked around. I searched the area for any vehicles I may have remembered from my first encounter with the Information Underground, maybe a black motorcycle or black van. I couldn't find either.

But I did see the sign on the simple one-story building. It said, "La Belle Baguette". The place looked like a bakery.

Joseph climbed out of the car and met briefly with officers from another police car. Then the other two started walking around to the back of the building and Joseph stood there, presumably waiting for them.

I stayed in the car and watched. There was no way I wanted to go in and face the bad guys again. Once was enough. Now I'll step back and let the professionals handle it.

As Joseph started toward the door, it occurred to me that he might be a professional policeman, but not a professional IT guy. It would be too bad if he missed something important, really too bad.

I opened the car door and ran after him. I caught him as he was entering the building.

Inside, to the right, there was a counter and behind the counter sat a very friendly, smiling blond with short curly hair. She greeted us in a high voice, "Hi! Would you like to make an order, or purchase some samples?"

I looked behind us, and there were some buns, bread, and other baking items.

Joseph said, "No. We would like to look around, if you don't mind."

"Of course! All of our products are right there." She motioned to the baking items behind us.

Joseph continued, "No. Around the building."

"A tour? I think I can find someone to give you a tour."

Just then another man walked in, looking just as happy. "Did someone say *tour*? I can do a tour right now. I'm Greg, the general manager." He reached out to shake our hands, but Joseph stood there, eyeing him up.

The policeman picked up his posture and said, "We have reason to believe someone in this building may be engaging in illegal activity."

Greg's smile narrowed slightly and he scrunched his eyebrows. "If this is about the cockroach incident, that was taken care of a long time ago."

"Involving computers!", Joseph almost shouted.

Greg's cheeks went red, and he shifted his eyes. "It's... it's not illegal to watch that stuff I watched, is it?"

The receptionist frowned. "What stuff were you watching, Greg?" she demanded.

"Never mind Lilly," Greg replied.

"Stop!", said Joseph. "We just want to look around ourselves. Is it OK if we go look around?"

"Yeah, sure you can," said Greg. "I'll go with you."

Joseph considered the short hall that presumably led to a few offices, and also considered the door that appeared to lead to the back, to the bakery proper. He said to me, "Stay here," then he and Greg went to check out the offices, leaving me in the entrance with Lilly.

I stood there, not saying anything.

"So, are you with the police?" she asked.

"No. I'm a computer programmer," I replied.

"Are you a crime-fighting computer programmer?"

"I... uh...", then I gave up and shrugged.

"It looks like you are."

I kept standing there.

She continued talking. "I'm not very good with computers. My computer went down earlier today, but Greg reset something and that fixed it."

I smiled. "He turned it off and on again, huh? That tends to fix a lot of things."

"Yeah. But it wasn't my computer. It was something in the back."

Joseph came back and Greg followed close behind. They turned and went into the bakery. I followed them.

I saw a large room with ovens, and racks, and other machines and equipment that served unknown purposes. Two people wearing white hats were busy working, but looked up when they saw a policeman eyeing them up.

Joseph walked slowly around the room, pressuring everything he looked at to confess, simply by staring at it. "How many people work here?" he asked.

"We currently have five employees," Greg replied.

"I count only four."

"Katie is off today."

"Does anyone here drive a motorcycle?" Joseph asked.

One person raised a hand. "I drive a moped."

Joseph ignored it and asked Greg, "What colour is your delivery van?"

"White. It's in the back. You can see it if you want."

Joseph looked around a little bit more, then walked back to the front. Greg and I followed him.

Joseph said, "Thank you for letting me look around. How can I contact you if I need anything else?"

GOD'S EMAIL ADDRESS

"Here's my card." Greg handed it to Joseph.

Outside the building, Joseph talked into his radio and waited for the others to come back from around the building. As we stood there, I said, "I don't think those people looked like the Information Underground."

Joseph guffawed. "No," he said and rolled his eyes. Then he looked at the number on the building as if to make sure we were actually at the right place.

"Maybe we got the IP address wrong," I said. "No, we triple checked it. Maybe..." Then my eyes got big and I drew in a breath.

"What is it?" Joseph asked, always alert.

I ran back inside.

Lilly beamed. "Welcome back! Did you forget something?"

I said, "You said your computer went down before. Was it your actual computer or your Internet connection?"

She hesitated. "It was Facebook. I think that's on my computer, right? But Greg fixed it."

"What did he do?"

"He reset something."

"Your DSL router?"

"I don't know what that is."

Then Greg walked in. I guess he could hear us. I said, "Did you reset your DSL router a while ago today?"

"Yes I did," he said. "Why do you ask?"

"Do you have a residential or business account with Tella?"

He said, "Um... which one is cheaper?"

"Residential."

"Then that's what we have. Why do you ask?"

"What time did you reset it?"

He looked up at the ceiling, "Let's see... it was after lunch I think."

"Can you get more specific on the time?" I asked. "It's

important."

Lilly said, "I replied to that new grocery store by email right after you did it."

I turned to her. "What time did you send that reply?"

"Let's take a look, shall we?" She bubbled as she opened her email program. "Let's see... this is the one right here... It says it was sent at 2:51 PM."

"And how long after you power cycled your modem did you send the email?"

"I don't know what that means, but it was less than five minutes. I did it right away."

"Two forty-six," I mumbled to myself.

Joseph had also come back. "What's going on?", he asked.

"I'll explain in the car."

4:44 PM

"So, what gives, kid?"

I had been taking some time organizing my thoughts into words while Joseph drove. I finally got them arranged.

"According to my logs," I began, "somebody accessed Adam's god account at 2:09 PM today."

"Yeah?" Joseph replied.

"And we found out the location of that IP address just before four o'clock."

"Are you saying Tella told us the wrong address?"

"No. It was the right address at the time, and probably still is. But it changed location."

"Why?"

"The bread shop uses a residential DSL account, which means every time they reconnect they get a different IP address. Commercial accounts have static IP addresses, but residential accounts are dynamic. And they reconnected at about 2:46."

"So we missed them?" Joseph hit his steering wheel.

"Yes." I continued thinking. "So if that really was the Information Underground at 2:09, they must have been smart enough to disconnect their Internet connection so someone else could connect and take their IP address."

"They're smart."

"Yes."

"Maybe someone tipped them off."

"What do you mean?" I asked.

"Maybe someone told them we're after them."

"But who?"

"Let's go through the list. Who all knows that you started spying at Adams?"

I went through the list. "Me..."

"Let's leave you off the list for now."

"Samuel Smith, VP of technology at Adams."

"His company is taking a beating, so it's probably not him."

"George Mannel, the System Administrator at Adams."

"I don't know him."

I chuckled at the thought. "He's a bit of a security freak. I can't imagine him doing anything less than a hundred and ten percent safe."

"Who else then?"

"People at Omniscient. My boss Randal, his boss Peter, who said I should report directly to him about this stuff."

"Their company might take the blame for this whole mess, so it's probably not them either."

"Then that leaves everyone else I work with. A lot of people."

"Who do you work closest with?"

"In our room there is me, Garth, Doug, and... and that's it I guess."

"You were going to say your friend Scott?"

I took a deep breath. "Yes."

"don't worry about that, Jeff. We'll get these guys."

"Thanks."

We drove in silence for a minute, then Joseph said, "Maybe someone you work with didn't just tip off the Underground. Maybe they *are* the Underground."

"What?", I said.

"Maybe the connection to Adams came from your office."

I considered that, then dismissed it. "No, our office uses a fiber connection. Completely different from a residential DSL connection. Different IP address range."

Joseph shrugged.

Soon we were turning into the police station, where I had gone to meet Joseph.

"Actually, I think we might have a DSL connection," I said.

"Yeah?", he replied.

"I think we have something coming into our building, like just into the server room, for testing connections from the outside going into our network."

Joseph put the car in park and looked at me. "Jeff, you need to consider the fact that someone at your company may be in on it. This is corporate espionage, after all. These people are spies, and spies could be hiding anywhere."

He got out of the car, and so did I.

On his way into the building, he said to me, "Let me know if anything else comes up."

"OK."

Walking to my car I admitted to myself that I didn't like the idea of someone I worked with to be a bad guy, especially if that meant that he had something to do with Scott's death. I just couldn't bring myself to believe it. I couldn't.

But maybe I had to.

GOD'S EMAIL ADDRESS

I got into my car and started thinking of how I could trap a spy. I would have to lay out a net. I drove back to the office.

I was going to lay out a net hoping to catch someone, and at the same time hoping it wouldn't.

CHAPTER 9

4:58 PM

Luanna, the receptionist, was packing up for the day.

I walked past her, into the hall, and bumped into the very person I was hoping to see. My stomach suddenly turned into knots.

"Ronja", I said.

"Hello Jeff," she said on her way past me.

I followed her back to the door. "Ronja, I need to ask you a question," I said, breathing hard.

She stopped. "What is it?"

"I... I need the root password for our server."

This got her attention. "Which one?" she asked. At least she didn't laugh in my face.

"The Omniscient server. The one that runs our email."

"For what reason?"

"I... I should probably not say."

"You are asking for the root password for no reason? This is not normal."

"Umm... yeah."

"You would need to talk with Randal first before I would share a root password."

Right. Randal. "Is he still in?"

"Randal left a few minutes ago," said Luanna, on her way out the door. Ronja followed her. I went too.

The two ladies stood waiting for the elevator.

"It's important," I said to Ronja.

The doors opened and they walked in. I followed them and the doors closed.

"Jeff," said Ronja. "Talk to me in the morning. We're going home right now."

"But I would like to work on it now. Before it's too late."

"Before what's too late?"

"I can't say."

"Then I can't give you the password."

The elevator arrived at the main floor and they stepped out. I followed them.

When they reached the main doors to the building, it occurred to me that I could call up Randal or even Peter on my phone. I could explain to them, and they could tell Ronja to tell me the password.

I stopped and pulled out my phone. I hate talking on the phone. Ronja and Luanna kept walking out the door. I got a list of my contacts and considered Randal or Peter. Peter would probably be better to talk to, since I'm reporting directly to him now. My finger hovered over the button to make the call. The thought of calling up the corporate CEO made all my muscles lock up. Who was I to interrupt such an important person? I looked up. The women were gone. It was too late.

I put the phone back in my pocket and sighed. Then I went and sat down on a nearby bench and stared out at nowhere.

I could have just called Peter. Why didn't I? I couldn't. It was just too hard. If I had, I would probably have the root password for the server right now, and I could start laying the net. But I didn't. I failed. And now I don't have it. They say good things come to those who wait, but I think good things come to those who jump on the phone. It would be nice if that could be me. Maybe I'll talk to God about that later. In the meantime, I should do something now. I checked the time.

5:07. Maybe I should get something to eat and replan my strategy.

I walked out to the Forks Market and stopped at Nuburger for some fries to go. I haven't had the courage to try one of their actual burgers yet, but I'll take a paper plate full of fries any day.

I took the food down to the river and sat there munching. I looked out at the muddy river and trees and birds. A goose paddled in the water and goslings followed it. I marvelled that all the parts of nature seem to fit together well, the water, plants, birds, bird food, sun. They all work together like they should. As a software designer, I also put different things together: the database back end, the web page front end, the logger, the POP requests coming in, the SMTP connections going out, and cron jobs that run in the background automatically. Everything needs to fit together.

I guffawed. Considering all the bugs we have, I'll bet nature is put together better than most software. But then again if God was the one who put it together, that would make sense. You know, considering he is God and all.

And speaking of God, I wondered if he had any advice for me. I shot him a quick email.

> To: god@heaven
>
> From: jeffd@omniscient.software
>
> Subject: Hi
>
> Hi God. How are you? Do you have any advice for me?
>
> --
>
> Jeff Davis

I finished my fries while I waited for him to reply. Normally he would reply right away, but now he took his time, and it wasn't an email that I received.

GOD'S EMAIL ADDRESS

5:36 PM

I sat there, watching the river, when I heard the notification sound that I had a voice mail message.

I checked. Yes, it was from God.

I pressed Play, and I heard his voice. I'll try to explain what it sounded like. His age was difficult to pin down. It had no strain of an older person, but it was certainly not immature either. He sounded grown-up, but with a youthful spirit. I was surprised by how there was absolutely no anxiety, worry, or fear. His voice was oozing with peace, gentleness, compassion, and love. Yet it was very strong. It sounded unlike any person I've ever heard before.

This is what he said.

> Hello Jeff.
>
> You asked me how I was doing, so I'll tell you. I'm large and in charge. I am large enough to hold you and your world in my hands. And I am. I am holding you close to me. Nothing can touch you. Nothing can get to you. I am protecting you on all sides. You are perfectly safe here in my arms.
>
> I am in charge. You have nothing to worry about, my son. I'm taking care of everything. Set all your worries and cares aside, for I am with you. Relax here in my arms. Stop stressing and straining. You don't need the acceptance of any other person, because I already accept you.
>
> I love you, my son Jeff. I love you very much. You don't need to do anything to earn my love, because

you already have it. You don't need to do anything to get me to like you, because I already do. I like your character, your style, your ways, the way you think. I like what makes Jeff Davis Jeff Davis.

You asked for advice, so here it is. Keep your eyes focused on me. Come to me, Jeff. Stop living life on your own, and come to me. Let me help you. Let's do life together. Stop living it on your own. Come to me. I am your father, and you are my son. Come to me, son.

Jeff, I am your real father. I provide for you more than your earthly dad does. I protect you more than he does. And I have given you more life than your dad ever has. I am your real father. And you are my son. You are mine, and I am yours.

I had never heard such words before in my life, ever. My own dad never said those things to me, not even close. My own mother who loves me didn't even say them. But now a God that I have never seen is saying these things to me. My mind could not wrap itself around this. Even my heart was having difficulty. For some reason, I felt something in my chest. It was a feeling of warmth or something that I had never known before. It was hard to explain. And why did I feel like crying? It made no sense at all. All I wanted was some advice on how to catch the bad guys.

I suppose I should send a reply. I hit the button that started recording my voice. I held the phone up to my mouth, but nothing came out. What can you say in response to such a message? I hit Cancel and put the phone down. Instead, I sent another email.

From: jeffd@omniscient.software
To: god@heaven

> Subject: Thanks
>
> Hi God. Thanks for that. It was nice.

After sending it, I took another look at what I just sent. *It was nice*? Really? God gushes his heart out to me and I respond with *It was nice*? Good grief. I have a lot to learn about this heart-to-heart stuff.

But then he replied.

> From: god@heaven
>
> To: jeffd@omniscient.software
>
> Subject: Re: Thanks
>
> You're welcome, Jeff. Any time. I love you. Whenever you want advice, or anything else, just come to me. I'm here for you.

So I replied to that one.

> From: jeffd@omniscient.software
>
> To: god@heaven
>
> Subject: Re: Thanks
>
> Well, I was hoping you would give me advice on how to catch the Information Underground, or something related to my work or life here.

God replied.

> From: god@heaven
>
> To: jeffd@omniscient.software
>
> Subject: Re: Thanks
>
> Jeff, I was helping you catch the Information Underground. In order to catch them, you need to do things with a full heart. An empty heart will keep you

from doing things you need to do, like making phone calls, or making difficult requests of people. If you don't have this foundation, you won't be able to do what you need to do. I'm helping you with the foundation. When you are full of love, you will do more for others.

But don't think I'm loving you just for the sake of others. I love you because I love you, and that's enough. If you were the only person on earth, I would still love you as much.

You asked for advice on how to catch the Underground, so this is it. I have given you an understanding mind, with the skill of creative problem-solving. Use this gift I have given you. Tap into it. Draw on it. If you use all that I have given you, I will give you more.

Also, don't be afraid to go for it. Don't hold back. Get out there and do something.

Also, don't be afraid to push yourself. The more you go talk to people, and make phone calls, the easier it will get. Keep going.

You also asked for advice on your life, so here is some fatherly advice for your life, son. Don't pursue a romantic relationship with Veronica, but you may pursue a friendship. Treat her like a sister.

I love you, Jeff. I want good for you. I am leading you into good.

I sat back and contemplated what I just read. There was not a lot of specifics there, except for that one thing, which I didn't really want to hear. Come to think of it, I didn't want to hear any of it. I wanted God to solve my problems, not push me into them. "Push yourself to make phone calls"? "Draw on your own skills more"? This isn't what I wanted to hear. I didn't want to work harder; I wanted my hard life to become easier! I wanted this God to tell me exactly which bush the bad guys were hiding behind, so I could sit back and pick them off.

But this message from God was basically, "Try harder." I was tired of trying harder! What good is this God if he doesn't give me actual answers? What good is it at all? I shoved my phone deep into my pocket and stormed off.

6:12 PM

I sat at my desk in my office, alone.

Everyone else had gone home for the day.

I sat doing nothing. It's not that I didn't know what to do. I did. I just didn't want to do it. I knew I needed to call Peter Steele and ask him to call Ronja and tell her to call me and give me the root password for the server. But Peter was probably having supper with his family, and what's worse than being interrupted while eating supper with your family? I didn't want to be that guy. And so I sat there staring at the phone.

And I knew what I wanted. I wanted God to make the phone lighter. I wanted life to be easier. If he really was God, he could just tell me the root password himself without me having to call anyone, without me having to talk to anyone at all. But I didn't feel like asking him. For some reason I didn't feel like talking to him at all.

And so I sat there.

Eventually though, I did find Peter's phone number. My breathing increased and my heart started pounding. I picked up the receiver on the desk phone and I watched my other hand punch in the numbers. Then I closed my eyes and waited for someone to pick up.

"Hello?" said a voice.

"Um. Hi. This is Jeff Davis, from Omniscient. Am I speaking with Peter Steele?"

"Yes, this is him. Hello Jeff. How is the fight going? Are we making progress?"

"Um. Maybe. Or not really. I would like to do some logging on our local network, to see if I can catch any activity going on here."

"What kind of activity?"

"Well, if the Underground is trying to hack into our network." I didn't mention *or if they are already inside our network.*

"I believe that sounds prudent to me. Are you calling to ask my permission?"

"I need the root password for the Omniscient server."

"I can't help you there, Jeff. You would need to talk to Randal for that."

"Ronja Wolff could tell me the password, but she won't unless you or Randal tells her she should."

"I see. You would like me to tell Ronja to give you the password for our server?"

"Yes."

"All right, I'll do that. I believe I have her number. I'll give her a call right now. Is there anything else you need, Jeff?"

"No. Thank you."

"Then have yourself a good evening."

"Thanks. You too. Bye."

"Goodbye."

I hung up the phone and took deep breaths to calm down. That wasn't so bad. No broken bones. Now I just need to wait for Ronja to call me with the password, and I can begin.

Pretty soon my phone rang. I answered it. "Hi. This is Jeff."

"Hello Jeff. This is Ronja."

"Hi Ronja."

"Mr. Steele just called me and asked me to give you the root password."

"Yes."

"I see you managed to convince him."

"I guess."

"Very well, the password is Main Fasten Earnest Governor, with no spaces, and the first letter of each word is upper case."

I smiled to myself. "Really? That's the password? 'Main Fasten Earnest Governor'?"

"Yes," she said seriously.

"Where did you find *that* password?"

"You have never heard of Correct Horse Battery Staple, by XKCD?" she asked.

"No."

"I am surprised."

"Oh, Ronja. One more thing. Do we have a residential DSL line coming into the building?"

"Yes we do, mainly for testing. Do you need it?"

"Maybe I do. Do you know when it last reconnected?"

"No, but it should automatically reconnect if it got disconnected."

"How could it get disconnected?"

"With the `ifconfig` command, or by unplugging the wire and plugging it back in."

"And anyone with physical access to the server room could do that?"

"Of course."

"OK, thanks Ronja."

"Yes, you are welcome, Jeff."

"Bye."

"Bye."

I hung up the phone and got to work.

For the next forty-five minutes, I installed the same logging software on our own Omniscient installation as I did at Adams. It was only slightly different because we were running version 4.1 beta whereas Adams was running 4.0. But in the end, everything I could reasonably think of was being logged, and I could access the logs whenever and wherever I needed to.

I sat back, pleased with my work. Now I was logging the IP address of our DSL line, so if someone connected through there, I would know it. I was closing the net around the bad guys. Soon they would make a mistake, and when they did, I would know it. I was doing so much logging that if they so much as breathed hard I would hear it. I looked at the time and saw that it was late. I had had a full day. I closed and locked the doors behind me, and went home. Tomorrow might be the day something interesting happens.

7:26 PM

I sat at home on my sofa. It may not have been a beautiful sofa, because I was a computer programmer not an interior decorator. Maybe none of my furniture matched, whatever that means. But my sofa was soft and my coffee table was fully functional, because it held my laptop, and that's what counted. I sat there and watched some guy comparing the weight and thrust of rockets, the Saturn V against Space X and Blue Origin. It should have been interesting, but my mind kept wandering.

Yeah, I got upset at God for that last message he sent me. I was hoping he could give me more help himself instead of telling me to use my own natural skills, but maybe he had a point there. And I didn't like what he said about Veronica. Who is he to tell me what I can and can't do, my father? Well, that's a good question. I suppose, in a sense he might be, but he's nothing like my own dad, that's for sure. This God-dad seems like a very nice person.

My dad used to slap my mom around. It was nothing violent. I don't think she ever lost blood, but still, it just wasn't nice. This God seems to be nice in a way that I had never experienced before. I don't know if *nice* is even the word for it. Kind? Loving? Something like that. If I had to choose, I'd rather have God for a dad than my own dad.

Even if he did tell me how to pick my girlfriends.

Maybe he was just a loving dad looking out for his son. That's a new idea. I've never had that before. My own dad abandoned me, so what did he know about having a son?

I pulled out my phone and went to chat with god@heaven.

I paused. I never know how to start a conversation with anyone, let alone God, so I finally just typed something.

"Hello?" I typed.

He replied, "Hi Jeff. It's always good to meet with you."

I took a deep breath and let it out slowly. Perhaps it was time to say something deeper.

"I just wanted to thank you for the kindness you are showing to me. You seem very nice. Thanks."

"I love you Jeff, my son. I love you with all my heart. From my heart to yours, I love you lots."

I sat there, not replying, not even thinking. I was feeling. For so long my heart had felt dry. It felt like it was dry ground that hadn't seen moisture in a long time. It was cracked and dusty, and so used to being that way that it seemed normal. But now drops of gentle warm rain were falling on my heart, and it was becoming moist. It was quite a feeling. I sat back with closed eyes and enjoyed it.

Soon I asked him another question.

I typed, "Why are you talking to me like this?"

He replied, "Because I love you. I am revealing myself to

you in these half dozen ways so that you can see my heart. I am showing you my heart, my child. I love you."

Then he said, "I would like to show you a video."

"Who is in it?" I asked.

"Me, you, your mom, and your dad."

Hang on! That last word made me stop. I... I wasn't sure I wanted to watch this video. I asked, "Is this going to be a happy video or sad?"

"It's going to be a healing video. It's good for you."

I still wasn't convinced. "And are you in it?" Maybe if this loving God was in the video, I might be able to handle it. Otherwise, I would probably pass. I didn't really feel a need to relive the past, if that indeed was what the video was about. I'm trying to avoid pain, not encounter more of it.

"I am," said God.

And as soon as he said it, I received an email, and it had an attachment which was a video file. I braced myself, then opened it. This is what I saw.

The scene was of a man and a woman at a table. They were arguing. I recognized them as my parents. Then the camera moved out to reveal a boy at the table and a man sitting next to him. The boy was me, and the man next to me was white and glowing. That would be God, I guess. My mom was sitting at the end of the table, and I was on her left. My dad was opposite me, and God was right next to me on my left.

Then my dad reached out his hand and slapped my mom across the face.

I remembered this scene from my childhood. I remembered all too well when my parents fought, but this day was different. Up until then, I had seen my parents fight, and I just knew they were fighting. But that day, I understood that my dad was in the wrong, and my mom was in the right. They weren't just fighting. He was fighting her. I remembered the scene well, so well that after he struck her, I knew exactly what was going to happen next.

For the first time in my young life, I spoke up against my dad. I watched and listened to the video. In it, the boy said, "Don't!".

Both mom and dad looked at their child. The mom, in fear of what might happen to her son if he got involved, and the dad in anger for rebuking him. The dad raised his hand back to slap his son.

I knew what was coming. That was when my dad hit me. It hurt. That was the day I learned to keep my mouth shut. I learned to not get involved, a reality that had been with me my whole life.

Until now.

Because as I watched, the strangest thing happened. As my dad brought his hand down upon me as if in slow motion, God himself leaned forward and took the force of the slap directly on his own face. The boy in the video felt nothing. The boy in the video, feeling fine, spoke again and said, "Don't hurt Mom!"

The boy in the video got off his chair and went to stand between his mom and the bad guy. The dad again tried to slap the boy, but God himself stepped in between and took the blow on his own body.

Then the dad left the room.

At this point in the video, the boy and the mom hugged each other and God turned around to face the camera.

"This is the day," he said, "that you learned to stand up for justice. This is the day you began to fight for what is right. This is the day you received your calling."

The video ended.

I sat there, kind of confused, trying to take it all in. I was sure that I had backed down that day, but here, right in front of my eyes, I clearly stood up. I felt conflicted as to who I really was. Was I someone who backed down, or was I someone who stood up? Was I really the loser, or was I actually the winner of the fight? I tried on this new identity for size, and I think I liked it. I think I could be this fighter. If this God who took the hits for me thinks I'm a fighter, then who am I to argue? Maybe I am. Maybe I will be this fighter, and just maybe I will win.

Thursday, 8:19 AM

An SQL query goes into a bar, walks up to two tables, and asks, "Can I join you?"

I read the joke on Garth's little whiteboard and laughed.

"Good morning Jeffery," said Garth.

"Hi Garth," I said. "Hi Doug."

"Morning Jeff," said Doug.

"And how is the life of the hacker finder?" Garth asked me.

"I'm doing pretty good," I said. "I had a good night's rest, so I'm feeling good today. How are you?"

"My life is what it is," he said.

"How are you, Doug?" I asked.

He turned around to me. "I'm doing OK. I did some gardening yesterday evening."

"What were you gardening?" I asked.

"I was just weeding the Thunbergia."

"That sounds interesting," I said. "What kind of plant is that?"

Veronica appeared. "Thunbergia are more commonly known as Black-Eyed Susans," she said. "They are annuals."

"That's right," said Doug. "Are you into gardening too?" he asked.

"No. I just used to work at a greenhouse," she replied. Then turning to me, she said, "Jeff, have you given more thought to what I suggested to you yesterday?"

"About giving up the fight?" I asked. "That's not going to happen." I wasn't about to tell her everything God has been talking to me about, especially not in front of everybody.

She was serious. "Well you should." She turned to see Ronja reading Garth's whiteboard.

Ronja laughed. "*Can I join you?* Yes, of course. SQL queries joining tables."

"Good morning Ronja," I said.

"Hello Jeff," she replied. "Hello Garth. This is a very funny joke you have posted. I like it. It is funny."

"Yes, it is," said Garth, his eyes not leaving his computer screen. "That is why I posted it."

"Agh. You are so serious," she said as she playfully hit his shoulder.

I smiled at her flirting. She'll have to try harder than that to win him.

"Jeff, did you accomplish what you set out to do yesterday?" Ronja asked me.

"Yes, I did, thanks"

"What was he doing yesterday?" Veronica asked.

"It was a secret," Ronja replied. "Jeff, why don't you tell us all what you were doing with the root user password on the Omniscient server?"

All eyes in the room focused on me.

I smiled. "Just trying to find the hackers."

"There's more than one of them, are there?" Garth asked.

"Yes," I said. "Didn't you hear what happened to me yesterday?"

"Men dressed in black surrounded his car," Veronica interjected. "And one got in his car and held a gun to his face."

"He didn't do anything to me," I said.

"But he could have!" she continued. "Somebody tell him to drop this whole thing right now."

Everyone looked to see how I would respond. I shook my

head. "I can't. I have to do this. These are bad people. They have to be stopped."

"And you think you are going to stop them?" she asked.

"I might," I said.

With that Veronica turned around and left.

Ronja said, "You be careful, Jeff." Then she too left.

Doug said, "Someone pointed a gun in your face, and you're still going?" He nodded to himself. "That's very courageous. Wouldn't you agree, Garth?"

"I'm just glad it's not me," Garth replied.

The two others turned to face their computers again, and so did I. It was time for me to look through the logs to see which one of us was the hacker I was looking for.

CHAPTER 10

9:15 AM

I found nothing.

I looked through all the logs on our local network that I had set up the night before. And I looked through all of Adams logs again. There was absolutely nothing interesting--nobody using the god account on either server. There was nobody doing anything they shouldn't be doing. It was piles upon piles of boring.

That's why I had come here to the server room. I was taking a peek into our own Omniscient database myself.

"I'm sorry if I've been too hard on you," came a voice from the doorway. It was Veronica. "I just don't want to see you get hurt."

I smiled. "I understand."

"So what are you doing now? Still hunting them down?" she asked.

"I'm looking through our own database of emails to try to find anything suspicious."

She looked concerned. "Have you found anything? You don't suspect anyone here, do you?"

I shrugged. "I hope not. I'm just making sure."

"Can you look through deleted emails, too?"

"If they are sitting in your Trash folder, sure. That's a folder like any other."

"Well, I'd love to help you, but I have an appointment."

"See ya," I said.

"Later", she smiled and left.

The terminal I was using was text only, of course. There is no reason to have a windowing environment on a server. I ran the database client and started querying the database. I quickly realized this thing was way larger than I could scroll through. There were many thousands of emails sitting here.

Pretty soon Veronica came back. "They didn't show, so I'm here to help." She grabbed a chair and sat next to me. I didn't mind. "So, what are we looking for?"

"Anything suspicious," I answered.

"And you're working only with words?" She gestured to the black screen containing nothing but white words. "Aren't there buttons or windows or something you can click on?"

"A text console is all you need," I said, trying not to be smug. "You can just run an SQL query right here, and it will show you all the results."

"What's SQL?"

"Structured Query Language is a way of querying a database."

"Ah! That's what you're doing."

"Yes. A Database contains a number of tables, which contain rows and columns."

"That's what Garth's joke was about."

"Yes. With SQL you often want to join two tables, such as the table of users and the table of emails."

"Ah." She smiled. "*Can I join you?* The SQL query is joining two tables. I get it."

"I don't know where he finds them all, but they're pretty good."

"So have you found anything incriminating in your querying?"

"No. I've searched for *Information Underground*, and I've searched for *Jade*, and found only the stuff I've sent or received. Nobody else is talking about it."

"Who's Jade?" Veronica asked innocently.

"The leader of the Information Underground. The ring leader, I guess. He's the guy who should be behind bars." I frowned. "Or worse."

"You should stay away from him."

"I should get him arrested."

"You're not the police. Why do you care?"

I looked at her to see if she was serious. She seemed to be. I thought of telling her my calling that God had given me, to bring about justice. I thought of telling her that this is what my life was made for. I thought of telling her that any decent human being should have a drive or at least a desire to see the good guys win and the bad guys lose. Instead I said, "Because. It's the right thing to do."

"Well, you can do it if you want, but I would leave it up to the police. That's their job."

"Yeah."

"Hey, you want to do lunch again? Are you going to be around?"

"I think I will. Sure." I smiled. But then I remembered what God said about Veronica. Treat her like my sister. My smile went away.

"Great! I'll come find you." With that, Veronica bounded out of the room, and I watched her go.

Ah, Veronica. I've never had a girlfriend before. I suppose I still don't; we haven't done anything except go out for lunch.

I sat and stared at the screen in front of me which could show me any email sent by anyone at Omniscient. I could search all the emails she has sent or received, to see if I am mentioned in any one of them. I wonder what she's been saying about me. It wouldn't be that hard.

It was very tempting to snoop, but I decided not to. It was too much like stealing. Let's keep this legit.

Luanna the receptionist poked her head in. She looked around at all the techy stuff, then said to me, "Jeff, there is someone here to see you."

"Who?" I asked.

"The reporter, Donald Roberts."

9:43 AM

As I walked towards the reception area to find the man, I wondered to myself what, if anything, I should tell him. Do I mention the Information Underground? The police involvement? Raiding the bakery? Well, no, not that. But what about Scott?

"Ah, Jeff!" Donald approached me, his hand outstretched toward mine, a large smile on his face.

I shook his hand. "Hi," I said.

"Can we find a place to sit down and talk?"

"Um... the board room is free," I said, glancing into the open door of the board room.

We went in and sat down.

"So," he began. "Anything new? Have you found the bug yet?"

I scowled. "We don't have any evidence that we even have a bug."

"But you might."

"Well, I can't say for sure we don't either."

"Have you been looking for one?"

"Yes."

"Have you found one?"

"No."

He wrote something on his pad of paper, something that will make us look bad no doubt. I tried to make us look better.

"We're doing everything we can to make sure Omniscient is fully trustworthy."

"Such as?"

These were hard questions.

"By looking for any security bugs. We haven't found any."

"Have you reviewed the Omniscient installation at Adams Corporation?" He asked.

I wondered who else this guy has been talking to. I answered, "Yes."

"And do you think someone else may have hacked into their network?"

I thought of the military way George handled his network. "Probably not," I replied.

Donald leaned back and put his arms out. "So how can you explain how their information got leaked?"

"Maybe someone at Adams intentionally shared it with someone."

"Oh come on, Jeff. Why would these executives leak their own information? They are the last ones who would want secrets to get out."

"Then I don't know."

He changed tactics. "Has anyone nefarious contacted you?"

I paused to consider if I should answer this. The answer, of course, is Yes, somebody with a gun got into my car and threatened me. I probably shouldn't mention it, but if not, what would I say? Lie? Give no comment? But by then my small pause was long enough for this investigative reporter.

"Did they offer you money?" He asked.

"No!" The idea of us taking a bribe was ridiculous! I would not stand for such an accusation. But by the time I had spit out the word, I realized my mistake. I just admitted that someone had.

"If not to offer you money, then what?" he asked.

I was flustered. I was losing control of this conversation, if I ever even had control. "I probably shouldn't talk about it."

"Did they threaten you?"

"I... I don't want to talk about it."

Donald looked concerned. "Jeff, if these people are threatening you, you need to tell me. You need to let the media know. Go public. They will back off. When we shine a light on what they are doing, they will scurry away like rats. Now tell me, who are these people, and how did they contact you?"

I considered his offer. Maybe it had some merit to it, but I wasn't ready. I shook my head. "I don't want to talk about it."

"OK, no problem. When you change your mind, give me a call." He gave me his card again. "And how are things here at Omniscient? Business is going well?"

There was another question I didn't want to answer. No, business was not well. There were rumours of layoffs, especially if this reporter starts spreading rumours that Omniscient is buggy software. What could I say that wasn't a lie?

"So far, business is fine."

But wording wasn't good enough for him. "So far?" He asked.

"Yes. Business is fine."

"But you anticipate business won't go well if people find out there are security issues with your software?"

"There are no security issues that we know of!" I stated, rather brusquely.

"What are the owners of the company saying? Omniscient Technologies is not a public company. The owners must be nervous."

"The owners are not nervous. They are... adequately addressing the situation."

"Oh! Great. How are they doing that?"

"They... assigned someone to... look into it and... fix it."

"You?"

"Yes."

"And you're doing a great job, Jeff. Thanks for talking to

me about this. I'm glad they are willing to talk now. You know, things just work out better when people are willing to talk about it. The people deserve the truth. That's what a free society is all about, wouldn't you agree?"

"Um. Yeah."

Donald was about to say something again, but he was interrupted by a loud alarming noise.

"What's that?" he asked.

"It's the fire alarm again."

10:02 AM

"Again?" he asked.

"Yeah, we had a false alarm a few days ago," I said. "It might be false again."

"I think I won't stay around to find out. It was good to talk to you Jeff," he said, and reached out to shake my hand. I shook it, and he left.

People were walking down the hall, toward the exit. I entered the flow, but in the opposite direction. I wasn't heading for the door.

I made my way down the South hall, turned left, then halfway down the East hall.

There in front of me was the server room. The floor was deserted of people. Only the sound of the alarm remained.

The door was slightly open, so I pushed on it and looked inside.

There sat Garth, one hand on the armrest of the swivel chair, one hand holding a Dr. Pepper. "Mr. Davis," he said to me. "Why are you in the server room when there is a fire alarm sounding loudly?"

"I just came to make sure it was safe."

"It is perfectly safe, as you can see. I am here, guarding it.

You may run along now."

I didn't move.

"I don't need help guarding this room. It's not that big." And when I still didn't move, he added, "And I don't need your help. You're not that big either."

He sat and stared at me, waiting for me to cave in and leave like I did last time. For some reason I didn't. I kept standing there, as if I now had some sort of strength inside of me that I didn't before.

"I would like to stay," I replied somewhat timidly, but at least I said it.

"This building might imminently collapse on top of us. I will not be responsible for your very painful death."

"We probably won't die from building collapse," I replied. "We'll probably die from smoke asphyxiation."

"I stand corrected. Instead the smoke will get us."

"There is no smoke."

"Why are you still here? As you can see, this room is being perfectly monitored by someone experienced. You need to go save yourself."

"I told Peter Steele that I would be the guy to solve the hacker problem. I'm keeping an eye on our server so nobody can hack in."

"There is nobody here to hack in, is there?"

I didn't answer.

Then Garth rose up from his chair. "You are accusing me of being the hacker?" he said. He was noticeably taller than me, and heavier, and the small amount of strength in my heart suddenly all but fluttered away.

"N...no. I'm just... covering all my bases. I'm just... doing my due diligence."

He sized me up, as if considering my words, and perhaps wondering at this new boldness of mine.

"In this instance, the due diligence is mine, since I am the designated fire marshal of the company. It is my job to keep everyone safe. But as it turns out, I am also guarding against hackers," he said, sitting down. "Perhaps we should guard together. That is, if you don't mind being choked to death by smoke."

"OK," I said. I had forgotten that Garth was the fire marshal, if I ever actually knew it. I found another chair and sat down.

We waited without speaking for a few minutes. Then someone's face appeared at the door. It was Ronja, followed by Randal.

"Ah, I was right about you two," Ronja said. "Here they sit in the server room, being close to the computers." She turned to Garth. "Are you all right, Garth?"

"Perfectly," he said, looking away.

"We noticed you two weren't at the muster point, so we guessed you were here. It's good to know you're both OK," Randal said. "This might be another false alarm. I'm going to go see if I can track somebody down." Then he left.

Just then the fire alarm stopped shrieking, and we all visibly relaxed. That thing was loud.

Randal popped his head back in. "I'm still going to find out." Then he disappeared again.

I got up to go back to my desk.

"We didn't catch anyone hacking, did we, Jeff?" Garth asked, also leaving.

"Nope," I said.

"Are you hoping to catch someone, or are you hoping to not catch someone?" he asked.

I thought about it on our way back to our office room. "I don't like the thought of one of us being involved with them."

"Being involved with whom?" asked Doug, also on his way back.

"The baddies," said Garth.

"Oh. Yeah. That's right," replied Doug.

Just as we sat down, my desk phone rang. Great. Who is it this time? The phone said, "Veronica Stansin," so I picked up immediately.

"Hey Veronica! Are you calling about lunch?" I said into the phone.

"Hi Jeff. No. This is strictly business. As a customer service rep, I'm on the phone with someone who has installed Omniscient, and they have a problem. I can't help them, but maybe you can."

"What's the problem?" I asked.

"They think they just got hacked, and they think it was because of Omniscient."

11:16 AM

I just turned my car left from Archibald Street onto Plinguet Street. This was an industrial area. There were empty train tracks out behind a number of old buildings. Some businesses had signs, but some didn't have anything.

I was looking for 750 Plinguet.

That's the address of Vandelay Industries. Apparently they think they got hacked and are blaming Omniscient. It might not be the software. It might be anything, probably their local network set up. No doubt someone just didn't install the latest security updates and left themselves wide open to attack, and now they're blaming us. They probably had been watching the news.

We didn't even do the install, but they insisted that we send someone to check it out, so here I am.

I found the place and drove onto their parking lot. It was a smaller building, and it could really use a coat of paint or two, but if they were going to pay for our support, we'll do it.

Besides, I needed to check it out just in case the hacking was actually true. That is my purpose right now, after all.

My first mistake was not seeing the name of a business anywhere. My second mistake was not recognizing the van parked outside.

I went in and didn't see anyone, but I heard someone calling from behind some doors, "Are you here from Omniscient?"

"Yes!" I called back.

"Right through here!"

Like an idiot, I walked through the doors and instantly regretted it.

In front of me was a man dressed all in black with a black balaclava on his head. He was holding a gun in his hands and pointing it at my face. His head was to the side, looking down the barrel as if he expected me to make some sort of quick move. My only quick move was to tighten my throat in fear. My eyes went wide and my breathing became laboured.

He spoke in the same deep gravelly voice I recognized from when he was in my car. "Have a seat, Jeff." He motioned with his handgun to a chair in the middle of this large room.

When I didn't obey immediately, someone behind me shoved me, or at least tried to. It wasn't very forceful. When I turned, I noticed another man dressed in black. He also had a gun, so I shuffled toward the chair and sat down. The guy behind me grabbed my wrists together behind the chair and tied me up. The rough ropes were tight as steel on my wrists. Only then did the man in front place his firearm back in his holster, underneath his leather jacket.

Despite the panic inside of me, I fought to remain calm. I tried, and failed, to take some deep breaths. I tried closing my eyes to relax, but they refused to close. I forced myself to think clearly about the situation.

I had never been tied up in a room of armed people before,

so it was natural that I was far outside my comfort zone, but still I had to regain control of myself. I had to stop and think.

Then a thought came to me. If he really wanted to kill you, you'd probably already be dead by now. Good thinking. Keep going, I encouraged myself. I realized that the last thing this man had told me, in my car last time, was a warning, and I had not heeded the warning. In fact, I had brazenly gone against it. Now he might follow through with his threat. That thought got me panicked again, so I had to think of something else. "What do you want?" I asked the man.

Not answering right away, the masked man brought a stool and set it down in front of me, then sat on it.

He took out his gun again and pointed it at the side of my head. "This is what I want," he said, nice and slow, "I want you to tell me you are going to give up chasing the Information Underground. I want you to speak these words to me, right here, right now. Say 'I will give it up. I will walk away.' Say it!"

I sat there, daring to look at him. I said nothing.

"Say it!" he screamed at me, pushing the end of the gun against my head, pushing my head over.

I sat there, my head at an angle, not saying anything.

"They said you were stubborn," he said.

I braced myself for what was coming next.

"They said threats wouldn't work on you," he said.

One click and it was going to all be over.

"They said we were wasting our time threatening you."

I wondered what it was like to die. Will I see God for real?

"Say the words, Jeff. You have until I count to three. One."

I remembered the picture of the young me sitting on God, my father's, lap. It seemed so peaceful. Something in me wanted that peace right now. I wanted it.

"Two."

But to get there, I had to die. Was I ready for that now? Did I really want to take a bullet to the head? No. No, I did not, because this was terrifying.

"Three."

I tried to yell, "Stop!" I tried to scream, but nothing came out. I could barely breathe I was so frozen in fear.

I heard the gun go *click*. It didn't bang or explode. It just simply clicked. I opened my eyes. The man backed off and sat down on his stool again. And I noticed I was still alive. Slowly I began to breathe again, and my heart rate relaxed down to only racing.

He holstered his gun again and sighed. Then he scratched the back of his head, stood up, and walked out of the room. I heard a vehicle outside start and drive away.

Even though I was still tied up, I began to relax a little. I was afraid he had mistaken my terror for courage, which may or may not be a good thing. At least I'm still alive. By then my stomach reminded me of my near brush with death and let out some anxiety. I leaned over to the side of the chair and emptied the contents of my stomach, which was not a lot.

I sat there for a while, wondering what was going on. Was I being abandoned? Left to die of natural causes? And where was the second guy? I called out, "Hello?"

A voice from behind me answered, "Just sit there and wait until he comes back."

So I sat there, and I sat there, wondering what was going to happen to me. Finally the man came back, and when he did, he did something I never would have guessed in my wildest dreams.

He placed two pizza boxes between us, then he reached up and took off his mask.

"My name's Max," he said.

12:01 PM

Max said to the other guy, "Untie him." He came over and did. I rubbed my sore wrists.

I continued to sit there, too confused to know what to do.

Max said, "Chip, get the drinks from the van. And we'll need a table too."

Max opened up the pizza boxes. Yes, they actually contained pizza. It looked good.

Pretty soon Chip was back and a table was set up.

Max shoved a box at me. "Have some pizza," he said.

I just looked at him.

"What, you don't trust me? You think it's poisoned or something? It's not poisoned. Here, look." He reached over and grabbed a slice, and took a big bite. "See?" he mumbled. "Not poisoned."

Not wanting to be rude, and not knowing what else I should do, I also took a piece and started nibbling. I finally asked, "So... what are we doing?"

"It was Jade's idea," Max replied between chewing.

"What was?"

"He decided that threatening you wouldn't work. I disagreed. I thought I still could. But..." He gestured to me, and kept on chewing.

"So instead of threatening me, you're... feeding me pizza."

Now Chip spoke up again. "We're hoping you will join the team."

I almost laughed. "What?!" I exclaimed, looked from one to the other.

Max answered. "Jade thinks You'll make a good addition. You're a smart computer guy."

"I'm also a computer guy," added Chip.

"He wishes," said Max.

"I am so!" he said to Max. Then turning to me, he said,

"Ask me a computer question. Anything at all."

I thought for a moment, then said, "What are the three principals of object-oriented programming?"

Chip looked blank. "I don't mean programming, I mean network stuff."

Thinking again, I said, "If you logged into a POP3 server using telnet, what is the first thing you'd say?"

Chip scowled, which made Max laugh. "Told you," he said.

Chip said, "I haven't memorized every communications protocol out there. Ask something a regular hacker would know."

At the word "hacker," I stopped. Was this the guy? Was this the hacker we're looking for? I sized him up. He might be. But then again, he might not be. The hacker we're looking for must be very good. This kid didn't seem to be that good. I'll ask him something a real hacker should know. "What is MD5?"

Chip brightened up. "It's a way of encrypting a piece of information, like a password." He pointed at me. "Ha!"

"That's pretty good," I said.

"Is he right?" Max asked.

I knew that MD5 is not actually an encrypting function; it is a hashing function, which is different. A real hacker would have known the difference between encryption and hashing. I said, "Close enough."

"OK, let's talk details," Max said. "First, your salary. You'll get four times what you're getting at Omniscient right now. And you'll get to keep your Omniscient salary of course."

I furrowed my eyebrows in confusion.

"You would still work there," Max said. "That's the whole point. You work there, and funnel information to us."

"And who is 'us'?"

"The Information Underground of course," said Chip.

"Of course", I replied. I paused and said, "So the hacker I'm looking for would actually be…"

"You." said Max.

"Me."

I sat and chewed. I didn't really know what to say. This was certainly a big change. My brain was busy processing it. I said to Max, "You did just almost kill me."

"No hard feelings, mate. It's just business."

Chip added, "Besides, Jade doesn't want to kill you right now."

"Why not?" I asked him.

"Never mind that part," said Max. "That's his business. We just do what he says."

I thought some more. "So if I joined you, what would I do?"

"You'd be one of the guys, a part of the team," said Max.

"And what do we do?"

Max put his pizza down. "Our business is information. We buy and sell information. We're an information company."

"Hence the name," I said.

"Hence the name," said Max.

"And you're underground." I added.

"The laws are very restrictive in this line of work, so we have to work under them. But business is still business."

"What exactly would you want me to do?" I asked.

"You would be in a very good position to find information. You would be a gatherer."

"And someone else would be a... distributor?"

"Jade is the salesman. He handles the sales."

"And how could I gather information, exactly?"

Max leaned closer. "You know the answer to that. We only need one thing."

Yeah, I knew what he wanted, but I still wanted to hear it. "What?"

"God's email address." He sat back up. "And password of course. For every site you can possibly get. The more the better."

"With that, we can get anything," said Chip.

"Yeah, I know," I replied to him.

Max continued. "If we had the god email address and password for every site you do an install for, just think of the information we would have." He hit the table for exclamation. "Business would be good."

"But the passwords are stored in the database hashed." I said.

"What does that mean?" asked Max.

"It means they're encrypted," said Chip.

"And besides," I continued. "I can't get into the database either. That's locked down too. And if the server belongs to someone else, I can't even get into the server."

Max looked at me and eyed me up. "You could find a way around all that, couldn't you?"

"He is a developer on the team," added Chip. "He could write some code that gives us everything we need, and sneak it into the official release code. Or, he could write a module that a customer service rep could tell the customer to install." Chip and Max looked at each other and smiled.

Then they looked at me, and I thought about it. Could I write custom code that steals passwords? Technically that wouldn't be difficult. But could I sneak it in and get away with it? That would be harder. But would it be possible? I nodded my head. "Yeah, I could."

"So will you do it, Jeff?" Max asked. "Are you in?"

I nodded my head. "I'm in."

12:46 PM

After discussing more details, they let me go.

We walked out of the building together. As he was getting

into his van, Max said to me, "It's good doing business with you, Jeff, but remember this." He pointed at my face. "Don't ever betray me. There is no forgiveness for betrayal. If you betray me, you will regret it, no matter what Jade says." With that, he got in and drove off.

Ah yes, that was my reminder that the bad guys are still bad guys. They don't magically become good people when you start working with them.

I had now missed my lunch date with Veronica, but I didn't want to stay on this yard a minute more than I had to. I drove down the road a ways and parked on the lot of a real business, then I sent her an email.

> From: jeffd@omniscient.software
>
> To: veronicas@omniscient.software
>
> Subject: Sorry about lunch
>
> Hi Veronica. I'm sorry I missed lunch. My excuse? I was kidnapped. Yeah, seriously. The Information Underground got me, but I got away unharmed. I'll tell you more about it later.

As I was pulling out of the parking lot, my phone rang. It was Veronica, so I answered it. "Hello?" I said.

"Jeff, are you serious?! You were kidnapped?" she said.

"Yes."

"And you're OK?"

"Yup"

"They just let you go?"

"Maybe they just wanted to threaten me some more."

"Well, you're OK, so that's what matters. I'm glad. Are you coming back to work?"

"Yeah, I think I'll be in yet some time today."

"Good. Take care of yourself, Jeff. I'll see you later."

"OK."

"Bye."

"Bye"

I hung up and thought to myself. Didn't I just say that all in the email? Why do you want to hear it all again with my voice? Women.

Yeah, I was going back to the office, but first I had a stop I had to make.

CHAPTER 11

1:55 PM

"Dear God in Heaven, I hope you agreed to it!"

"Of course I did," I said.

"And I hope you're not actually going to follow through?"

"Of course I won't," I replied.

I was talking with Detective Joseph Wakefield about my encounter with the Information Underground, and about their offer.

He leaned forward on his squeaky wooden chair. "You be careful Jeff. These are bad characters, and if you cross them, they can make you disappear like your friend Scott. Are you sure you want to do this?"

"Scott is the reason I'm doing this. I have to. I have no other choice."

"Well, you're in pretty deep at this point, so be careful."

"I will be."

"Good. Threatening to kill someone while brandishing a gun is a felony, so we could get this guy Max with that, if we had proof. If your story holds up, there are also some other misdemeanours we could throw at him, again if we could arrest him." Then he said to me, "How would you feel about setting up a meeting with him, and inviting me unannounced?" He smiled.

"So you could arrest him?" I asked.

"Exactly."

I considered that. "Then he'd go to jail?"

"Yes. And if convicted, he would go to prison for a while

too."

"Only for a while?"

"Depends on which charges we could get to stick."

"And what about Jade, the leader?"

Joseph shrugged. "We don't have much on him. Again, we need hard evidence if we want to put him away."

Just then it occurred to me that we might have some hard evidence. I had forgotten that I had wired up my car with cameras. I told the detective this, then ran out to my car to collect data. In a few minutes I had the videos of all three cameras on my phone, and I was back watching them with the detective.

"That's Max right there", I said as I pointed to a man on my screen walk past my car.

"That might not be enough to convict him, but we can place him at the scene of the crime, and at least we have his picture now. Will you send these all to me?"

"Yes. I'll email them, or send you a link to them."

"Our next step is to bring this guy in. If your camera could have picked up his license plate, that would make it easier. But once we bring him in, we can question him. Do you think you can set up a meeting?"

"I'll try."

"Good. Stay in touch, Jeff. I'll be ready."

I stood up. "Thank you, Detective."

"Thank you, Jeff."

2:51 PM

I sat in our server room, staring at the screen.

I had run an SQL query on the database to find the god email address and password for our domain, omniscient.software. The email address was simply god@omniscient.software, and the password was 2C6528C3C933207AD341165BF493B497.

It was hashed, not encrypted. If it was encrypted, it could be decrypted to reveal the original password. But hashing is one-way only, so there was no way to get it back. To find out if a user entered the correct password, you have to hash what the user entered and compare hashes. If they are correct, it must have been the right password.

I let my mind wander. What if I did, in fact, find out this password and give it to the Underground? They would probably pay me a lot of money. I could pay off my student debt, move out of my apartment into a real house. I could help out my mom, give her a vacation for once in her life. My life would be different.

Scott would still be dead though, and his warning would have been for nothing. Instead of warning me to stay away from them, I would have joined them. That would make me an accomplice in his murder. The thought was unthinkable.

But now I found myself in this place where I promised them exactly that, and they are expecting me to deliver. Could I betray Omniscient Technologies, my own employer? Could I betray the trust of my colleagues and friends here at Omniscient? Could I betray every single company that installs Omniscient, expecting it to keep their information safe? No, I honestly could not do that.

And besides, hadn't God himself told me that he made me to be a fighter for justice? How could I turn my back on him? How could I betray my own destiny? A fighter for justice is who I am. It is the core of my God-given being. I can't just stop being that.

No, the way I see it, there is only one path in front of me. The only thing I can do is to set up a meeting with Max, bring Joseph along to arrest him, and pray to God that he does. Because if the meeting goes bad, and Joseph doesn't arrest

Max, Max is not going to forgive me, and then I don't know what I'll do. I got the impression he really didn't want to be betrayed, and betrayal was exactly what I was planning to do. If he doesn't get caught, all his threats might actually turn real. And that's not something I wanted to think about.

But with Max behind bars, we can tell the news people that the bad guy was caught, and Omniscient Technologies will be the hero, and life will continue as normal. Our investors will love us. Adams will love us. Even Donald Roberts will love us for giving him a good story. It will work. It will have to work. We have no choice.

And just as I was contemplating the future, I received a chat message from my mom that made me consider my past. As much as I had tried to leave my past in the past, it was coming back. First God himself was reminding me about it, and helping me deal with it, now my own mother was bringing my past to meet me face to face.

> Mom: Jeff, you won't believe who talked with me today. It was John, your father. He says he is in town and wants to meet you. He's coming over for supper. Please come too. 5:00 at my place.

I had to stare at the screen for a few minutes. My father? My father, whom I haven't seen in thirteen years? The man who deserted us? Just at the time God himself visits me and calls himself my father, and I'm his son, my own flesh-and-blood father comes into my life again?

I didn't want to go.

I had no desire to meet this man again. What, was God making me deal with my past in real life now, not just with a safe video? When I just thought about my father, a wide range of emotions came to me, and I didn't know which one to go with. I felt connected to him, since I do get my DNA from him. But I also feel disconnected. I was also feeling some distrust and anger for what he did to us. It was complicated. I hoped God wasn't expecting me to forgive him.

I read the message again. Mom really wanted me to come over too. I think she doesn't want to be home by herself with him. She probably shouldn't be. I would have to go, just to be there with her, for her sake.

I replied.

> Jeff: I'll be there. In fact, I'll be there early.

4:30 PM

"Jeff! It's good to see you!" Mom gave me a hug at the door of her apartment.

"You too, Mom," I replied. "Is he here yet?"

"Your father? No. You know, you can call him that."

"What?"

"Father. Dad. You can call him Dad, because he's your dad."

"Is he really?"

I stepped into my mom's small apartment. It wasn't the most beautiful place in the world, but it was taken care of. The kitchen counters weren't the latest style, but they were clean. The floor may have had stains on it, but it was swept and tidy. She did what she could do.

"Of course he is," she said. "A parent never stops being a parent."

"They do if they leave you," I said.

"You don't know why he did that. Maybe he was going through some hard times and was overwhelmed. Maybe he wants to just see his son again, and see how he turned out. Look at you, Jeff. You turned out great."

"Thanks." I sat down at the small table. "You know, I

wouldn't have thought it at the time, but I wonder if it was a good thing he left us."

Mom sat down too. "Jeff, how can you say that?"

"He... wasn't always nice. He hit you, mom. Dads shouldn't do that."

"That was a long time ago, Jeff. You need to let go. You need to forgive."

I raised my eyebrows. "I don't think I need to, and I don't want to."

"You would feel better. Forgiveness isn't about the other person. It's about you. If you went fishing and your friend got his hook stuck in your arm, wouldn't you take it out?"

"I don't go fishing."

"You wouldn't want to live with the pain your whole life, would you?"

I shrugged. "He doesn't deserve to be forgiven."

"It's not about him. It's about you. You need the hook removed from your arm."

I said nothing.

"Wouldn't you like to have a father again?" she asked.

I was about to say, "Not one like him," but I had already made my point.

"Try it, Jeff. Try it, you might like having a father."

When she said that, I remembered back to someone else who told me to try something. It was the plant lady who told me to try God's email address. That turned out pretty good. I looked at my mom. "OK, I'll try."

She cheered up. "Very good." She stood up. "You can help set the table. We're having chicken."

I helped set the table for three. Then I swept the floor. Then I sat around, waiting for the mystery man to show up.

Soon Mom's phone rang and she answered it. "Hello?... Hi John... Yes, come on up." Then she pressed a button on her phone. She said to me, "He'll be right here," and she went to her door. Soon there was a knock. She took a deep breath and opened it.

There stood a man who looked too much like an older me. His dark brown hair was greying, and his face was starting to show some age. At least he was wearing a shirt and tie. And he was holding a bouquet of red roses.

"Hello John," my mom said.

"Hello Julie," he said. "These are for you."

She smiled and said, "Thank you. I'll find something to put them in." As she walked toward the kitchen, I tried to read the expression on her face, but I couldn't. She was just being polite to her guest.

Then the man walked in, and I stood up to greet him. He stuck out his hand to shake mine. "Hi Jeff," he said and smiled. It wasn't one of those *I like you* smiles, it was more like a *I'm trying to make you think I like you* smiles.

I shook his hand and said, "Hi."

"You must be twenty-eight years old by now," he said.

"Yup."

"Your mom tells me you are a computer programmer."

"Yup."

"Ah, well done, Jeff."

I was surprised by how deeply those small words hit me. There is a place in a man's heart that is specifically reserved for praise from his father, and when my dad said those small words, that cold, dark place began to glow with warmth ever so faintly. And when that happened, it occurred to me that this feeling was not new to me. It was the same feeling that came over me whenever I talked with God and he continually said, "I love you, Jeff. I love you. I love you. I love you." Maybe these two fathers in my life were not so different.

Mom came back. "Well, let's sit down, shall we?"

We sat as we always had. Mom at the end, me on her left, and my dad opposite me. I could almost imagine God here to my left, protecting me from everything, just like in the video he sent me. I relaxed a little.

We ate our chicken as if we were a real family, which we were not.

At one point, the man, John, dad, asked Mom, "So what do you do for work, Julie?"

"I work at a hotel nearby, cleaning rooms."

"Oh, that sounds interesting. It must be rewarding work," he replied.

"It's hard," Mom said. "But it pays the bills."

He turned to me. "And you are a computer programmer. Where do you work?"

"Omniscient Technologies."

"Didn't I hear about them in the news today?"

I was surprised. "Did you? What did you hear?"

"It was something about your company searching for a bug that might be related to the Adams Corporation email leak."

I had just talked to the reporter that morning. I must have missed the report he put out. And now I didn't know how to respond. I said, "I must have missed that article."

My mom and dad continued talking with each other about small things, and about me. I ate my food. My dad never showed any signs of anger. Never once did he even raise his voice. I don't know if that means he got rid of his anger issues, or he is just covering it. Call me cynical, but it's probably the latter, which means it will probably come back yet. I wasn't really interested in being there when it happened, but I knew I had to be here with my mom in case it did.

When we were done, Mom cleared the table and I sat there with my dad. He fidgeted with his napkin, then finally said, "Jeff..." I waited for him to continue. "You know that when you were young, I didn't always treat your mom the way I should have. I know now that you need to treat people a certain way in order to get them to respond a certain way, and I didn't do that right with your mother. And because of it, you may not have had the best upbringing. It was a mistake."

He looked at me, and when I didn't respond, he continued. "And so, I just wanted to start off on the right foot here, so to speak, and put the past in the past. All right?"

He looked at me as if this pathetic excuse for an apology could magically erase years of the pain he put me and Mom through. If it wasn't so tragic, it would almost be laughable. No, I wasn't going to forgive him right now, but in order to answer his question, I could agree with him that yes, he did want to start off on the right foot here. I agreed that that was what he wanted, by saying, "OK".

"Good." He smiled as if he had gained a victory.

Mom came back. "Well, why don't we go sit in the living room?"

"I would love to do just that," Dad responded, "but I have to go. But I do hope you two have a lovely evening."

He walked to the door and Mom followed. Soon he said his final goodbyes and was gone.

Mom relaxed and leaned against a wall. "Well, that didn't go as badly as it could have. How are you, Jeff?"

I shrugged.

"And what do you think of your dad now?"

I shrugged again. "He's older."

"Yes, I guess we all are."

"What do you think of him?" I asked.

"He seemed very polite, but then again he could always be that way if he wanted to, especially to strangers." She shook her head. "We didn't see the real him today."

"Does that mean you're not going to get back together with him?"

She shook her head. "I don't think so." Then she walked up to me and placed her hands on the sides of my head and looked into my eyes. "Do you want us to?" She let go, but continued.

"Of course you do. Everyone wants their parents to be together, don't you?"

I shrugged, but then added, "Not necessarily. Not if they're bad for you."

"Well... that's in the past. And now, I have the whole evening free, but I don't feel like doing anything. I think I'm going to snuggle into the sofa and watch something. Want to join me, Jeff?"

"I think I'll go home and do the same."

"OK. Have a good evening, Jeff."

"You too, Mom."

I gave her a hug and headed out the door. All I wanted was to go home and relax.

7:13 PM

I lay myself down on my sofa, pondering supper with my dad. Then I took out my phone and wrote an email.

> From: jeffd@omniscient.software
>
> To: god@heaven
>
> Subject: My dad
>
> Hi God.
>
> I guess you know that I had supper with my dad this evening. He seemed nice enough, and he kinda asked me to forgive him. Mom doesn't trust him though. Do you have any fatherly advice for me?

I soon got this reply.

> From: god@heaven
>
> To: jeffd@omniscient.software

Subject: Re: My dad

Hi Jeff, my son, my friend. It's always good to talk with you. I love when you come to me and share your heart and your life with me. I love to live your life with you.

Forgiveness is not about the other person, it is about you, and your heart. You need to forgive your dad for your sake, to cleanse your heart. You need to wash out the resentment and bitterness that is living there. Only when you forgive will the pain start going away. Forgive, Jeff. Forgive your father for what he has done both to you and your mom. But there is a difference between forgiveness and trust.

Jeff, no matter what you do, I am your real father. I love you with a never-ending, undying, unconditional love. You will always be my son, and I will always be with you, no matter what.

If you seek me, you will find me, if you search with all your heart. I promise.

I wasn't sure if this message of forgiveness was something I really wanted to hear. On one hand I wanted to hold on to my hurt, but on the other hand, I did want to be free of it. And what was this about seeking God? Hadn't I already found him? Wasn't I talking with him right now? What did he mean by that? I composed another email to ask him.

From: jeffd@omniscient.software

To: god@heaven

Subject: Re: My dad

Thanks for that, but what do you mean about searching for you? Haven't I already found you?

When I hit Send, something strange happened. I got a little message window on my phone popping up saying "Error: The address 'god@heaven' in the 'To' field was not recognized. Please make sure it is a properly formed email address."

I sat up straight. This can't be happening. I tried sending again. Same error. I tried shaking up the address by adding characters then removing them again. Same error. I tried composing a brand new email instead of replying. Same error. It must be something I'm doing wrong. I kept trying ideas. I restarted my phone. Same error. I tried it on my laptop. I tried through a web browser instead of the email client. I tried sending from different email addresses. I even went online and found a way to send an email from a new email account, like I had when I first discovered God's email address. Everything failed.

I sat down on my sofa, breathing hard. What could this mean? Why is God not talking? Did I do something to offend him? Am I not seeking him hard enough? What's wrong?

It occurred to me that I was now in the same place I was a week ago, disconnected from God, so what's the big deal? The big deal is that in the last few days, my life had been changed. I had been touched deeply. I enjoyed, I needed, this deep encounter with God, and I couldn't go back. I couldn't.

I reread the last thing he said to me. "If you seek me, you will find me, if you search with all your heart. I promise." I was going to take him up on this promise. It was time to get serious. I suddenly had become desperate, as desperate as a drowning man needs a gulp of life-giving air.

I looked at the time, then headed toward the door. The answer was out there, and I was going to find it.

7:59 PM

When I got outside, the clouds had grown dark. The wind had picked up, and it was starting to rain. I hurried to my car and started driving. I had no address, but I knew what I was looking for when I found it. After a few minutes, I pulled into a parking lot next to a large building. Through the darkness, I saw that the building had a cross on it.

I got out and jogged my way through the rain to the little roof covering the door. I didn't really know what I was going to say, but I thought surely this must be a place I could find answers.

As I got to the large doors, I saw a man significantly older than me come out and close the doors behind him. I hope he wasn't locking up for the night. When he saw me approaching him, he turned his attention to me and smiled. It wasn't one of those small smiles I give people instead of saying "Hello." It looked like he was actually pleased to see me.

"Hello," he said to me and stuck out his hand. I shook it.

He waited for me to say something, so I said, "Hi. Do you... work here?"

His grin increased as if I made a joke. I didn't know what lingo these people use.

"I do. I am Paul. Can I help you, young man?"

"I...", I searched for the right words to say. I couldn't find any, so I searched for any words to say at all. I finally chose these. "Is it possible to talk with God?"

"Well, I am just locking up for the evening," he said, then asked, "Do you mean you want to talk with God yourself alone, or do you want to talk with me?"

"Umm... You I guess."

"Then let's come into my office." He opened the doors again, and we walked inside. The building was spacious, but completely empty right now. He walked to a hallway, then into an office room. I followed. He sat on his side of his desk, and I on mine.

"You have the look of a troubled man. What troubles you so much that you would seek me out in the middle of a storm?"

I said, "Do you think it is possible to talk with God?"

"Of course. God hears our prayers, no matter where we are."

I rephrased the question. "I mean... I don't mean us talking to God. Is it possible for God to talk to us?"

"It appears as though he has in the ancient past, to the great men of old, yes."

"Can he, does he still, today? With our technology?"

"I don't see how technology makes a difference, but are you asking if God still speaks today?"

"Yes."

"In that case, of course he does." I was about to get my hopes up, but he continued. "He speaks to us through nature. His handiwork can be seen by everyone." The man reached over and picked up a large book and placed it in front of us. "But primarily, this is how he speaks to us now." He tapped the book with his finger. "With this."

I pondered the large book, and how much it didn't resemble the email client in my pocket. "But what about to us, individually? Like to me? Doesn't God do that?"

"I'm sorry, my son. The words of God have been written down for us here. You and I are not going to add to them, are we?"

"Well, no... but can't he speak still today, and we just won't put it into there?"

"I'm sorry. The canon is closed, as we say."

I sat there, not knowing what to say. If my only hope, this man who is supposed to know how God works, says It's not possible, what hope was there? I said, "So it's not possible?"

"God has chosen to not speak directly to us now, because

he has already revealed himself to us, and that was sufficient. No more is needed."

This spark inside me refused to die, and out of desperation, I spoke the thoughts of my innermost heart. "But wouldn't you like it if God spoke directly to you, and talked to you about who you are and what you were going through, and gave you his perspective on what you were doing or thinking of doing? He could give you fatherly advice, and he could give you encouragement and direction. Wouldn't you like that?"

The man shifted in his seat. "Of course, in an ideal world, that would be of great benefit, but it doesn't happen, does it? Do you know of anyone who can have a telephone conversation with God? It would be a miracle!"

"Maybe God can still do miracles."

He was ready for that argument too. "Yes, he can do miracles, but he chooses not to. There is a difference between God's ability and his will."

"But why wouldn't he want to?" I asked, somewhat exasperated. "Isn't he a God of love? Isn't he powerful?"

"He doesn't because he doesn't need to. He has already done great and mighty works, and these are recorded here."

Ah yes, back to the book. I looked off to the side.

"What is it, exactly, your heart is searching for?" he asked me.

I looked at him, and the frustration in me came out in a burst of honesty. "I'm looking for a God who is relevant to me, in my situation, a God who knows me. Me. Jeff Davis. With all due respect to your book, sir, I wasn't alive then. I am now. I need a God who can meet with me now. And if your God can't, then I'm not interested." I stood up.

"Wait," he said with genuine concern. "You can still come to God..."

I shook my head and moved toward the door. He didn't say anything else, so I let myself out.

I walked slowly to the car, letting myself get wet in the rain. By the time I was there, I felt so alone that I placed my arms on the roof of the car and buried my head in them. When God first started talking to me, it rocked my world. Now he's gone and I feel even more rocked by this loss. Or wasn't he gone? Was this man just wrong? I didn't know. And I was too tired to think.

I felt a hand on my back and I whirled around to see Paul quietly standing in the rain with me.

"Jeff," he said to me. "You are searching. I pray that you find what you are searching for."

I could tell from the compassion in his eyes that he meant it. "Thanks," I responded to him, and I meant it too.

CHAPTER 12

Friday, 8:00 AM

"Hello Jeffrey."

"Hi Garth."

"Hi Jeff."

"Hi Doug. So, anything interesting happening around here?" I asked as I sat down at my desk.

"Negative," said Garth.

"Not really," said Doug, but then he added, "Oh, Susan says we will each get an extra two thousand five hundred dollars on our next paycheck."

I said, "Oh. Right. The hacker payment. I had forgotten about that."

"You forgot about what you were tasked to do?" asked Garth, glancing my way.

"Um. No. Just the payment part. That's all."

"What exactly have you been doing, then?" he asked. He swivelled his chair to face me and I got a look at his shirt. It was another Star Wars shirt. It showed a picture of Darth Vader, with the caption of "Come over to the dark side."

That startled me a little. Was this a subtle hint that Max wanted me to join him? Did he tell Garth to wear this shirt to put pressure on me? Was Garth already on the dark side? I had no evidence of this, only doubts. "I... uh..." I started to speak but had nothing to say. What was the question again? Oh yeah. "I've been setting up logging on servers to try to catch the bad guys."

"And are you getting closer?" He looked at me.

"I might be," I said, looking away. "I should look over the logs to see if there is anything there." I sat down and got to work.

I examined the logs from Adams and from our own server, and found absolutely nothing. It's as if the bad guys knew I was looking for them and went underground. Yeah, good choice of words.

I went out to the kitchen and grabbed a cup of coffee. I sat down at one of the tables and looked through the large windows. I spied the river in the distance. It looked so peaceful out there, as if nature didn't care what was going on. The birds couldn't be bothered with the fact that there was a man out there with a gun who expected me to give him passwords. Oh, to be free and at peace like a bird.

I remembered when I sat beside the river reading emails from God. That did give me peace. That felt good. But now he's gone. And I don't know if I'll get that back.

I took a sip of coffee and continued letting my mind wander. And my dad is back. I wonder if he will want to get together with me more. I wonder if I even want that. God said I need to forgive. Maybe he's right. I took a deep breath and let it out.

"What's up, Jeff?"

I turned around to see Veronica getting herself a cup of coffee. She came and sat down at my table.

I smiled at the company. "I was just contemplating life."

"Oh, don't do that too much, you'll get in trouble."

"Why?"

"Because you'll realize that it sucks. Better to just live for the moment."

I'm not sure how much I agreed with that, but it kinda felt good to have someone to talk with. "I saw my dad yesterday."

"Oh! How long has it been?"

"Thirteen years."

"That's a long time. I'll bet it feels good to have a father in your life. Unless he's a jerk of course. Then tell him to take a hike."

I shrugged. "He seems nice enough, but my mom doesn't trust him."

"My dad is nice enough. Well, he's my stepdad. My mom married him when I was twelve."

I said to her, "So you grew up without a dad, then had one at twelve?"

"Yup."

"And I grew up *with* a dad until he left when I was sixteen."

She smiled. "Between the two of us, we could make almost one normal person. I guess we should get together then, huh?"

I looked at her to see if there was some underlying meaning there. Yes there was. I wanted to say, "I would like that," except that God told me to treat her like a sister. So I looked away.

"Unless you're not interested in me?" I couldn't believe she had the nerve to ask that. This was one gutsy lady. I admit I was drawn to that.

I met her gaze and nodded. "I am," I said. Yeah, God might not have liked that response, but I was just being honest here.

"Let's do lunch?" she asked.

"OK," I replied.

"Unless something comes up again," she added.

"Yeah."

"Good!" She got up, and patted me on the shoulder on her way out. I sat there and finished my coffee, then went back to work. Maybe a new idea will come to me.

GOD'S EMAIL ADDRESS

8:24 AM

On my way back to my desk, the new idea I was hoping for suddenly came to me. I must have still been in a talkative mood from my conversation with Veronica, because I said out loud, "Oh, I just had a thought."

"Just one?" quipped Garth. "I have several on a daily basis."

"Good thoughts are hard to come by," Doug added. "They are valuable."

"And do you also get several a day?" I asked him.

"I don't know if I'd say that," he said. "But you have to take them when they come to you."

"Yeah, I've noticed that you can't really cause a good idea to come to your mind," I said. "It kind of just comes to you."

"Normally on the way to the restroom," said Garth.

"Is that why you drink so much Dr. Pepper?" asked Doug.

"I refuse to divulge the secret of my extreme success," he replied. We chuckled and got back to work.

My idea was that I should look at some of the IP addresses of the computers connecting into Omniscient, and check their locations to see where they were coming from. So I began looking at IP addresses connecting in to our local server. Most of the locations were right here in the city, but one was odd. It was 203.186.69.98. When I looked up its geolocation, it said it was located in Hong Kong. That was odd. I don't think anyone here on staff was currently in that part of the world. So I looked up who's account was being accessed from Hong Kong and I read his name. This wasn't good.

Just then my phone rang. I answered it. "Hello?"

"Jeff this is Peter. Can you please come see me in my office? I would like an update on how things are going."

"OK"

We hung up, and I walked out there.

Sitting down in his office, he leaned forward and said, "Well Jeffrey, tell me the progress you are making. Are we any closer to catching the people we are looking for?"

I said, "Yesterday the Information Underground threatened me again."

"Oh, Jeff, do the police know?"

"Yes, I've told them. I've visited the police a number of times already. Anyway, after they threatened me, they tried to get me to join them."

"Join them!"

"Yeah."

"I expect you turned them down."

"Well, I didn't turn them down right there. I kinda played along."

"For what purpose? Jeff, these are dangerous people. Go to the police and be done with them."

"Well, you see sir, we need hard evidence. I was hoping we could catch them, and for that to happen, I need to play along."

Peter scowled. "I don't like it. I think it's too dangerous."

"We want them caught, don't we?"

"Well, yes."

"Then the next time I see them, I will bring the police, and the police will arrest them. Then when that happens, we can tell the media, and they will tell everybody that the hackers have been caught. Then people will trust Omniscient again, and we can get investors, and everything will be back to normal."

My boss paused and furrowed his eyebrows. "Well, that is what we want, yes." He scowled again. "I still don't like putting one of my men in harm's way."

"The police will be there."

"Very well then, follow through. But still, be careful, Jeff."

"OK, I will."

Peter sat back in his chair. "This certainly is an interesting turn. If all goes well, this might all be over sooner than we know it. Very well. Good. Is there anything else we need to discuss?"

"Yes actually. Just as I came here, I noticed that someone in the office has been accessing his account from Hong Kong."

"Hong Kong!? I don't know of anyone travelling there right now."

"No, the person is right here in the building."

"Who is it?"

"Garth Fonte."

"And he's at his desk right now?"

"Yes"

Peter consulted a piece of paper by his desk, reached for his phone, and hit three quick buttons. Before I knew it, Peter Steele was asking Garth to come join us in this office. When he showed up, he sat down beside me, two chairs away. The chairs didn't have armrests.

Peter began. "Jeff here tells me that your account, Garth, has been accessed from Hong Kong."

"Hong Kong?" Garth asked. "Clearly not, seeing as I'm in your midst as we speak."

"It might not be Garth doing it," I interrupted. "We might be hacked by someone out there. They might have gotten his password."

"Unlikely," Garth snorted. "I keep all my passwords incredibly secure."

"It might not be anything you've done," I said. "It could be our server."

"Are you suggesting our own server has been compromised?" Peter asked me.

"It would seem so," I said.

"That is unfortunate," he replied. "What do you recommend we do?"

"I think there is only one thing to do," I said. "Reinstall our installation of Omniscient, and change everyone's passwords."

Peter looked distraught. "Is there no other way of fixing it? Do we have to change everyone's password? If we do this, then everyone will know. Word would get out."

Garth added, "Fixing a major security breach will certainly require changing passwords."

"We need to keep the bad news to a minimum," said Peter, "or morale will suffer. If word got out to the outside that our own server has been compromised..." He didn't finish the thought. He didn't need to. Then turning to Garth he said, "Thank you, Garth. Unless you have anything else to add, you may go."

"I do not." He stood and left.

Peter said to me, "Admitting we have a compromised server is something I am loath to do. Our disposition must be that we trust Omniscient explicitly. We must be sure of this before we take action. Will you look into this, Jeff, and prove it is true?"

"OK," I said. "And I should tell Ronja too, since she is the system administrator."

"Do what you must," he said. "Thank you, Jeff. You are dismissed."

8:48 AM

On my way to Ronja's office, I thought to myself. Who hacked us? Was it the Information Underground? If so, how? Through the security bug we haven't found yet? And if so, why are they asking me for our god account password if they are already in? Are they just testing me to see if I'll give them the right answer? That thought made me feel even worse. Maybe they already know the password and are seeing if I will give them the right one. But I don't have to worry about that, because the police will get them.

But what if the Information Underground isn't the only organization out there who can hack? Maybe someone else has hacked us. Maybe Ronja will have some ideas.

I was at her office and knocked on her open door.

She looked up at me. "Hello Jeff. How is the email server?"

"Fine. No, there might be a problem."

"Do you need another password, or do you need me to fix something?"

"Maybe. I think the..." I stopped and closed the door, with me on the inside, so nobody could listen in. "I think the email server might be hacked."

She looked serious. "Why do you think this?"

"Because someone just logged in from Hong Kong."

"So?"

"So he's not in Hong Kong. He's right here."

"Who is it?"

"Garth."

"Garth? We should talk to him." She got up and opened the door and started down the hall. I followed.

When she got there, she said to him, "Garth, Jeff says there is a problem with your login."

Garth kept staring at his screen. "There is no problem, Ms. System Administrator."

"Because if there is, I can take a look at it for you."

"There is nothing to look at."

"Alright, Garth. But if you have a problem, you may come see me in my office. I will help you."

"Understood."

I looked over at Doug, who was watching and smiling. So was I.

When Ronja finally left, I heard Garth say under his breath, "That woman! Give me some peace."

Ronja and I went back to her office, and I said, "I don't

think Garth had anything to do with it. I think the server is hacked."

"Or perhaps Garth's password has been hacked."

"Mmm... probably not. He seems the kind of guy who would take security seriously."

"Still, we should ask him to change it."

"Yeah, probably," I agreed.

"I'll call him and tell him," she said, reaching for her phone.

"No, I'll do it. I'm going there anyway."

She put the phone down. "OK."

"But the question is," I started, "how can we verify the server is actually hacked? Can we test something?"

"First of all, I will change the root password, and the god password while I'm there. Since Peter asked me to share the root password with you, would you like the god password as well?"

I had to think about that. This is exactly what Max wanted me to tell him. If I get the god email address and password from Ronja, then I will know it, and I can tell Max. Maybe it would be a good thing to know. But then again, maybe he will beat it out of me, and if I didn't actually know it, there would be nothing to tell. It would be easier to not accidentally leak it out if I didn't actually know it.

I shook my head. "No, don't tell me the god password. But I do want the root password again."

"OK, I will do it right now." She went to a website that generated passwords, clicked some buttons, then told me, "It will now be 'PlentyLoyaltyThereforeDecrease'. Upper case first letters, no spaces."

"Thanks," I said. "And what should we do if the server is actually hacked?"

"Then we should rebuild it from scratch, and everyone must change their passwords."

"That's exactly what Peter doesn't want, because then word will get out that our server got hacked, and people will no longer trust us."

"Yes, I can see that. I will look for evidence that the server has been compromised, and hope there is none."

"Good. Thanks Ronja."

"You're welcome."

8:53 AM

When I got back to my desk, I told Garth that Ronja wanted him to change his password.

He said, "Already done," without looking up.

"Something secure?" I asked.

"My password is a thirty-two character long string of random upper case letters, lower case letters, numbers, and symbols. It is stored in my password vault on my personal VPS, which only I have access to. All communication to and from said VPS is encrypted with the latest industry recommended encryption scheme. Accessing this password vault by me requires two-factor authentication, both another password which is unimaginably difficult to hack, as well as a text message sent to my phone. Is that secure enough for you, Mr. Davis?"

I could have guessed half of that, but it didn't really surprise me. "Yes," I said.

"Jeff, do you have a minute?" I turned to see Veronica standing in the doorway to our room. "Kaleisha said I should talk with you."

"About what?" I asked, but Veronica wasn't listening. She was examining Garth's little whiteboard of jokes, which displayed these characters:

(2b || !2b)

"Are you enjoying today's witticism, Ms. Customer Service?" asked Garth.

"Hilarious," she replied. Then to me, she said, "Can I talk to you in my office?"

We walked to the other side of the building, and as we sat down, I decided to stir her up a little. I said, "Your office is actually a cubicle, not an office."

She looked hard at me and said, "I like to think of it as an office."

I enjoyed her stare and grinned. "OK"

She restarted the conversation. "Our customers are not happy. They have been hearing about us in the news. They have been asking if we support a migration path to other communications products."

"And Kaleisha asked you to talk to me about it?"

She smiled. "It was my idea. I thought that maybe you could calm their fears. Tell them there is nothing to worry about. Everything will be fine."

I sat there, pondering this idea. I didn't know how to respond. I didn't know that everything would actually be fine. And I didn't like the idea of phoning people and talking to them, especially when I wouldn't know what to say to them. I was a computer programmer just so I didn't have to talk to people. I shrugged. "I don't know what to say."

"Just say you'll do it. We need to do something. Customer confidence is very low."

"I mean I wouldn't know what I would say to them."

"Tell them... tell them we are working to find any bugs we might have."

"We always find and fix bugs. Constantly. Nothing has changed there."

"Good. It would mean a lot more coming from an actual developer. Please, Jeff, we think this could help us out a lot."

I looked at her. It was hard to say no, so I said, "OK."

GOD'S EMAIL ADDRESS

"Great! I'll email you some people you can call."

"OK," I said again and stood up.

"Oh, by the way, what does Garth's joke mean? The two b and the other two b?"

"It's not *and*, it's *or*. Two vertical pipes mean *or*. Well, logical *or*, I mean. One vertical pipe means bitwise *or*, but you don't need to know that.

"And the exclamation mark?", she asked.

"Not"

"And the parenthesis?"

"Nothing. That's just for show."

I watched her face do the calculations. "Right. Got it. Yeah, funny. Thanks Jeff. I'll get that email to you."

"Thanks," I said, and went back to my desk.

9:06 AM

After many minutes of emotional anguish, mental gymnastics, and bodily sweating, I finally was able to make the first call.

"Hi, this is Jeff Davis from Omniscient Technologies. May I please speak with Rajesh Mukherjee please?"

"I'm sorry. Did you say Rajesh or Ramesh Mukherjee?"

"Um... The first one. Rajesh. You have two people with that same last name who work there?"

"Three. The third is named Dev. They are not related. One moment please."

I waited a minute before hearing, "Hello, this is Rajesh Mukherjee."

"Hi, this is Jeff Davis. I'm a developer from Omniscient Technologies. I heard you were having a problem with your installation of Omniscient?"

"Hello Jeff. No, we do not have a problem, but perhaps

199

you have a problem."

"What is the problem?"

"What is the problem!? The problem is that we don't trust your software. Too many people are breaking into it."

"We are actively trying to fix all known bugs."

"Well you had better hurry up and fix this bug, because we are looking into changing email software."

"Do you have evidence you have been hacked?"

"No we do not, and we want to keep it that way."

"Maybe Omniscient is fine and you should keep on using it." This was my attempt at telling him there is nothing to worry about and everything is fine.

"Are you telling me, Jeff, that Omniscient doesn't have any security bugs at all? Is that what you are telling me?"

"There's none that we know of."

"What about the data breach at Adams Corporation? They are blaming that on you."

"I... I don't think they are."

"They had leaked email messages. How could they have leaked except through their email program?"

"Perhaps their server itself got hacked. Or their database. Or a desktop. Maybe one of the executives' desktops got a virus. That happens."

"You are covering up the fact that a hacker contacted you about a security bug, and you paid him for it. This is a sign of guilt."

"It is a sign of responsibility. We were doing the responsible thing."

"So you admit that you paid him off?"

"There is nothing wrong with paying for bug reports."

"So have you fixed the bug he reported yet?"

I paused. He got me there. "He never left a bug," I said.

"And that is why we are looking for other software, because you have a security bug that you don't know about."

"Maybe he didn't leave a bug report because there is no bug."

"Do you want me to base the security of my company on your word of *maybe there is no bug*? I will not do this."

I paused, thinking of something to say, but then he continued. "Goodbye, Jeff." Then he hung up.

I hung up too.

Well that didn't go well. I got up and went for a walk down the hall. I suspected every other phone call I was supposed to make would end the same way. Was this the beginning of the end? Would people just start leaving and never come back? Were we hemorrhaging customers and soon nobody will want us at all, and soon we'll all pack up and go home? Then a thought occurred to me. Perhaps there was some way we could still win this. Maybe we won't go down without a fight.

I stopped walking and stood there outside someone's office. I thought to myself. What is the problem here? The real problem is that people don't trust us anymore. In that case, how do you fight lack of trust? Well, the best thing would be to announce to the world that the hackers have been caught. Let's hope that works. But maybe there is another way. I had an idea, and I had to go talk to Peter.

CHAPTER 13

9:19 AM

"Jeff!"

I heard my name being called and realized it was coming from inside the office I was standing in front of. The office belonged to Andy, who did graphic design, sound design, and some UX (User eXperience).

"Jeff, come look at this", he repeated.

I went inside his room. Andy had an outside room with his own door instead of a cubicle, not because he was higher up the corporate ladder than anyone else, but because he worked with sound and people tended to be annoyed by all his sound making.

"I just made a new sound, and I want you to see it," he said.

"Don't you mean *hear it*?" I asked.

"Nah, this sound needs to be *seen*. You can practically see what's going on when you hear it."

"OK," I said. Maybe another reason we kept Andy in his own room was because he was so much unlike a developer. He didn't have black and white Dilbert comics on his wall. Instead, he put up large colourful posters. There was one that said, "Blood Brothers", with two hands grasping each other. Another one was a stylized big red dot with the words, "I'm sorry Dave, I'm afraid I can't do that." A third was a giant poster of a Campbell's Tomato Soup can. He also decorated himself with a tight-fitting flowery shirt, a tattoo of something abstract on his left arm, and a beret on his head. And somehow all the colours in his room went together well, including the bowl of saltwater taffy on his desk. Artists care about such things--colours, not salt water taffy.

Andy turned some dials on some speakers he had in his office, clicked a few buttons on his mouse, and I heard a kind-of chirping binging sound. His eyes were wide. "Isn't it awesome?", he said.

"Yeah," I said. "Great. What is it for?"

"It's the new Beginning Conversation sound. Can't you just see someone waiting for you to talk?"

"I guess so."

"It's confident, but not overly aggressive. It's a request to engage in human conversation. You can almost see it in his eyes that he craves human interaction." He scrunched up his eyebrows and waved his head while he played the sound again. It went chirp-bing again, the same as last time. "Do you see it?" he asked.

"I hear something."

"Come on. Close your eyes, Jeff."

I closed my eyes. He continued talking. "Now imagine you are in your house, at your front door, and there is someone outside it, and he presses the doorbell." Andy played the sound again. "Now you open the door. What do you see?"

I opened my eyes. "A person?"

"Yes! Close your eyes again." He played chirp-bing again. "Can you see his expression? How is he feeling?"

I said with my eyes closed, "He... he is pleased to see me and wants to come in, but is cheerful."

"Perfect!" Andy shouted. I opened my eyes. "That's the scene I was painting. I think you're seeing it, Jeff."

"I didn't even know you could see sounds," I said.

"Of course you can. Everything is connected." He gestured around his office. "Some of these posters are loud, some are soft. *Loud* and *soft* are volume adjectives used for colours. Colour and sound are connected. Everything's connected."

I pondered that, then added, "When I'm on the phone with a bad connection, trying to listen closely, I close my eyes."

"Exactly," he pointed. "You do that so what you're seeing with your eyes doesn't contradict what's going in your ears. And when you're watching someone play an instrument," He moved his one hand over the other like a violin. "You open your eyes and watch closely to make it sound better."

"That's interesting," I said. "But are we discussing this for a reason?"

"Nah," He waved a hand at me. "I just wanted to show off my new sound. You can go if you have to. Have a taffy."

"Thanks," I said, grabbing a piece from the bowl. "It's a very nice sound, Andy."

"Thank you. I worked hard at it."

I stood up and left his office as I popped the taffy in my mouth and the wrapper in my pocket. Mmm. Root Beer. I still had to talk to Peter about my idea. But before I got there, my phone rang. I looked at it and didn't recognize the number. I considered not answering it, but then reasoned that it might be important, with everything going on. So I answered it.

"Hello?" I mumbled.

"Jeff." I would recognize that deep gravelly voice anywhere. "Do you have the password?"

I quickly swallowed the taffy. "The god password for our office here?" I asked.

"That's the one."

"Yes," I lied.

"Good. Meet me in Traders Lane, beside Dragon Express, in five minutes."

"At The Forks Market?" I asked.

"Yes. And come alone."

I started to protest, but he hung up. I looked at the time. It was exactly 9:30. At 9:35 I had to be out the building, across the way, and into the Forks Market building, and inside a little dark hallway to meet with a very dangerous man, probably armed, who doesn't want me to call the police first. There was no question in my mind whether I would call the police or not.

9:35 AM

I stood outside the Forks building and looked around. I couldn't see the person I was hoping to see before meeting Max, so I decided to stall. I thought I could push two minutes. If I would show up at 9:37 and give some excuse about being late, I could probably get away with it. And it would help if I came into the meeting breathing hard, so I ran up and down the sidewalk for a minute or two. Then I went inside.

The main area in the middle of the building was full of tables and chairs for people to eat at. It was surrounded by small businesses selling culturally diverse food. Near the back of the building, connecting the eating area to another area was a small, dimly lit hallway. It had the words "Traders Lane" lettered above it. I advanced toward this hallway.

It was empty.

I went and stood in the middle of it, so anyone could see me.

"You're late!" I heard the voice say. I turned to see Max walk out from an open doorway that led into an adjoining restaurant.

"Sorry. I went looking for a piece of paper to write down the password on, for you. Then I ran to get here as soon as possible." I said, trying to breathe hard without it looking fake.

"You said you had the password."

"I had it on my phone. I just wrote it down for you." I examined him, looking for his gun, so I knew if I should feel nervous or not. He could easily be hiding it under his leather jacket. And even though I didn't see it, I decided I should still feel nervous anyway, especially considering I didn't actually have a password to give to him.

"Hand it over," he said.

As I reached into my pocket, I used my peripheral vision to look for the police I had called. There was nobody. I had to stall.

"Ah... what will you give me in exchange for this? I want to know before I betray my company."

"You already made that decision. You'd be part of the team, with lots of money coming in."

"How much money, exactly?" I asked, glancing behind him.

He glanced behind himself, then turned back to me. His countenance turned angry. "You're stalling," he said.

"I'm not stalling," I said, subconsciously backing up. "I'm just trying to get a picture of what I'm getting myself into here, that's all."

"Give me the password right now." He walked toward me with his hand out.

I started sweating. Memories of this man holding a gun to my head came flooding back. It was a mistake messing with him. What was I thinking? My brain started shutting down. I pulled something out of my pocket and held it out.

He took it and looked at it. "What's this?" he turned it around looking for writing and found nothing. "A candy wrapper?"

He crumpled it in his strong fist and threw it down. Then he started coming to me. "Are you messing with me?" he demanded. My feet were glued to the ground in fear and my eyes were wide. "Are you trying to play me?" He grabbed my shirt with his left hand. "Do you know what happens to people when they think they can mess with me?" He drew his strong right arm back.

I braced for the worst, expecting to feel the pain. I may have lifted my hands to protect my face, I don't remember. But before his fist landed, we heard a shout.

"Freeze! Get down on the ground!" We both looked and saw a policeman holding his gun out at Max. It was Joseph Wakefield, and he was breathing very hard. It was about time he got here.

Max brought his right hand swiftly toward my face, but instead of striking me, he grabbed me and spun me around so I was between him and the policeman. And his arm was around my neck.

"I said get down! On the ground!" Joseph shouted.

"Or what?" Max asked. "You'll shoot? You'll hit this innocent bystander here. Or should I say *guilty* bystander?" He flexed his right arm to make me cry out in pain. He was backing up, dragging me backwards out of the hallway.

"Backup will be here any minute and you'll be surrounded," Joseph said. "There is no way you can get away with this. Give up now."

"Ha! I have a hostage." By now we were out of Traders Lane.

In the midst of my panic, my brain still managed to send me an idea. I took a breath and lifted my knees as far up as I could. This, of course, made me very heavy. For a second I was hanging by my neck, completely unable to breathe.

Max swore and threw me off to the side.

"Now get down! On the ground!" Joseph yelled again, still pointing his gun at the man.

Max didn't. He said, "You wouldn't shoot. Look at all these people. You'll hit one of them." He moved himself side-to-side like a moving target.

I looked around and saw people gawking and staring at what was taking place right in front of them. It's as if they had absolutely no thought that anything bad might happen to them. It was like they were watching TV, and they now had something to tell their friends or family when they got home. Some even had their phones out, recording proof of police aggression, as if the policeman that just saved my life was somehow the bad guy.

Joseph yelled at the people. "Everybody get down!" Then he made his only mistake, the mistake Max must have been waiting for. He pointed his pistol up in the sky and was about to fire a warning shot, when he remembered he was inside a building. He looked up. And when he looked up, Max made his move.

Max sprang forward and landed low in front of Joseph. With his left hand, he grabbed Joseph around his right knee. With his right hand, he reached up between Joseph's outstretched arms, toward his chin. Then he stood up quickly, moving forward. Joseph got pushed backwards and was unable to regain his footing. His arms flailed uselessly. As he came down to land on his back, Max's right hand pushed Joseph's head up and back so that both their weights combined drove the policeman's head onto the concrete floor with a sickening thud.

Max got up. Joseph did not.

I lay on the floor, watching in horror as the man who just knocked out an armed policeman now came toward me. My eyes were wide, and my breathing was shallow.

He pointed his finger directly at me and said very clearly, "I don't care what Jade says. I'm going to kill you. I'm going to kill you, and I'm going to enjoy it."

Then Joseph moaned and started moving.

Max turned to see him stirring, then immediately ran away, leaving me on the floor trying to recover from what just happened.

9:44 AM

I tried standing and found that I still could. I rubbed my neck. It was sore but fully functional. Joseph was up too, leaning against a wall. "Are you OK?" I asked him.

"I'm fine," he muttered. "Just a bump to the head." He winced. "Stupid. Rookie mistake. I should know better."

"He's dangerous," I said.

"Yeah."

Then two other policemen came running in. I guess Joseph wasn't bluffing about the backup. He pointed to where Max ran off to. "He's gone. He went that way. You might be able to catch him. Black leather jacket." They ran off.

Turning to me again, he said, "You'll need to come in and make a statement."

Then he went and talked with some people who recorded the video. He got their contact information and he gave them his card and asked them to send the video to him as evidence.

Then he came back and said to me, "Meet me at the station in fifteen minutes?"

"Umm...", I replied, "can I get a ride with you?"

He looked at me. "I don't want to bring you back here. Don't you have a car?"

I looked away.

He continued. "Oh. you're afraid you'll meet him again."

"He's still out there," I said.

"Listen, Jeff. When people like this have a run-in with the cops, they usually get scared and go into hiding."

"He threatened my life," I said. And besides, he didn't exactly lose this run-in with the cops. He won. It will only give him more boldness to keep going.

He said, "I'll take you to your car. You'll be fine then."

"OK."

The two other policemen came back and reported not seeing anyone. Joseph thanked them for their help. Then we walked to his police car parked outside, which was still running.

He drove me to my car where I switched vehicles. I looked all around and inside my car first before I got in. You never know.

At the station, I filled out a report of what happened and signed it.

I put it on Joseph's desk, sat down opposite him and asked, "So, what happens now?"

He leaned back in his squeaky wooden chair and put his hands behind his head.

"First thing, watch your back, Jeff."

"Thanks!" That didn't make me feel better.

"And second, assaulting an officer is an offence that can get him up to five years in prison. And we have it on tape, so it should be easy enough to convict him. He'll probably fight it, but he'll lose."

"But we need to catch him first."

"Yes we do. So if you see him again, let me know. I'll also share his picture around the city. It will be hard for him to hide. Maybe he'll leave the city."

"Yeah," I said, but I wasn't convinced. I tried to hang on to that thought for hope, but it didn't really stick.

"So what do I do now?" I asked.

"Go back to your regular life, and if you see him again, call 911."

"OK. Thanks." I stood up to leave.

I had a feeling I would see him again.

10:50 AM

I parked my car back at the parking lot and got out. I looked around for Max, but couldn't find him, so I started walking.

On my way to the Johnston Terminal, I thought about what to do now.

I couldn't tell the news people that the bad guys were caught, because they weren't.

I couldn't tell either of my bosses that the bug is found and fixed, because we haven't found anything, let alone fixed it.

I couldn't tell the police where Max was, nor where to find him.

I couldn't tell my co-workers everything was going to be OK, because if we didn't get more funding, the whole company might go under.

I couldn't tell myself everything would be OK, because I wouldn't believe it.

I sighed. There was more.

I couldn't tell Veronica I liked her, because God said I should treat her like a sister. And besides, I probably didn't have the guts to anyway.

I couldn't even tell God what has been happening recently.

I was halfway to our office building. I looked around for anyone suspicious, and not finding anyone, I sat down on a bench. I took out my phone and composed an email that probably wouldn't go through.

> From: jeffd@omniscient.software
>
> To: god@heaven
>
> Subject: Lately
>
> Hi God. It's me. I think you won't get this, but I just wanted to tell you what's been going on.

We thought we could catch Max, but he got away. And he threatened me. I admit I'm scared. I would love to see a picture of you putting your arm around me and telling me everything will be OK, like a loving dad. I could use some of that right now.

I'm trying to be the justice person you said I was. I'm trying, but It's hard. It's very hard, and there is no guarantee anything will work.

I remember sitting by the river and reading messages from you. I liked that. That was nice. If this email doesn't go through, maybe I'll go review some of those.

I don't know why I can't email you anymore. It used to work. But then again, I don't know why it started working in the first place. It's all very strange. I hope I can get you back one way or another. I would like that. In the few days I've been able to communicate with you, God, I have been moved more deeply than I ever have in my whole life. You touched my heart. I'm like a different person now. If all I get is a few days of you, I'll take it, but I want more. Something in me is drawn to you and your words and your everything else.

I talked with a guy who said you don't speak anymore. Obviously he was wrong. But then again maybe he was right. We'll find out when I try sending this.

Anyway, that's what I've been up to. I don't know if I'll see you again. But here's hoping.

--

Your son,

Jeff Davis

I pressed Send, and got the same error message, "Incorrectly formed email address." I stood up, put the phone in my pocket, and found my way back to work.

11:11 AM

From the moment I pulled open the large glass doors leading into Omniscient Technologies, the receptionist couldn't stop staring at me. I even said, "Hi Luanna" to her, but she kept on staring.

When I entered the common area of cubicles, I saw Veronica dash out of her room, run down the hall, and look into the room where my desk was. I couldn't hear what she said to the other guys, but I saw her put her hand on her head as if in distress.

I was almost there when she turned around and saw me. Relief rushed over her and she ran and embraced me. That was strange, not that I minded it. I'm a computer programmer, so I don't get a lot of women hugging me. But it was still odd social behaviour.

"What's wrong?" I asked.

"What's wrong?! Did something just happen to you at the Forks Market this morning?" Now she was almost upset.

"Yes. How did you know?"

"Social media. Someone took a video of someone choking you and beating up a cop. Jeff, are you OK?"

"Yeah, I'm OK."

"Who was that?"

"Max, from the Information Underground."

"Is that the same man who threatened and kidnapped you?"

"Yes."

"Jeff..." She walked away then came back. "You need to be

more careful."

"OK."

"The whole office is going to find out. The newsman is going to find out. You're probably going to make the news. And what are you going to say to them?"

I shrugged.

She threw her hands up in the air and walked away. Women.

I made my way to my desk and sat down again.

"A little birdie told me you had a run-in with a hacker this morning," Garth said.

"I'm OK," I replied.

"There are dangerous people out there," said Doug. "You need to be careful."

"Thanks," I said.

Garth spoke up. "You don't strike me as a dangerous kind of person, Mr. Grimm," he said to Doug.

Even though his back was to me, I saw Doug take a deep breath and let it out. "Maybe you shouldn't make comments," he replied to Garth. This was unusual for Doug. He's usually a nice guy.

"Why not?" said Garth, not backing down in the least.

"Because you don't know everything," Doug replied. With that, he got up and left the room.

"We are a bit touchy this morning," said Garth.

Just then Veronica poked her head in the room. "Jeff, can I see you in my office please?"

"You sure can," I said.

We walked to her cubicle and sat down.

She said, "I don't like the idea of you being threatened by people, or hurt, or kidnapped. There isn't much I can do about most of that, but I can do something about you being kidnapped."

"What?"

"I found an app you can install on your phone. It tracks your location and reports it to people."

I thought about that. "So you would always know where I am?"

"That way if you get kidnapped, we can know where to find you."

"Couldn't I just call the police?"

"You could let them in on it too. You've talked with a police officer, haven't you?"

"Yes. More than once."

"You could let him know too."

I didn't say anything.

"Jeff, I'm trying to help you. This is something I can do to help you. I don't want to see you hurt."

This idea of a digital leash around my neck did chafe me a little, but I had never had a girlfriend before, so a woman baring her heart to me was a new experience. I gave in.

"OK, I'll do it."

She perked up and smiled. "Good!" She showed me the app, I installed it, and told it that she could see my location.

Then I sent an email to Detective Joseph Wakefield.

> From: jeffd@omniscient
>
> Subject: Tracking App
>
> Hi Detective.
>
> In case I ever get kidnapped again, I have installed an app that can be used to track my location. I hope we'll never have to use it, but here it is just in case.

Then I pasted in the link he could click on to get access to my location, and I hit "Send." I put the phone back in my pocket.

"Done," I said to Veronica, still in her room.

"Good," she said. "Now let's go try it out."

CHAPTER 14

11:31 AM

"Are you going to answer that?" Veronica asked me.
"I wasn't planning to," I replied.
"It might be important."
I reluctantly pulled out my ringing phone and looked at the number. "It's nobody I know," I said, and started putting it back in my pocket.
"Jeff Davis, answer your phone this minute. You can't just ignore the world around you."
"It's worked for me so far." We paused outside the Johnston Terminal and I answered the phone. "Hello?" I said.
"Jeff, this is your dad. I got your number from your mom."
"Hi."
"I'm going to be in the Forks area and I was wondering if you'd like to do lunch. I think that's where you work, right?"
"Yes, I work here."
"Then why don't we grab something to eat? We can do some catching up."
I didn't want to. I didn't like people that much, and sitting across a table from someone I'd only met once in the last thirteen years wasn't my idea of a good time. But then, he was my dad, and if he was anything like God had been to me, it would be a good idea. "OK," I said.
"Very good. I'll pick you up in twenty or thirty minutes. Does that work for you?"
"Yes."
"Good. I'll see you then Jeff. Bye."

"Bye." I hung up.
"What was that about?" Veronica asked.
"That was my dad."
"And?"
"And he wants to go out for lunch."
"And you agreed?"
"I agreed." Then I asked, "Where do you want to go?"
"Well, I was going to suggest we drive somewhere to go for lunch, seeing as how you stood me up yesterday." She smiled at me.
"It wasn't entirely my fault," I said.
"And it seems I won't get you for lunch today either."
I shrugged.
"Then let's go for a walk," she said. "How about down by the river?"
"OK," I said and we started walking. I should have been more nervous than I was, considering what Max said to me, but the bright, warm sun and a beautiful woman next to me melted that all away. I walked happily with Veronica, a relaxed smile on my face.
"You don't need to be nice to him," she said.
"Who?"
"Your dad."
"Why?"
"don't take this the wrong way, but you're a nice guy, Jeff, and you will try to be nice to your dad, even if he doesn't deserve it. He left you. He doesn't deserve you. He doesn't deserve anything. You don't have to be nice to him."
I pondered that. "Still, it would be nice to have a dad."
"Oh of course it would be nice. Everyone wants a good dad. I would love it if my own dad stayed around and loved me too. We all want someone to love us and shower us with good things. We all want God to be a loving heavenly father who will give us love and sunshine every day. But then we have to wake

up, grow up, and realize that sometimes life sucks. You can't have everything you want. You have to play the hand you're dealt, and sometimes you don't get good things. Sometimes you don't get love. That's just the way life is."

I didn't respond right away to that. I considered the words, looked for truth in it, found some, and finally said, "I'm sorry you didn't get love."

She stopped and looked at me as if I said something strange, but then slowly nodded. "Thanks," she said. We continued walking.

Soon we stopped under an overhanging tree right next to the river. Veronica pulled out her phone and tapped. "I see your location," she said. "you're right where you're supposed to be." She put her phone away again. "Good. It works."

"We should probably start heading back," I said, and we turned around.

After a minute I said, "So I guess you don't believe in God, huh?"

She snorted. "I would love it if God existed. It might give this life some meaning. But no, if there is a God, he's not a nice guy, at least not to me."

"Maybe... maybe he does exist and he is a God of love, and you just haven't found him yet."

She smiled a tired smile with a touch of sarcasm. "Are you going to introduce me to him, Jeff?"

Come to think of it, if his email address wasn't working, I didn't think I could. His email address was my only connection to him. So I shrugged. "I don't know."

Soon we were back at the building. She stopped and said to me, "Hey, you know what they say about nice guys finishing last?".

I turned back to her and said, "Yeah?"

"I hope you don't finish last." She took a step closer to me, and for a brief instant I thought she might lean in and kiss me, but then she looked up and her eyes got wide. "Is that your dad?" she asked.

I turned. "Yup."

11:52 AM

My dad was wearing a suit. He looked important. He shook my hand and said, "Hi Jeff." As he turned to Veronica, he said, "And who is this?"

"This is Veronica," I said. "I work with her."

They shook hands. "Hello Veronica. I'm John," my dad said.

"Hello John. I'm Veronica," she said. I noticed they were very polite and formal. I supposed customer service people and salesmen were that way. I wouldn't know.

"So Jeff, are you ready to go?" he asked.

"Sure."

We left Veronica and walked out to where my dad parked his car. It was silver and looked expensive. "Nice car," I said.

"Mercedes makes good cars. That's why I drive them."

We got in. It was nice on the inside too.

"What are you driving, Jeff?" he asked.

"A Honda."

"Honda, eh? Not a bad car. Not bad, but you could do better, Jeff. You could do better."

"Yeah?" I asked, trying to sound interested.

"But we'll get into that later. There's something I want to ask you, but not yet. Let's eat first. Is there somewhere you like?"

"Um. Anywhere I guess."

"I'll pick something then." We drove away from the Forks, and soon were on Ste. Mary Avenue and then we pulled into Garry Street. It was only two days ago that Max invaded my car and threatened my life right here on this street. When we parked, I looked around nervously. My brain tried to tell me Max was nowhere around, but I couldn't hear it over the thumping of my heart.

"Are you OK, Jeff?", my dad asked.

"Yeah. I'm fine."

"Oh. This is the street where you encountered those men. I forgot about that."

I looked at him. "How did you know?"

He got out of the car, then said, "Your mom told me."

I didn't think Mom would have talked to him about that, but I guess they have been talking more than I expected.

We went into the same restaurant as I went into with my mom and sat down at a table. I looked at a menu and soon a waitress came to ask what we wanted. She didn't look that pretty, and the scowl on her face made her look a little grumpy too. I said to her, "I would like a chicken Caesar salad please."

My dad said, "I would love some eggs. Can I get a plate of eggs on toast?"

The waitress replied, "We only serve breakfast until noon. Can I get you something else?"

My dad looked at her name tag and said, "Jesayda. That's a great name!" He flashed her a winning smile. "Listen, Jesayda, I don't want you to get in trouble. Seeing as it's still very close to noon, the chef probably still has the eggs and toast out. And you seem like a very capable, beautiful, and resourceful young woman. Do you think there is any way you could still get me this order?"

Her countenance and body language relaxed and her face lit up a little at the compliment. She probably didn't get them that often. "I'll see what I can do."

"Thank you Jesayda. I appreciate that. I knew you could." my dad said. The waitress left and he said to me, "And that, Jeff, is how you win friends and influence people."

"Well, you certainly got what you wanted anyway."

"Isn't that what life is about? Everybody wants something. That waitress works here for the money. We come here for the food. Everyone's happy. That's life I think."

"Life is selfishness, huh?"

"Hey, It's more than just taking; it's also giving. People give to charity for the warm feelings they get from giving. You might enjoy giving affection to a girlfriend because of the feelings you get from her."

That last one hit too close to home. Did I like Veronica simply for the feelings it gave me? I didn't know. I might have to give that one some more thought later.

"That's why I'm in sales," he continued. "I get what I want when I help other people get what they want. Win win. It's like this." He pulled out his phone. "Do you think the people who made this phone and sold it to me did it because they cared deeply about my well-being, or because they cared about their own bank accounts?"

"Probably their own bank accounts."

"Exactly. They found a need and filled it. They wanted money, so they did something for me. I'm happy. They're happy. It all works out. And it all works very well."

That certainly sounded good on the outside, but somehow it didn't quite sit well inside me. "What about justice?", I asked.

"What do you mean?"

"Some things are just wrong, and some things are just right. Where is the selfishness in that?"

He sat up and looked at the ceiling. "Well… a government lawyer wants to win a case, so he argues for it. And your defence attorney also wants the win, so he argues for you. Both sides are being selfish, and justice is done… maybe."

The waitress came back with our food, and we started eating. Well, I started eating and my dad flashed his smile at

Jesayda first and said some more words to influence her.

Halfway through my chicken Caesar salad, I asked, "So if you only do things for yourself, why are you taking me out for lunch?"

He smiled. "I'll get to that in a minute."

After another minute, I asked, "How much are you going to tip for this meal?"

He looked up and studied me, amused by my question. "You tell me."

I tried to think about it from his perspective, then replied. "I would say *nothing*, because you don't get anything from it, although if you plan on coming back here and they remember you, you should tip well, so you get better service next time."

He looked satisfied. "Jeff, you have learned well."

12:45

"What about that black one?" my dad asked the salesman.

"That's a BMW 335i with xDrive, and the M-Sport package, I believe. It has a 3.0 litre turbo inline 6 cylinder engine, arguably one of the best engines ever built."

"I'm a Mercedes guy myself, but my son might like one of these", my dad replied.

"I certainly think he would. It's a very nice car. We only sell the best here. Would you like to take it for a test drive?"

My dad looked at me. I said, "Sure."

"I'll be right back with the keys." The salesman ran off.

I said to my dad, "Are you... are you buying me a car?"

"Well, I can't have my son driving around in a Honda Civic, can I?"

I was tempted to believe that this man was being a good dad and caring for his son out of the goodness of his heart, but then I remembered the conversation we had. I remembered his motivations. "And what do you expect from me?" I asked.

"Ah, now we get down to it. Yes, there was a reason I invited you for lunch, and yes, this car does come with a condition."

"What is it?"

The salesman came back with a key. He handed it to me and I said "Thanks," as I took it.

"Please feel free to go for a little drive," he said. "It's a good car. Test it out. Come back, then we can talk."

"Thanks," I said.

"Thank you," my dad said.

The two of us got in, me in the driver's seat, and my dad in the passenger's seat. I looked for a place to put the key, but then realized it wasn't a key at all, it was just a key fob. My dad said, "It doesn't matter where you put that thing. Anywhere inside the car will do. Then just push the start button."

I put the key fob down between the seats and pressed the start button. The engine roared to life with a lot more power than my car. I slowly pulled out of our parking spot and onto the road.

I turned right on Nairn Avenue and pressed the gas. The vehicle accelerated rapidly. "Wow," I said. "Nice! It has a lot of pick up." I pressed the gas some more, but we were already at the speed limit, so I slowed down, just so I could do it again. I pressed the gas, and my whole body pressed backwards. I couldn't help but smile. I had no words to describe the feeling. I just grinned.

"Work for me," my dad said.

"What?!"

"Work for me," he repeated. "I want you to work for me. I want to hire a computer programmer, and I want you."

"Um..." There were red lights up ahead, so I came to a stop. "I... I'm kind of in the middle of something right now where I'm working."

"Ah, Omniscient can hire someone else easily. I can't hire another son so easily"

"I guess," I conceded. "But there is something there I'm in the middle of, and I would like to see it to the end."

"The hacker business?" he asked.

I glanced at him. "How did you know about that?"

"I read the news, just like everybody else. Jeff, remember what we were talking about before, about motivations?"

"Yeah."

"Well, there is nothing for you at Omniscient. There is no reason for you to pursue that. They might pay you well, but I will pay you more, including this car."

The light turned green so I drove.

"Wouldn't you like to work with your dad?"

"I guess."

"Well, you could. You would have family, you would have lots of money, you would have new friends. Think what you could do with more money. You could get a better place to live, a better car, like this one. Wouldn't you like to own this car?"

"Sure."

"We'll call it a signing bonus. What do you say?"

"How did you know I drove a Civic?" I asked.

He looked confused. "Didn't you tell me?"

"I just said I drove a Honda."

"Agh," he waved his hand. "I just assumed."

"OK."

"But what about my offer?" he asked.

I thought about the friends I worked with. Did I want to leave them? Not really. I thought about Veronica. Did I want to leave her? No, but God told me to treat her like a sister, so maybe I should. I thought about Scott, and I thought about God calling me to justice. Could I walk away from those? Absolutely not.

"I'll think about it," I said.

"Good. You think about it, and then say *Yes*. It's the only reasonable answer. I'll be expecting it."

"OK."

"Oh, and I hope you'll be a better employee than a driver."

"Why's that?"

"Because you drive like an old lady, Jeff. Pull over and let me drive. I'll show you how it's done."

12:56 PM

I pulled into some random business beside the road, and we switched places.

My dad threw the vehicle into reverse, backed up, threw it into drive, then put his foot down. We took off like an unleashed animal, off the parking lot, and onto the road. Some people may have honked their horns at us. It was hard to hear over the roar of the engine.

We ducked and weaved through traffic as if the cars were standing still. He generally stopped for most red lights, probably just because he didn't want to get hit, but besides that, he just drove wherever, however he liked. We took some side streets, and cut some corners through parking lots.

Pretty soon I noticed my neck muscles were getting sore because I had been holding my head up. That's not something I had to deal with in my car. But in this one, I decided to rest my head back against the headrest at all times. It was just easier that way.

At one point he made a U-turn where there was a break in the boulevard. He barely slowed down as he cranked the steering wheel around. The back end of the car swung around obediently, and we took off again in the other direction.

He may have been talking, but it was hard to hear over the sound of my brain screaming for its life. As I gripped the armrests, and whatever else I could grab, he said casually, "That's the x-drive system. It puts sixty percent of the torque on the back wheels and forty percent on the front. That way it still handles like a rear-wheel drive."

My eyes were wide and my mind was busy not hitting things, so I may not have caught everything he was saying.

"Are you following me?" he asked.

"Um... I'm not sure," I replied.

He laughed. "I thought it was the children who were the rebellious ones and the parents who were boring." He palm-turned the wheel hard to the right, and we went sliding around an intersection, narrowly missing some cars coming from the left. "Not in this family. Jeff, you need to learn to have some fun."

"I... I think I'm good, thanks."

"Come on, if you want to work for me, you need to be about to handle some adventure."

"I thought you wanted me to be a programmer."

"I'm speaking metaphorically of course."

A truck ahead of us suddenly slammed on his brakes hard. My dad swore and veered to the left to avoid him, causing us to bump up onto the boulevard. We came down hard on the other side and kept going the wrong way. Thankfully we didn't hit anyone.

He gunned the engine, spun all four tires, then stopped. "Good. The tires are all still seated. It's the low profile tires."

We heard the siren before we saw the flashing lights.

As I slowly looked around for the police car, my head was jerked to one side as the car bolted into a sprint. My dad had chosen to drive into oncoming traffic, because that intersection was closer, and it brought us farther from the flashing lights. The cars ahead of us parted to make way for us, amidst blaring horns. Soon we were at an intersection, and we tore across it and plunged into a road leading to a large parking lot.

I looked behind us and reported, "He's following us."

"Yeah, I thought he would be."

"We could pull over," I suggested.

He rolled his eyes. "Jeff, you don't get out much, do you?"

We went swerving around cars, and at one point we drove down a narrow lane behind a building. My dad quickly looked to see if the police car was coming to follow us. It wasn't, so he swerved the car around and came back out. "He thinks we're going to come out the other side."

That manoeuvre gained us some distance, but as soon as we were back in the open again, the police car came straight for us again.

My dad started monologuing. "Know thy enemy. What are his weaknesses and strengths? In this case, his strengths are that he can make traffic get out of his way and he can call for help. As for vehicles, I'd say we are evenly matched, or at least close enough. But he also has weaknesses. Firstly, he doesn't know where we are going, which gives us an advantage. But secondly, and more importantly, his weakness is that he is unwilling to put other people at risk of harm."

"Um... what are you saying? You are willing to?"

"It's all a matter of confidence level, Jeff. Confidence, and risk tolerance." He turned a corner into oncoming traffic again. There were two lanes coming at us, so cars dodged either direction to get out of our way. We were going up a hill. At the top of the hill, he picked up speed. "Now people can see us coming a long way off." We were going more than highway speed, but the cars were still dodging us. We had enough room between them to speed through.

I looked behind us. "I don't see him."

"That means he has either fallen far behind, not wanting to take the risks we are, or he has given up, hoping that we will also stop driving like this and endangering peoples' lives."

We kept on driving recklessly, against traffic, and through

traffic for a few more minutes, until there we were sure the police car was gone.

Finally he slowed his dangerous driving, and began blending into traffic again. "Let's say we have lost him. It was a wise choice on his part to call off the chase, because he wanted us to stop, and he got what he wanted. Another win-win situation."

"Avoiding the police is illegal. And you could have gotten us killed," I said.

"It was unlikely. It was a matter of risk assessment. I was willing to take the risk. He wasn't. So we won. That's how you play the game. Always play to win."

Soon we were back on Nairn avenue, at the car lot. My dad returned the keys to the salesman and said, "don't sell this one for a while. I have a feeling my son will want it. I'll get back to you."

We got back into his Mercedes and soon we were back at the Forks where he dropped me off.

"I'll be in touch with you, Jeff," he said as I was getting out. "I would like you to start as soon as possible."

"OK."

"OK, you'll do it?" he asked.

"OK, you can get in touch with me again," I replied.

He drove off, and I went back inside to work. I still had work to do.

CHAPTER 15

1:41 PM

"Jeff, can I see your phone?"

I turned around in my chair to see Veronica. She looked as good as ever. "What for?" I asked.

"I'm trying to help a customer, and they have the same kind of phone you do. I just thought I should look up something on your phone to see if it's working the same way."

I stood up and took my phone out. I unlocked it, opened the Omniscient app, and handed it to her. "What feature are you interested in?", I asked.

"The friend search," she replied, as she grabbed my phone, grinned, and walked away.

"Hey!" I called out. "I need my phone."

"I'll bring it back," she shouted back at me. I was also going to say I was running 4.1 beta and her customer probably wasn't, but she was long gone.

As I sat down again, Doug said, "I think Veronica just did her friend search, and found one."

Garth chuckled.

"People are allowed to be friends," I said.

"I keep my best friends near me at all times," Garth replied. Doug and I both turned to him in surprise. Was he implying we were his friends? It was almost shocking.

Garth grabbed his bottle of Dr Pepper, waved it at us, and threw back a large gulp. Ah yes, his friend Dr Pepper. That's the Garth we know.

Suddenly I needed a cup of coffee, so I went to the kitchen

and got myself a cup. I sat down in the kitchen, looked out the large window, and contemplated my next move. I should check the logs on Adams' server. I should check the logs on our own server. Maybe there has been some more suspicious behaviour. Oh yeah, and I was going to suggest to Peter that we could hire a security firm to do an audit. I should also ask Joseph if he has matched Max's face to any known criminal. I should tell Samuel Smith from Adams that I found activity and that the police and I checked it out. Why haven't I done that yet? I'm not going to remember this all. I should write these things down.

Oh, but I don't have a phone. Wow, it's amazing how dependent I am on that thing. What did people ever do before phones? Write stuff down on paper? Hmm... I just had a thought. I should write these ideas down on paper. A paper to-do list. What an idea.

I got up and went looking for paper.

Holding my cup of coffee, I asked in my office. "Does anyone here have paper and a pen I can borrow?"

"Sorry," said Doug.

"A computer programmer asking for paper," said Garth. "Please describe to me this task you desire to perform that cannot be done with software. Where is this glaring hole in productivity software that still requires you to use paper?" Turning to Doug, he continued his rant. "Doug, start searching the Internet. Jeffrey here needs paper because he can't find software that will do what he wants to do. So, what is it, Jeffrey, what do you need paper for? Wait! Let me guess. Origami."

"I don't have my phone," I said.

Garth turned to his keyboard and spoke loudly as he typed. "I... don't... have... my... phone", then pressed Enter. "Oh!" he pointed to his screen. "I found a search result. It says, 'don't give your phone to girls, idiot.'"

GOD'S EMAIL ADDRESS

I turned and walked away without saying a word. I didn't have time for Garth right now.

I went to see the receptionist. "Luanna, do you have any paper and a pen I can have?"

"What for?" she asked.

"I need to write down a To Do list of items before I forget them."

She looked around. "I might have something here for you." She opened a drawer, then another one. "Aha!" She pulled out a pad of paper that said, "Webber Printing" on it. I'd never heard of them, but that didn't matter. Then she handed me a pen.

I took the objects in one hand, because my other was busy holding a cup of coffee. I said, "Thank you!", and left.

Back in the kitchen, I started writing and sipping coffee. There was: check Adams logs, check our logs, ask the police if they matched Max's face, tell Samuel Smith about the raid on the bakery, and… I couldn't remember anything else. There may have been one more, but I forgot it.

Just then Peter Steele walked in. He smiled at me politely as he went to the coffee maker. I thought there was something I was going to say to him. I checked my To Do list. Nope, nothing on there. I watched him take a mug out of the cupboards and pour himself a cup. I wracked my brain. What was I going to say? He ripped open a package of fake sugar and poured it in. Then he took a stir stick and stirred.

I continued watching.

Then I gave up trying to remember anything.

But as he was walking away, I blurted out, "Peter!"

He jumped, almost spilling his coffee. Then he turned to me. "Yes?"

"Do you have a minute?"

He looked a little confused. "I was just standing here for a full minute."

"Yeah, well, I only remembered now what I was going to say to you."

He came and sat with me. "You know, you could write your idea down when it first comes to you. That way you won't need to surprise people when you remember."

"OK. I'll do that." I held up my paper. "This is my To Do list."

"Good. Now what can I do for you?"

"We should hire a software security firm to audit Omniscient. If they find something, we can fix it and tell everyone it's fixed. If they find nothing, we can tell the world that there is nothing wrong."

He sat back and considered the idea. "That is a terrific idea, Jeff," he said.

I smiled.

"Will you please do a bit of research and find a good security firm for us? I will consider whomever you recommend."

"OK."

"Good," he said, getting up. "Keep up the excellent work."

I wrote down on my paper to research a security firm. Then I went back to my computer, because now I had a lot of work to do.

4:21 PM

For the past two hours I had busily worked on my To Do list, and I had done it alone. Garth and Doug were not there, so I had the room to myself. It's easier to get work done that way. When I had finally finished, I rewarded myself with a free trip to the washroom. On my way back, I stopped at Veronica's office to get my phone back.

"Hi Jeff," she said. "Did you get your phone?"

"What? No, that's why I'm here," I replied.

She looked shocked. "What are you talking about? I only had it for five minutes. I tried finding you, but couldn't, so I put it on your desk."

"I've been at my desk for two hours. It's not there."

"I put it there two hours and five minutes ago, when you weren't there."

I scowled. "I'll go check." I walked back to my office, planning to scour the place from top to bottom, when I saw Garth sitting on my chair, mousing with my mouse, and reading stuff on my screen.

He swivelled around and questioned me. "What is this? What are these logs?", he demanded.

I looked at what he was referring to. "That's the Omniscient install at Adams Corporation."

"You have access to all their email?" he continued.

"Well, I was searching for the hacker."

"The hacker who got access to Adams' email?"

"Yes."

"It turns out you are the one who has access to Adams' email, Mr. Davis."

"What are you saying?"

"What am I saying?" Garth rose out of his chair. He was taller than me and a lot wider. I admit he could be intimidating.

"I'm saying I have just put some things together."

"What?"

"Adams said their email got hacked. It turns out you have access to it. You said you were kidnapped by the Information Underground, but you don't have a scratch on your body. You said they threatened you, but you have no proof. You have said a lot of things that you want us to just believe. Well, I'm done believing you Jeff."

Peter walked into our room. "Does there seem to be an

issue here?" he asked.

"Yes, Mr. Steele, there is an issue here." Garth turned to the CEO. "On Tuesday, when we evacuated because of the fire alarm, I stayed around because I'm the office fire marshal. I saw Jeff here sneaking around the server room."

"I wasn't sneaking!" I said.

"And during the second fire alarm, he was sneaking around the server room again."

"I believe he was just being diligent," Peter replied.

"If by diligent you mean gaining access to email servers, then yes, that's exactly what he was doing. He even talked you into giving him access to our server room, didn't he?"

Peter glanced at me, almost a little nervously. "Yes, I did give him access, but I trust him."

"I don't see why you should," Garth continued. "This whole thing was his idea. He made it all up."

"Come on!" I said.

"Who did the supposed hacker talk to on Tuesday morning? Jeff. Who volunteered to talk to the media and the police? Jeff. Who did Adams hire to keep an eye on their own server? Jeff."

"That's ridiculous! What about Scott?"

Garth didn't even slow down. "Who did Scott supposedly send an email to before he disappeared? Jeff."

"That was a real email!" I shouted.

Garth spoke to Peter but looked at me. "This guy specializes in email. He could have made that up in five minutes."

The desire in my heart for justice boiled over into anger. I pointed at Garth and shouted, "That's not true!"

He pointed right back at me. "Give us the ten thousand dollars back."

"What?!"

"We paid you ten thousand dollars in bitcoin. Give it

back!"

"I don't have it!"

"That's right you don't have it." Turning to Peter, he continued. "Do you know why he doesn't have it? He spent it on a down payment for a new BMW." Turning back to me. "Tell Peter where you went today."

"I...", I stammered.

Garth finished. "He went to a car dealership and test drove a BMW, didn't you?"

"Well, yes... how did you know?"

"I followed you. It turns out that Jeff here doesn't tell us everything, do you?"

Peter looked at me with knitted eyebrows.

"Don't listen to him," I said to Peter.

"I'm not sure who to listen to at this point," Peter said.

"He stole my phone!" I said.

"What?" said Peter.

"What?!" said Garth.

"Veronica dropped off my phone here hours ago, and now it's not here. I think Garth took it."

"You're crazy!" said Garth.

"And you're a thief and a liar!" I replied.

"Gentlemen, please." Peter stepped between us. "Our emotions are running high. We need to settle down before we can accomplish anything constructive." He looked at his wristwatch. "It's now about quarter to five on a Friday. Let's all go home and have a relaxing evening. On Monday morning I will do what I have to do. Let's settle down and go home, right now, all of us."

With Peter standing right there, Garth went to his keyboard, locked his screen and got ready to go. I also shut down my computer and got my things ready. My phone was still nowhere in sight.

Garth left.

As I walked out too, I said to Peter, "You do believe me, don't you?"

He sighed. "I'll see you on Monday, Jeffrey."

4:46 PM

My heart was still pounding with emotion when I left the Johnston Terminal.

When I was halfway to my car, I had cooled down somewhat and the pace of my walking had slowed considerably. Now my mind kicked back in, and the question most at hand was this. Was Garth serious in his rantings of me, or was he just trying to get me fired? Was he the hacker trying to get rid of me, or was he not? And if not, could it be that the hacker was still among us? If I wanted to discover who it was, I would have to redouble my efforts, but I might not be able to do that now that I had lost credibility in Peter's eyes.

I stopped walking and sighed. It had just gotten a lot harder.

"Jeff!" I heard my name and looked around for where it came from. Perhaps I should have just run, considering the number of people who had it in for me, but instead I tried to find the source.

"Jeff!" It was Doug. He was calling to me from the other side of the street. I crossed the street to him.

"Hey Doug."

"Hey Jeff. Do you have a minute?"

I was curious, so I said, "Yup. What's up?"

"I have something for you," he said, and he led me to his car, deep in the heart of a parking garage. It was dark and there was nobody else around. It was exactly the kind of place I should be taking great pains to avoid. As I looked around, I could just imagine Max stepping out from any corner, lifting his gun to my face and pulling the trigger. I started breathing hard again.

Anxious to get going, I asked, "What is this thing you have for me?"

"You've been doing a lot of dangerous things recently, haven't you?" he asked me.

"Yes."

"Someone like you needs to be careful he doesn't get hurt."

"Yeah," I replied, agreeing, but inside I wondered if that sounded like a threat. Was Doug threatening me? I stopped walking and stood in my tracks. Had I been looking in the wrong place this whole time for the hacker? Maybe it wasn't Garth. Maybe it was Doug, this innocent-looking guy who doesn't talk a lot, who has been planting malicious code into Omniscient. Could he do it? He sure could. And like a fool, I followed him to this dark place so he could finally get rid of me.

I should have run, but when I get scared I freeze up. He motioned for me to come to him, but I didn't. I just stood there. Giving up on the motioning, he walked to the trunk of his car, got out a shoebox and came back to me with it. Yeah, I could guess what was in it.

As he walked up to me, his expression changed. He was normally quite down or even depressed. Now, he squinted his eyes and became angry. "Do you know how my wife died?" he asked.

I shook my head, and now I wondered if they had a fight and Doug did her in. When he opens the box and takes out a gun, we'll know.

He opened the box and took out a gun. "In a sense, you could say I killed her."

This idea of Doug killing his wife seemed crazy. Doug was a nice guy. Even after he admitted it, it was still hard to believe.

He put the gun back in the shoebox and leaned against a

nearby vehicle. He closed his eyes and took a very deep breath and let it out slowly. Then his chin quivered. "We had been married for twenty-four years."

I had no idea what he was about to tell me. Was this guy schizophrenic? He certainly seemed sad about his wife's death. So why kill her? I kept my mouth shut and listened.

"We were making plans for a twenty-fifth anniversary when we got a knock on our door. It was Denise's ex-boyfriend, Manuel. Manuel was just let out of jail. He had been there this whole time and now he wanted to get back with Denise. She said no of course, but Manuel didn't take no for an answer. In the days and weeks following that day, he approached her when she was shopping, when she was doing yard work, anytime I wasn't around. Then he started getting violent. I found bruises on her. We were both scared. When he threatened her life, I finally bought this."

"What happened?" I asked.

Doug took another long breath. This seemed to be hard on him. "One day I went outside, and I saw them both. I ran back inside to get my gun. When I came out, he was on top of her, and he had a knife."

I stood there, my mouth almost gaping at this story. I had never heard this. I only heard that Doug's wife had died a few years ago. I assumed cancer or something, but never in my wildest dreams did I imagine this.

He continued. "I pointed the gun at him and yelled at him to stop, but he didn't. He looked up at me and grinned this... evil... the man was just evil. He called my bluff. He killed her right then and there and then ran away."

"You... you didn't shoot?" I asked.

Doug stared at me with eyes filled with anger mixed with deep grief. "No," he said. "I didn't. My cowardice and fear kept me from it. It's because of me, because of my inaction that my wife is dead today. And that's something I have to live with the rest of my life."

Not knowing what to say, I said, "Wow."

Then he asked me. "You have a mom, don't you?"

I nodded. "Yeah."

"And maybe other family, or a girl-friend?"

"Yeah."

He put the gun back in the box, took a step toward me, and pushed it against my chest. Leaning in close to my face, he said, "Don't make the same mistake I did."

I held onto the box by instinct, and he turned and walked away. Then he got in his car and drove off.

And there I stood, in the middle of a parking garage, armed with a gun.

5:10 PM

As I walked back to my car, I was very conscious of the fact that I was carrying a handgun. It made me feel powerful. Too powerful. I would have preferred to submit to the powers that be out there, instead of challenging them. What if a bad guy with a gun also saw my gun? He might consider it a challenge and shoot me first. If I'm not careful, this thing will get me killed, or arrested. I'm quite sure this is illegal. Which side of the law am I on here? Maybe I should get rid of it. That would be easier--less conflict.

I walked to where I thought I parked my car, but it wasn't there. It must be in the next row or two.

But maybe sometimes conflict is necessary. Maybe someone should purposefully stand up to the bad guys and forcibly change their behaviour. And maybe, just maybe, that person should be me. Hadn't God called me to stand up for justice? And can't I do that a lot easier now that I have some way of manipulating other peoples' behaviour? Maybe God was providing me with a way of following his command.

My car wasn't there either. I turned around, scanning the parking lot. It wasn't anywhere. I stood up on a small fence, but I still couldn't see it. It was just gone. Stolen. Someone had stolen my car.

I'm sure it was Max. But why would he steal my car? Then it dawned on me, and I could only think of one reason. He knew when I would be leaving work, and at what time I would be here. And now that I'm here without a car, I'm a sitting duck.

I immediately ducked down between two vehicles. I crouched there, thinking of what to do. I'm sure Max was out there, probably with a gun trained at my head right now. I peeked above the car next to me, and I searched the area for anyone who might want to kill me. I didn't see any obvious assassins, but there was one man walking directly toward me. I ducked down again, and tried to watch him through the windows in the cars. He came closer, so I crouched on the ground between the cars.

And then he reached the spot between the cars where I was hiding. He looked down at me. I clutched the shoebox gun to my chest, thinking that I should pull out the contents.

The man took a few steps toward me.

I told myself to take out the gun, but my hands didn't respond. Deep down I knew I was just like Doug--coward to the core, and it would get me or my family killed.

Then the man opened the door of the car on one side of me. He got in, started the engine, and drove away.

I felt like such a fool. I wasn't just a coward, but an armed, embarrassed, fool of a coward as well.

Just because this guy wasn't out to get me, doesn't mean Max wasn't still out there. My hiding spot was suddenly a lot bigger, and I was more vulnerable. I looked around for any Maxes out to get me. Still seeing none, I wondered what to do next. Then I heard something that answered that question. It was the sound of a bus.

I left the safety of my hiding spot and sprinted toward the bus. Hopefully Max won't be able to hit a moving target. He probably could, so I ran back and forth a little, to make it harder for him. Even though I haven't seen any evidence of him, I don't want the first evidence to be a bullet crashing into my skull.

Just before I hopped into the bus, I realized that I'm probably not allowed to take a gun on the bus. I hated breaking the rules. Maybe I should ask the driver to hold it for me. No, dumb idea. I paid the fare with some coins in my pocket and sat down in my seat. Soon the bus would start driving, and I might be able to relax a little. Probably not, but maybe.

CHAPTER 16

5:24 PM

I sat on the moving bus, wondering what in the world I was going to do, when the last thing I ever imagined happened. The guy next to me started talking to me.

"Do you regularly take this bus?" he asked.

I shook my head. "No."

"I don't either. I just got on a few stops ago with no destination in mind." He chuckled softly. "You look concerned about something. Is everything alright?"

I glanced briefly at this man. He appeared to be fifty or sixty, shorter than me, with a short beard, and peaceful eyes. Something about him told me he was safe to talk to, so I went through my list of problems and picked one to share with him.

"I think my car was just stolen," I said.

"Oh! That's too bad. That's why you're taking the bus."

"Yup."

"My name is Mark, by the way," he said to me, holding out his hand.

I shook it. "I'm Jeff."

"Do you work around here, Jeff?"

"Yeah, I'm a computer programmer at… at a place around here." I didn't want to mention Omniscient, just in case this guy reads the news.

"A computer programmer! You must be a very smart person."

I shrugged. Wanting to change the subject, I asked him, "What do you do?"

He said, "I'm a minister."

I was surprised a politician would be taking public transit. Maybe he's meeting the people and buying votes. That would explain his friendliness. "Minister of what?" I asked.

He chuckled again as if I made a joke. "I'm a minister of the gospel."

"Oh, sorry. I thought you meant politics. You're a... priest?"

More chuckling. "No. I used to be a pastor, but now I'm just a minister. I write books, run a university, and I travel around the world teaching people."

"What do you teach?"

"There are a number of things I am passionate about. Health, inner healing, but I mostly teach about how to hear from God."

Everything else in my world just fell away. The only thing left were me and this mystery man beside me. A million thoughts swarmed through my head. I thought of the plant lady giving me God's email address and I thought she was crazy. This man must be just as crazy if not a lot more. I should probably run away right now, but something kept me there. I thought of the night God stopped talking to me, when I went out in the rain to find someone to help me get him back. The man I found couldn't help me, but he did say "I pray you find what you are searching for." Maybe God answered his prayer by sending this man, Mark, to me. But the greatest thing I thought of was the feeling I got deep down inside me when I read the words God sent to me. They touched me so deeply, like nothing I had ever experienced. That thought is what kept me in my seat, and even drew me to respond to this man.

"You... teach people how to hear from God?" I asked.

"Yes I do. I teach it, and people learn it."

I had no idea what kinds of crazy things might be involved in getting God to talk to you, maybe animal sacrifices or throwing a virgin into a volcano. OK, maybe not that, but something in me still had to ask. "Can you teach me how?"

He looked at me. "Probably. Children seem to learn quicker than adults. I can teach a child to hear from God in twenty minutes, but grown-ups seem to require a ten-hour course." He laughed again, as if what he said was funny. It may have been, but my heart was hanging on the line here.

I kept looking at him, expecting him to continue.

"You mean right now?" he asked.

I nodded my head.

"OK, right now then. I have discovered four keys on how to hear from God."

"Four keys," I said, listening closely.

"The first key is to go to a quiet place and still your thoughts and emotions. There is a deep inner knowing in our spirits that each of us can experience when we quiet our flesh and our minds. It's harder to hear from God during the busyness of the day."

I'll agree with that. When my dad was driving the car, I was so stressed I couldn't hear a word he was saying. I suppose in a quiet place It's easier to hear. This first step didn't sound so hard. I said, "OK."

Mark continued. "The second key is to look for vision. I have learned we need to open the eyes of our hearts."

This guy sounded like Andy who made me close my eyes and try to see the guy at the door. Come to think of it, that worked. Maybe this would work too. "You mean imagine something?" I asked.

"You could call it that."

"OK"

"The third key is recognizing that God's voice in your heart often sounds like a flow of spontaneous thoughts."

"Thoughts?"

"Yes. You probably won't hear a big booming voice in your

ears. A thought will just come to you. That's what God's voice sounds like."

So far these keys didn't sound that bad. In fact, they were almost familiar. I remembered the conversation that Garth, Doug, and I had the other day. I had said, *I've noticed that you can't cause a good idea to come to your mind. It kind of just comes to you.* I don't know if those thoughts are God speaking to you, but I've always been a believer in spontaneous thoughts. So far so good, but there was one left. "And the fourth key?" I asked.

"Write it down."

"Just write it down?"

"It helps you stay in flow. Otherwise God will get two words out of his mouth and You'll wonder if you heard from God or not. If you write it down, you can write down whole paragraphs and pages, before coming up for air. And besides, you're only human and will likely forget what he says otherwise."

Yeah, that last thing was definitely true. I had to write my To-Do list down on paper or I would have forgotten everything. Writing things down sounded like a good idea. If hearing from God was just a matter of these four things, it didn't sound so hard at all.

"Would you like to try right now?" he asked me.

Of course I wanted to hear from God again, but for some reason I felt resistance to it. Maybe it was still just a bit too strange or too easy, but when I thought about it more, I had to agree. I nodded.

"Good. Then do this," he began. "Close your eyes. Relax. Take some deep breaths." I did. "Then picture God in front of you." That was not hard for me, because he had already sent me his picture and video.

"Are you seeing him?"

I nodded.

"Now we will take our hands off the picture and let him take over. So watch what happens, and tune into spontaneous thoughts." After a few seconds, he continued. "Did something happen? Or did some thoughts come to you?"

I opened my eyes. "Nothing," I said.

"Nothing at all, or nothing that makes any sense?" he asked.

"Well, I'm sure it was just my imagination, but it looked like he was poking his finger at a keypad."

He chuckled. "Let's honour that vision by writing it down. Do you have some paper and a pen? Maybe in that box?"

I looked down in my lap and saw a shoebox. "No... this is... something else." I reached into my pocket and found a piece of paper with my To Do list on it. Mark handed me a pen and I wrote down, "5426". Giving the pen back, I said, "You really think this is a message from God?"

Just then I looked out and saw something I wasn't expecting. We had travelled far from the Forks. In fact, we were exactly at my apartment and the bus was getting ready to leave. I blurted out, "I have to go," as I scrambled for the front of the bus. The bus driver let me out, and I stood there in front of my apartment, and in front of my stolen car.

5:53 PM

I walked around my car looking for external damage. There was none.

I opened the door and looked in. On the seat was my phone. I examined it. There was no damage. It seemed to work fine.

I saw that the plastic panel under the steering column was lying on the passenger seat. Where the panel should have been were car parts dangling down. I tried starting the car. It didn't work. When I examined the stuff hanging down I found something that looked like the thing that actually starts the car. Using my key, I twisted the insides of that thing. Sure enough, the car roared to life.

I slammed the door shut and drove away. Now my emotions were kicking back in, but this time I was just mad. These people stole my phone! And they stole my car! And they wrecked it! Now it's personal. They deserve justice. I drove straight to the police station.

6:18 PM

I was met at the door by Detective Joseph Wakefield himself. He didn't look very happy, probably due to the bump on the head he suffered earlier this morning.

"Please come this way," he said to me. Instead of going to his desk, he led me to another room. It was more like a booth where I sat with a plexiglass window with holes in it to another booth. Joseph sat on the other side. "I will be recording this conversation," he said.

"What for?" I asked.

"I'll ask the questions."

"Detective, I came here to report my car stolen. You're treating me like I did the stealing myself."

He momentarily looked at me when I said that, but then continued what he was going to say. "Where were you at 3:15 PM this afternoon?"

"What?! Working! Why are you asking this?"

"Working where? At the Omniscient headquarters, or on the road?"

"At the office."

"Are there people who can corroborate this?"

"What? Well, I work with people there."

"Did they see you at 3:15 this afternoon?"

I stopped and thought about it, then said, "Normally Garth and Doug are in my room, but they weren't right then."

"So nobody can testify to your whereabouts at 3:15."

"I was working! At my desk."

"Not according to this." He pulled out his smartphone and started tapping. "According to this person locator you sent me, you were not in fact at your office, but you were on the road." He held it out to me. Sure enough, there was a map of where I had been that day. I could see the walk I took with Veronica, and when I went for lunch with my dad, and the drive afterwards. Oh. That shouldn't be shown to a policeman. And in the afternoon when I was working, the map showed me driving around town.

"My phone was stolen," I said.

He humphed. "Convenient."

"It was not convenient! It was very inconvenient!"

"Convenient or not, the evidence says you were not at your office."

I thought briefly. "I can prove I was there. I sent some emails. They should have the time sent in them."

Joseph thought about this, but then said, "Can't you email from your phone?"

"Well... yes... but I didn't."

"Couldn't you set an email to be sent in the future at any time?"

"Well... yes... but I didn't."

"Your alibi is not looking very good, Jeff."

"Alibi?! Why do I need an alibi? For what?!"

When he didn't immediately reply, I continued. "Somebody stole my car. I came here to report it. Did something happen? Detective, tell me. We're on the same side."

He leaned back in his chair contemplating, then sat back

up. "You haven't heard, huh?"

"Heard what? What happened?"

"At 3:11 PM this afternoon, Adams Corporation received an anonymous phone call that if they didn't hand over a million dollars, more emails will be leaked. Then the caller said that they would drop off a copy of what would be leaked to their main headquarters in five minutes. At 3:19 PM a white Honda Civic showed up on their security cameras outside their building, and a folder was thrown out the window. We got a clear view of the plates. They are yours, Jeff. It was your car."

I sat there, stunned. "Well... they stole my car. It wasn't me."

"You have no alibi."

As I sat there and fumed, I told myself to calm down and think. I won't be able to do anything with all these emotions in the way. I took some deep breaths. Then I thought of it. "My car has video cameras installed. We can take a look at them."

Joseph raised his eyebrows. "Let's do that right now."

6:33 PM

We walked outside to my car. As I was walking around to my side, I saw Joseph open the passenger door, grab something off the seat, and sit down, resting the thing on his lap.

When I got in and sat down, my heart almost stopped when I saw what it was. A shoebox. With a gun inside. My gun. My instincts told me I had to get it as far away from him as possible. I was going to offer to take it from him, but he was already examining the car.

He pointed at the two cameras in front. "This one points forward. This one points this way." He turned around. "That one points back."

If he opened that lid, that would be it for me. I would be arrested, charged with something gun-related, and also charged with that information stealing incident. The Information Underground was pushing me to get in trouble with the police, and it was working. Not only was I sweating about the gun, I had to control myself, because this detective can probably spot fishy behaviour. I concentrated on breathing normally.

He pointed to the car parts dangling under the steering column. "Well, your car theft story checks out." Then he looked at me, then looked me in the eyes.

Act normal. Look back at him. don't panic. Maybe smile a little. His detective's eyes drilled deep into me. "Of course you could have done it yourself," he said. Then he added, "Something about you doesn't add up, Davis."

I didn't know how to respond to that, so I finally just said, "Should we take a look at the video?"

After an eternity, he nodded his head.

I took out my phone and connected wirelessly to the three video cameras I had mounted in my car. Reviewing the video, we saw that at 3:13 PM the car jostled as if someone had sat down in it.

It was immediately apparent that the driver was not on camera.

"You call this security surveillance?" Joseph asked.

"It was designed to catch people breaking into the car and sitting in the passenger seat and pointing a gun at my face."

Pretty soon the car drove away.

"That was enough time for someone to hotwire it, if they're good." He looked at me. "You might not be that good."

I didn't know if he was insulting me, but I replied, "I've never hotwired a car in my life."

"How did you drive here?"

"I tried something and it worked."

"Uh huh." I'm not sure what he meant by that, but it probably wasn't good.

At 3:19 PM the car pulled up to the curb of a sidewalk. The passenger side window rolled down electrically, and an arm could be seen reaching toward the passenger side window and throwing something out.

"Aha!" I said. "Did you see that?"

"What?" he asked, but he probably already knew.

"That arm had no sleeve, but I'm wearing long sleeves." I motioned to the long-sleeved button shirt I wore to work."

"So?" he said.

"And his arm is redder than mine, and hairier, and his hand is bigger." I rolled up my shirt sleeve to show off my pearly white, thin programmer's arm. You don't build up a lot of muscle by pushing a mouse around all day.

He examined my arm. "Play that part again," he said. I did, and he paid close attention.

We continued watching my car drive away and park outside my apartment building. The video wiggled as presumably the driver got out. After that nothing happened until I arrived at 5:53 PM.

The detective pointed his finger at me as he continued to rest his other hand on my illegal firearm. "There's something you're not telling me, Davis. I don't know what it is, but you're right about the arm. It wasn't yours."

That made me feel a little better, but he continued. "But still, evidence is evidence, and I have enough to take you in. I could, but I won't. Instead, I want you to cooperate with us so we can take down this Max or maybe even Jade. Will you cooperate with us, Jeff?"

"Yes, absolutely I will."

"Good. Then send me these videos as soon as you can. For your own sake." He opened the door and put one foot out. "Oh, and it looks like Max is still around, assuming that was him, so be careful." As he put the box down between the front two seats, the gun in it shifted position and knocked against the side like only a gun could. Joseph reached his hand to open the lid as if to examine it, but I grabbed the box and held it on my lap.

"Thanks for that advice, detective. I'll keep that in mind."

He got up and closed the door.

I breathed a massive sigh of relief, put the box down on the passenger seat again, and drove away.

6:51 PM

As I drove home, I thought.

Whoever stole my car knew to not walk up to it from the front or the back or from the passenger side, but only from the driver's side. I have to assume it was Max, and probably Jade told him to. And not only that, they had my phone, which means the Information Underground already had someone on the inside of Omniscient. I had to start trusting people less.

But why would they do this? I can only guess that they are trying to get me in trouble with the police. They tried getting me to leave them alone by threatening me. That didn't work. Then they tried to get me to join them. That didn't work either. And now they are trying to get me to go to jail. I hope that wasn't going to work.

There was only one thing I could do. I would have to catch them before they caught me. Yeah, easier said than done. I remembered the weapon in my car, but I didn't want to think about that. It scared me.

What else could I do? I needed to gather hard evidence. This means recording a confession in audio or video. With

Omniscient you can make video calls. That might be a way of recording video. Maybe I need a way of quickly activating a video call, maybe with some sort of shortcut on my phone. I pulled the car over and set that up. Now I was ready to record when needed at a moment's notice.

Pretty soon I pulled into my parking spot at my apartment. Just as I turned the car off, I got a phone call. I wasn't in the mood to talk with anyone, but then I looked at who was calling. It was Peter, my boss. A few hours ago he was doubting if he could trust me. Maybe he changed his mind. Maybe if I told him about my stolen car, he might trust me again. I answered it.

I said, "Hello?"

"Jeffrey, this is Peter Steele."

"Hi Mr. Steele."

"Listen Jeffery, I received a phone call from someone just now telling me to read a news report."

"OK. About what?"

"Apparently someone tried to blackmail Adams Corporation. They wanted a million dollars or they would leak private, confidential email."

I threw my hands up. I couldn't believe this.

He continued. "And then someone matching your description pulled up at their office and threw a print-out of said confidential email messages out the window of your car."

"It wasn't me, sir! I wouldn't do that."

"I called Adams and they confirmed it."

"It wasn't me."

"The police confirmed it too."

"My car was stolen. And so was my phone."

"Regardless, I did authorize you to have access to our server. And I know you have access to Adams' server."

"I didn't abuse your trust, Mr. Steele. I'm not the bad guy here."

"Thank you for that, Jeffery. It means a lot to me, and I hope we can get this all sorted yet, but until then I have no choice."

"What are you saying?"

"I'm saying that effective immediately, you are suspended."

"You're firing me?"

"No, not yet. Not so hasty on a Friday evening. Let's give ourselves some time, but you are suspended, so don't come in to the office until you hear from me again."

I didn't know what to say, so I didn't say anything.

"OK, Jeff?" he asked.

"OK." What else could I say?

"Good. Goodbye, Jeff."

"Bye."

I ended the call and rested my hands in my lap and my head against the headrest. What in the world do I do now? After a minute of thinking, I couldn't come up with anything, so I got out of my car and started walking toward the apartment building.

Halfway there I stopped. If the Underground could steal my phone and break into my car, what could they do to my apartment? I didn't want to find out. And Joseph did tell me to be careful.

I took out my phone and made a call. When it connected I started talking. "Hi Mom, it's me."

"Jeff! It's always good to hear from you. How are you doing?"

"I've been better. Can I come over?"

"Of course! Is something the matter?"

"I... I'll explain when I'm there. Can I stay for night too?"

"Yes, I think so. Is everything all right? Tell me."

"I'll tell you when I get there. I'll see you soon."

"OK."

"Oh, and Mom?"
"Yes?"
"Don't tell Dad."

CHAPTER 17

7:12 PM

I knocked on my mom's door and waited for her to open it. There was so much going on that I just needed someone to talk to. I just got suspended, I was interrogated by the police, my car got broken into and stolen, my phone was stolen and used against me, and a guy I worked with loudly accused me of being the hacker, the very person I was trying to bring to justice and failing miserably at. Oh, and I couldn't go back to my apartment, so I have nowhere to live. Soon I will be safe with my mom.

But then the door opened and I looked straight into the eyes of my dad.

"Hi Jeff," he said, and opened the door to let me in. I froze. "Please, come in," he said.

I looked past him and saw my mom. "Your dad just showed up," she said. "But please come in, Jeff."

I stepped inside and I walked to the table and sat down.

"Are you hungry? Have you had supper?" my mom asked.

"Ummm... Yeah. I.. haven't eaten yet."

"Sit right there. I'll get you something."

My dad also sat at the table. "Have you considered my offer?" he asked.

His offer. I had already forgotten about it.

"I wasn't planning to," I said.

"Come on, Jeff. Are you going to work at Omniscient forever? You know, the business may fail. They might lay everybody off. If word gets around that Omniscient is insecure, nobody will use it, and there goes the business. You may as well leave now while you have a choice, because soon you may not have one."

My mom set a glass of water in front of me. I drank it.

He continued. "By the way, how secure is your job there right now?"

I considered the question. "Fine," I lied.

"Oh, that's not what I've heard."

"Yeah? What have you heard?"

"I've heard you're in trouble - with your boss and with the police."

"How did you hear that?"

Mom came in with a plate of leftovers. I started eating.

My dad looked up at my mom and said, "I offered Jeff here a job at my company today."

"Oh," she said. "Did he accept?"

"No, he hasn't yet, but I think he might. I even offered to buy him a car as a signing bonus."

"Oh wow," she said. "He might like a new car. He could get rid of that one he's driving, since it holds bad memories of something that happened to him the other day."

I looked at my mom. Then I looked at my dad. He was glancing between me and my mom.

"I'm going to make some coffee," she said. "Would you like some coffee, John?"

"Yes, I would. Thank you."

I continued eating. "What would I be doing?"

"Oh, any number of things. We have a few small projects around that could use some custom software. I'm sure you would be great at that, wouldn't you?"

"What kind of business do you do, exactly?"

He sat back. "We... buy and sell mostly."

"Import export?"

"Yes! Exactly!"

"With warehouses?"

"Yes, we have a warehouse."

"What software do you use to keep track of your stuff?"

"We... ah... put everything in spreadsheets. It works, but It's terribly inefficient. It's an ugly solution. You could make us something that works a lot better."

Mom came back and brought the coffee. Neither of us touched it, but she poured herself a cup and sat down.

"A minute ago you said you had a few small projects for me. A complete warehousing solution is not a small project. It sounds rather big to me."

He smiled that big broad smile. "Hey, I thought it would be small. I thought you could handle it easily. Something like that should be no sweat for you, should it?"

"I specialize in email," I said.

"Ah, a good programmer can program anything, couldn't you?"

I took a deep breath. "No. I'm not interested."

"But why not? It's a great opportunity, with great pay. And you're all but fired at Omniscient as it is."

Mom interrupted. "Now hold on you two. John, if Jeff doesn't want to, he doesn't have to."

He replied to her, "Julie, Jeff is being difficult. Could you help me out here?"

Turning to me she asked. "Jeff, why don't you want to work with your father?"

I replied to her. "I don't trust him."

She turned back to her ex-husband. "John, Jeff has a very high level of morality. If you want him to trust you, you will have to stop beating around the bush, stop being mysterious, stop lying, and start telling the truth, the whole truth, and nothing but the truth. You have to be completely honest and transparent with him."

That made him stop. He sat there for a long time. In the

meantime my phone alerted me with an unusual sound. I quickly checked it, because you never know what might be happening, but it was only my new tracking app advertising some fancy new feature. I closed it, quickly tapped some other things, and stashed the phone in my shirt pocket, because that's just easier when you're sitting down.

My dad looked at me and said slowly, "OK. I'll tell you everything. Let's go for a walk."

I almost believed him, and in my curiosity to know what he was going to say to me, I agreed to the walk.

7:35 PM

"As you know, I left when you were sixteen."

"Fifteen," I corrected, as we walked down the sidewalk. The sun was going down and a cool breeze had picked up.

"Yeah. So I continued in sales for a while. I tried furniture, cars, but found my niche in drugs."

"Illegal drugs?"

He waved his hand. "Ah, nothing really bad. It's just a product like anything else. I was pretty good at it, until I got hooked myself."

So that's what my dad has been doing this whole time. He was a drug dealer, and a druggy himself. Why was I not surprised? Maybe it was a good thing he left us. "So it *was* illegal drugs."

"Ah, the government doesn't know what the people want." He continued. "So I tried to break the habit by leaving the situation."

Yeah, he was good at leaving.

"I joined the army."

That I didn't know.

"It was hard kicking the habit, but I did. I also got in shape and learned to fight. I learned to take care of myself, learned to make good decisions. I realized that the source of all my problems was me."

That we agree on.

He continued. "It was me. I was the reason I had sunk so low. But with this realization came the knowledge that I was also the only one standing in the way of success. I started reading self-help books, and business success principles, and anything I could find. When I quit the army, I was ready to do great things."

"Yeah?" I was cynical, but tried not to sound like it.

"Yes I was. I started a business."

"What business?" I'm pretty sure I already knew, but I asked it anyway.

"Buying and selling."

I looked at the sidewalk, but I could sense he was looking at me, as if trying to read me, to know how much he could tell me. I didn't want to hear what he was about to say, but he had to say it. I needed him to say it.

He shifted tactics. "You know when I was in the army, they started by calling me John, because that's my name of course. John Davis. Then they called me by my initials, JD."

I stopped walking and leaned against a tree for support. He continued. "Then they shifted the accent from the D to the J." He looked at me again, but I continued to look at the ground. I wasn't happy.

"And then they started calling me just..."

I interrupted him. "You're Jade, the leader of the Information Underground."

He paused, then asked, "How did you know?"

"It's your green tie," I said. "You always wear green ties, to match your name I guess."

He looked down to examine his tie. "Really? That gave it away?"

"Not really."

"Then what?"

I looked at him. "Mom never told you about the incident on Garry Street. How else would you have known about it? It was your idea. You called it." If I was angry, it was under control.

"Hey, it was nothing personal, Jeff. It's just business. I just wanted you out of the way, so you wouldn't get hurt."

"Wouldn't get hurt?! Do you know what it's like to have someone come into your car, point a gun in your face and threaten your life? It's like rape. That's what you did to me."

He walked around, in a little circle, then came back and said, "OK, I may have gone too far there, but I didn't know you would be so stubborn about this. After all the threats, you persisted in going to the police to try to take us down. Why? Why not just give up?"

"It's the right thing to do."

"The right thing to do, Jeff, is what's right for you. If something will get you killed, it's not the right thing for you, is it?"

I looked away and didn't answer. He must have mistaken my silence for agreement, because he continued. "When I saw that you were adamant about not quitting, even at the cost of your life, I changed tactics and tried to recruit you instead."

I looked at him again.

"That offer still stands, Jeff. I still want you to come work for us. It is a high paying job. I would rather offer positive incentives than negative incentives."

"What does that mean?"

"Let me explain." He found a vehicle's hood to sit down on, and proceeded to explain to me how life worked. "If you are a parent, and you want your kid to behave himself, you reward his good behaviour with good things, and his bad behaviour with..." he paused, looking for the right words. "with unpleasant situations."

"Spankings."

"Something like that. That way the child will associate good behaviour with pleasure and bad behaviour with pain, and will choose good behaviour."

"I'm not a child."

"Let me continue. The same is true with employees. If you want them to act a certain way, give them raises. If you don't want them to do certain things, demote them."

"Yeah?"

"The same is true for anyone else in life whose behaviour you want to modify. For example, you could make a contribution to a politician, and they will be more likely to do things in power that you want them to do."

So now my dad is bribing politicians. How much worse could this get? Maybe I shouldn't ask. "Bribing?"

This accusation didn't slow his monologue in the least. He continued, "And if positive motivations don't work, you have to use negative motivations. This is what we did with George Mannel."

This got my attention. How did he know the system administrator at Adams? "What?"

"George couldn't be bought either, so we had to think of something else."

"What did you do?" I suddenly felt concern for my fellow techie who seemed to be under the thumb of the Information Underground like I was.

"It was Max's idea." My dad's smile returned to his face when he thought of this wonderful memory. "He snuck up to George's front door when his wife was inside. He took a picture of himself waving his gun with George's wife in the background, inside through the glass in the door." He smiled and shook his head. "It's amazing what people will do with a little negative motivation. We paid him the money too, but that's not what turned him. It was his love for his wife." He shook his head as if George was the stupidest man on earth.

"Is that how you treated Scott too?"

He looked at me. "I started with a positive motivation. Ferrari 812, I believe. Nice car."

"He didn't take it."

"No, he didn't."

"So you killed him."

He pointed his finger at me. "No, I didn't!"

Then Max did, whatever. I rolled my eyes. "And when you were done with him, you went for me."

"Well, I am in the information business, just like Omniscient is. I wanted another person on the inside. It would be a match made in Heaven."

I was confused. "Another person besides Scott, or another person besides the other person already in Omniscient?"

He smiled. "You'll find out who this other person is as soon as you take my offer and we can trust you."

It wasn't hard to guess who this other person was.

He got up and took a step toward me. "So, will you accept our offer? It would be easier for us both if we didn't have to resort to negative motivation. I know you're not married, but there might be someone else you have feelings for."

I looked at him, hoping he was bluffing. He was not. I backed away. "I'll think about it," I said, then kept on walking. My car was on this street, not far away. I felt the need to get away.

"We will be in touch, Jeff. You can count on that."

I pulled out the phone in my shirt pocket, checked to make sure everything was functioning as it should, turned it off, then put it back in my pants' pocket.

I heard my dad talking behind me, "Jeff! What did you just do? What were you doing with your phone?"

My heart was beating fast. I ran to my car, got in, and

drove away as fast as I could.

8:11 PM

On my way to the police station, I let myself start hoping.

I started believing that it would soon be over. I would tell the police everything, they would start arresting people, and soon my life could get back to normal. The news man would publish the truth, Omniscient would be trusted again, investment money would come in, I would be hired, and life would go back to normal.

I tried not to think that the bad guys were still on the loose. I tried not to think that the main bad guy was my father, and that I was on my way to rat on him. Part of me didn't like that thought, but part of me did. There was still a part of me that was holding on to offence, to hurt, to unforgiveness, to anger. On the outside I didn't let my emotions out, but on the inside, there may still have been some hurt that turned into bitterness that turned into anger that turned into hatred. That part of me looked forward to my father wasting away in jail to pay for not being the father I always needed.

I slowed the car and turned into the parking lot of the police station. As I pulled into a spot, my phone rang. I examined it to see if I knew who it was. There were not many people who could stop me at this point. In a minute it would all be over, and even if the CEO of Omniscient himself called, I wouldn't answer. It was Veronica. I decided to answer.

"Hi, this is Jeff," I said.

"Jeff! It's me, Veronica." She sounded stressed.

"Hi Veronica. What's going on?"

"Jeff! I've been kidnapped! They tied me up. He has a gun! Jeff, help!"

"Where are you? I'll call the police."

"No! don't! They said they'd kill me if you do. don't! Please! Come yourself. No police. They'll kill me! Please, help me, Jeff! Help me!"

"Where are you?"

"750 Plinguet. An old building."

I immediately recognized that address. It was the same place they held me and almost killed me.

"OK, I'll be right there."

The call ended.

Now I had a decision to make. I looked out my window at the building that would solve all my problems. Then I remembered how I felt tied up in the building Veronica was in at that moment. I would have given a lot to have someone know I was there. Now Veronica was there. Would I do everything I could to help her? Of course I would. What about Max's threat to kill Veronica if I tell the police? I couldn't take the chance. It may have been a bad decision, but I backed up my car and drove out to 750 Plinguet.

8:22 PM

The last time I pulled up to 750 Plinguet, I thought it was called Vandelay Industries. I had no such notion this time. I knew what I was getting into, but this time I had no choice. If doing the right thing means anything, it means to rescue the princess. I'm not exactly sure how I will do that, but at least I can try to make sure she doesn't get killed.

As I approached the door, it opened for me. Chip did it. He motioned me inside.

Inside the building, in the middle of the room, sat Veronica on a chair. She was tied up. It was probably the same chair I sat in. I knew how she felt.

Max stood behind her, pointing a gun at her long black

hair.

Chip closed the door and pushed me farther in.

"I'm here. Let her go," I said, displaying some small amount of courage.

"You don't call the shots here, I do. Never forget that."

When I didn't reply, he continued.

"I will consider not killing your girlfriend if you cooperate."

"What do you want?"

"To begin, I want god's email address and password."

For a very brief moment, I thought he wanted God's actual email address, god@heaven, but that thought didn't last long. "For what server?" I asked.

"Omniscient, idiot."

"I don't know it."

"I think you could find it, couldn't you?" Max tapped the side of Veronica's head with the end of this gun. "Right now. No more waiting."

I thought about it. Ronja did tell me the new password to our server, so I could get in to that. And then I could get into the database. I admitted, "I might be able to."

"Get busy." Max pointed me to a table off to the side where Chip had a laptop running. I went and sat down. I thought of all sorts of things I could do to stop this. There must be some way of rescuing Veronica without giving away access to our server.

"Passwords are not stored as plain text," I said. "They are stored MD5 hashed."

"What does that mean?" Max asked.

Chip spoke up again. "Like I said last time, hashing is like encryption." Then to me, he said, "I don't care. Get us the MD5 hash then."

That I could do, because it wouldn't help him anything. Hashes are one way only, so even if you had the hash, you still wouldn't have the password. I would be happy to get that for them.

I connected in to our server and logged in with the root password of PlentyLoyaltyThereforeDecrease. Then I looked in the database. I ran an SQL query to find the god account, then I pointed at the screen. I said, "The god email address is god@omniscient.software and the password is that." I pointed at a blob of characters, which were 2C6528C3C933207AD341165BF493B497.

Chip pushed me out of the way and started doing something on the laptop. "You can't decrypt it," I said, "because it's not encrypted."

"Is it salted?" he asked.

"What?" I replied, confused.

"Now who's the idiot?" he said to me. He looked a little irritated. "The last time you were here you made me look like a loser with all your questions, but I can do research as good as anyone. It turns out that if you don't salt your MD5 hashes, you can look them up in a big table called a rainbow table." He turned back to the laptop and did some stuff. "See? There it is right there." He pointed to the screen where the god password was staring me in the face in plain text.

My face grew pale. I just gave everything away.

"You're the idiot!" Chip laughed in my face. "I'm smarter than you!"

Max asked Chip, "Are you really in?"

I saw Chip open the web site where we check our email and log in as the god account. It was successful. "I'm in!" he said. Max came over and stood beside Chip. Both men smiled.

In a daze, I walked over to Veronica. "Did you really let them in?" she asked.

I nodded. Feeling defeated, I sat down on the floor.

"What are you going to do now?" she asked.

"I don't know." I looked at this beautiful woman tied up. "I don't know if I have a choice anymore. If I don't cooperate with them, if I try to turn them in, they'll kill you. What can I do?"

"You can stay safe, Jeff. You can choose to stay safe yourself."

"You mean 'Do what is right for me'? Jade would like that answer."

"What else is there besides what is right for you?"

"I could do the right thing."

"You need to think about you."

"No! I need to think about doing the right thing."

"It's too dangerous."

"It has to be done. I'm sorry you got dragged into this, Veronica. I should have just gone straight to the police."

"Gone to the police with what?"

I looked at the men to see if they weren't watching us. They weren't. "I recorded my dad, Jade, on my phone confessing to everything. I was on my way to hand over the video to the police when you called. But I'm going to do it now."

Her eyes grew wide. "But... but they'll kill me!"

"I don't think they will. They're just using you to get to me, to scare me."

"Don't do it, Jeff. You have to believe them. These are dangerous people."

We both heard the door open, and turned to see Jade, my father, walk in.

9:06 PM

Jade looked around and saw us, and saw his two men. Ignoring us, he asked, "Maxwell, did he cooperate?"

Max smiled. "Yes he did."

Chip added, "And I got in to the god account for

Omniscient."

"Well done, Christopher," he said. Turning to me, he said, "Good choice, Jeff. Very good choice. It's too bad it had to come to this, but it had to be done. Next time don't be so stubborn."

I didn't say anything. I despised this man. He was evil.

"Jade," said Chip with eyes still on the laptop, "Jeff has been emailing the cops. Oh, and there's one from Scott, after the other night. You'll want to see this."

As Jade walked over to read it, he said, "*After* that night? That little sneak!"

While they were distracted with Scott's email, I reached up behind Veronica's chair and started working on the ropes that bound her hands together and to the chair.

"What you doing?" she asked.

"Setting you free."

"They will notice."

"They're busy with their jackpot. Just keep your hands behind the chair as if they were still tied up." I worked while keeping an eye on the men. To my relief they never noticed, and soon she was free. She still looked rather anxious. "It's OK," I said. "We'll be alright. We just need to get out of here."

We waited a while for something, anything. It would be great if there was some sort of distraction right about now. I tried to think of something, but nothing came to me.

Just then we heard a thump coming from somewhere, outside maybe. The other men heard it too. Jade said to Max, "Go check it out." On his way out, Max said to me, "If you brought the cops, you're both dead. Both of you." I was almost getting used to his death threats by now.

As soon as he was outside, I started walking to the door to see where he was. Glancing at Jade, I saw him look at me, but then look down again. I guess he figured he had me, and there was nothing I could do, so I didn't pose a threat to him. I opened the door and couldn't see Max anywhere, but I could see my car. I walked back to Veronica who was untied but still sitting there as if she wasn't. I said, "When I say 'run', we run for the door."

"I don't think we should."

"Don't worry. It will be fine."

"Max might be there."

Just then we heard a gunshot come from what sounded like outside, on the far side of the building. Max must have found something. I said to Veronica, "Run!" I took her by the arm and we ran fast for the door. I didn't stop to look back. I heard my dad yelling "Hey!", but I didn't look back.

We burst through the door, scrambled into my car, and we were soon speeding away.

"Wow," I said, while driving. "That was almost easy."

"What did you say about recording your dad?"

"Oh, it turns out Jade is actually my dad. When he told me that, I was recording him with my phone in my shirt pocket." I gestured to my pocket. "I had made a shortcut to open Omniscient and record a video to send."

"Did it work?"

"It sure did." I tapped my pants' pocket." The evidence is right here."

Veronica still looked nervous, so I smiled at her. "Don't worry. As soon as we bring this to the police, it will be all over and we can return to our normal lives."

My phone rang. It was Jade.

CHAPTER 18

9:31 PM

I answered the phone while driving. "Hi."
"Jeff, this is your father."
"Hi."
"Where are you going?"
"I'm going for a drive with Veronica."
"You're not going to the police, are you?"
"Why would you think that?"
"Because I saw you doing something with your phone when I was talking with you. You weren't recording our conversation by any chance, were you?"

I paused, thinking of what to say. He continued. "Is Veronica with you?"
"Yes"
"Let me talk with her."
I looked at her, then asked into my phone, "Why?"
"I just want to talk with her."
I gave Veronica the phone. "Hello?" she said.
I couldn't hear Jade talking, but I heard Veronica say, "Yes he did... Yes he is... Really?... Are you sure?... OK... Bye" Then she said, "It's getting hot in here," and rolled down her window. She turned around to look behind her, and said, "Do you see anyone back there?"

I looked in my rearview mirror, then turned around too, looking for that black van or Jade's Mercedes. I saw nothing.
"Oops!" Veronica exclaimed.
"What?"

"I dropped your phone out the window! I'm so sorry."

"you're kidding!" I hammered on the brakes and we came to a stop beside the road. We were just past the Provencher bridge over the Red River. "I hope it didn't go over the bridge," I said. "That would be not good. Not good at all."

We ran up the bridge, looking for the phone. Very soon I saw Veronica bending down to grab something, but it was just a rock. We kept going. Soon I saw it and pointed. "There it is! Good, it didn't go over the edge." Veronica ran over to it as fast as she could.

Then I saw her do something strange. She lifted the rock that was in her hand over her head and brought it down. Why was she doing that? Just getting rid of the rock or something. Maybe there was a bug or rodent next to the phone she was trying to kill. Then a terrible accident happened. The rock missed the bug or rodent. By a stroke of rotten luck, it hit my phone, cracking it terribly. I stopped in my tracks, wondering if it could be saved. Maybe we could extract the memory card where the video was stored on.

Then something even stranger happened. She lifted the rock up again and brought it down on the phone a second time. And then she did it a third time. I stared at it and at her, completely speechless.

"What?... What are you doing?" I gaped.

She picked up the mangled, broken pile of electronics and looked at me.

As I looked at her, my head shouted things at me that my heart didn't want to hear. My heart refused to listen.

Finally she said, "You know Jeff, I kind of liked you."

I couldn't believe the thoughts my head was telling me. There had to be some other explanation, so I mumbled, "Why did you break my phone?"

"Jade just told me to. I have to do what he tells me to do, you know. Job security, and all that."

Slowly my heart started listening to all the thoughts swarming around inside of me. I thought about when Veronica started work how eager she was to go for lunch with the developers, instead of the other girls from Customer Service. Then when Scott died, how eager she was to develop a relationship with me. I thought about the time she supposedly met my father. That was right after she almost kissed me. I felt myself growing cold on the inside, like the time I lost my best friend. Now I was losing my girlfriend.

"You... you're the other person at Omniscient. You've been working for him the whole time." I wasn't asking, I was just talking out loud.

"Well, a girl's gotta do something for a living."

I stood there for what seemed a long time while my heart and mind were turned upside down and inside out. At one point she lazily tossed the broken phone over the railing and down into water.

"You should be going," she said. "They'll be here soon. They will know your last location because of the GPS tracking app on your phone."

"That you installed."

She nodded.

"And you stole my phone."

She nodded again. "And then I gave it to Max to take to Adams in your car."

"I thought Garth..."

"Garth is a first-class jerk, but he's not the Underground."

"You know, you almost got me fired? And arrested?" I didn't know if I was angry or just grieving.

"We had to get you to either leave us or join us. Neither of those were working, so we framed you."

"And I can't even go to the police now, because I have nothing to show them."

"Yeah, I don't know what you're going to do."

"What are *you* going to do?"

"Me? I don't know. Whatever Jade tells me. Probably not work at Omniscient anymore."

I should have been angry. I should have been furious that this person messed me up so bad. But love doesn't die so quickly. I said, "Then it's goodbye."

She took one last look at me, then said, "Goodbye, Jeff. Take care of yourself." She turned and walked off toward the other side of the bridge.

I also turned around and started walking slowly toward my car. On my way I realised there was absolutely nothing I could do now. I was stuck between a rock, a hard place, and something else immovable as well. When I got to my car, where would I even go?

Then it hit me. There was still one thing I could do, I should do. I had just given the god account to some bad men. Maybe I can undo that.

Before I took another step, a black van came to a screeching halt right in front of me, and two men got out. They were Jade and Max.

10:04 PM

I probably should have run, but instead I stood there as they approached me. Max had his gun out, of course.

My dad started talking. "Jeff, Veronica told me you recorded our private conversation."

I shrugged. "Yeah."

"For the purpose of taking it to the police?"

I shrugged again. "What does it matter? It's gone now. Veronica smashed my phone with a rock and threw it into the river."

"It matters because it is an indication of your intentions.

You have not been altogether forthright with us, Jeff, have you?"

I didn't answer. They kept walking toward me.

"Max here gave you pizza and asked if you would join us. You agreed. Then he asked if you had the god email address and password. You said 'Yes', but you didn't deliver. Instead you called the cops on him. That's not good business, Jeff."

In my nervousness I didn't answer, but I did back up slightly.

"And just now you did give us access, but then you took off. you're mixing your signals, Jeff. Are you in or out? No, don't even bother answering, because we wouldn't believe you. You have lied to us before, and you'll probably lie to us again."

I had backed up until my back was against the bridge railing. There was nowhere else to go. I briefly considered jumping in, but they would probably grab me before I could get over. And even if I did get over, I would probably have a bullet in me by the time I hit the water.

Jade continued. "But out of curiosity, Jeff, please tell us. Would you like to now join us? Or do you want to turn us in?"

I decided to be honest. "What you're doing is wrong."

Both men chuckled, and Jade said, "What does that have to do with it?"

"You shouldn't do what is wrong," I replied.

"I'm not asking if you think what we're doing is legal or not. I'll tell you right now it is not. It is highly illegal." Then he paused. "You're not recording me now, are you, Jeff?"

"No. My phone's in the river."

"Max, check him out."

Max gave Jade his gun and came to me and patted me down all over, none too carefully either. "He's clean," he said, then took his gun back. Max seemed to enjoy pointing that gun at me.

Jade continued. "We do a lot of illegal activity. Some

people would say it is wrong to do this. And it might be wrong for them, but It's not wrong for me. I rather enjoy the idea. Now I'm asking you, Jeff, if you think joining the Information Underground would be wrong or right to you."

I took a deep breath and answered. "Wrong."

"Then what am I supposed to do with you?" He threw his arms up. "I've tried positive motivation and negative motivation. If I let you join us, you're just going to escape to the cops. If I let you go now, you'll do the same thing. What else can I do?"

I wondered if Scott had this exact conversation with these same people. I looked around me. It was dark, and we were above water. Was this how Scott met his end? He was down by the Assiniboine River. I'm over the Red River. If Scott couldn't escape, then I probably couldn't either.

Then my dad started monologuing. "You know, Jeff, when I started getting my life together, I read lots of books and listened to many successful people. They all said the same thing. Do you want to know what they said?"

I nodded.

"They all said to follow your dreams. Don't let anything stand in the way of your dreams. In life, you will come across obstacles. You need to get over them or around them or through them. Don't let anything stand in your way. Nothing. I have done this. One by one I have removed obstacle after obstacle. And now there is one left. And do you know what it is?"

"It's me."

"Yes, it is. And do you know what I'm going to do with you?"

I took a shaky breath and nodded.

"I'm going to remove you out of my way. So far Max here has told me he doesn't like you. You haven't been very kind to him. He wants to get rid of you. And do you know what I'm going to tell him to do with you?"

I nodded.

Then he said it. "Max, kill Jeff."

10:14 PM

Max's face broke out into a wicked smile, and his low voice said, "With pleasure, boss." As he raised his gun to me, I should have run. I should have jumped. I should have done something. But I just stood there, heart pounding and eyes squinting against the pain of being shot.

Then we heard a car honking, coming over the bridge toward us. We all looked. It didn't slow down. It kept coming and honking, and it was out of its lane, racing along the side of the bridge near us. Jade and Max panicked and started moving. Max fired a few bullets into the windshield, but it did no good. It was dark, but it looked like the driver was leaning over, hiding from the bullets.

I watched as the grey car struck both men, sending them flying. Jade went right over, first striking the front bumper, then the hood, the windshield, and finally falling to the ground. Max got hit on the side of the car as he was jumping out of the way.

And then the car raced away, leaving the three of us there. Jade was grabbing his right knee, in obvious pain. Max was on his side, doubled up as if he couldn't breathe. He must have got the wind knocked out of him.

Out of the shock and horror of seeing people get driven into right before my eyes, a thought came to the surface of my mind like a ray of sun peeking through the clouds. The thought was *Run!*

I took off running and didn't look back. I ran around the black van and toward my car. I briefly considered disabling the van somehow, but I didn't think I had the time. I got in my car, started it, and drove off fast.

When I was some distance away, I looked in my rearview mirror and thought I could see Max standing up. That wasn't good. I knew he would waste no time tracking me down. I immediately turned into a side street, in an attempt to hide. I drove down several side streets for a while, trying to get lost. If I didn't know where I was, he couldn't find me either.

At one point I parked in a dark spot beside the road and sat there, but pretty soon my thoughts came to bother me. How was it possible that a random car could lose control at just the right time to save my life? Wow. I wonder if God had something to do with that. I'll try to remember to ask him about that if I manage to live out the night.

Then I thought about Chip. He's probably still in the hideout, helping himself to our server. He's probably downloading every email we have ever sent. That got me mad. I don't know if I was more mad at Chip for stealing our private information, or more mad at me for letting him. But I was mad, and I had to do something about it. I briefly considered going back and confronting him and confiscating his laptop. No, I don't think that would work. I considered it again just to be sure. No, I was right--there was no chance of me being successful at that. But there was one thing I could do. If I could make it to the Forks and into our server room, I could change the appropriate passwords so Chip no longer had access. That was something I could do. And not only could I do it, it was the right thing to do.

I started my car again and made my way to the Forks, hoping the Underground wouldn't spot me, because I'm sure they were trying to.

10:58 PM

It took me longer to drive to the Forks than usual, only because I had gotten myself truly lost and I couldn't get unlost since I didn't have a phone. I took a mental note to get a new phone first thing in the morning, if I lived through the night.

I didn't park in the distant parking lot. I parked close to the building, because it was late and I didn't want to be too exposed walking around.

When I got out of my car, I looked around me, hoping to not see a black van. I didn't. But after starting to walk to the Johnston Terminal, I did see a man wearing a dark hoodie standing around in the shadows. I stopped and looked at him, hoping he didn't see me. He turned to look at me, which made me nervous. I was already almost shot once this evening, and I wasn't in the mood for more confrontation. And besides, this person might very well be Max. He probably took off his leather jacket and put on a dark hoodie so I wouldn't suspect him. He was wrong. I certainly did suspect him.

I went back to my car. I sat down in it and noticed that he was walking toward me. That was enough to get me going. I started the car and drove away. I decided to park in the parking complex and walk from there. Perhaps I could walk around to the other side of the building and avoid the hooded Max.

When I parked the car in a free spot, it occurred to me that this was pretty close to the exact spot where Doug had given me his gun. I looked behind me to the back seat. There was the shoe box, resting right there. What should I do with it? Did I want to get into a gun fight with Max? Absolutely not. Should I still try to get to our server room to disable it? Yes I should. Would I have a better chance of doing that if I carried a gun? I sighed. Yeah, probably.

I looked around to make sure nobody saw me, then I

opened the box lid, pulled the gun out and held it in my hand. It was heavy. It scared me. What scared me most was that it was forcing me to be a person who carries a gun. It was forcing me to be a gun-carrying person. I now had the ability in my hands to take someone's life, and with that ability came the weight of responsibility. I could kill someone or I could let them live. This gun was forcing me to judge, it was forcing me to come into confrontation with people and make a decision. I didn't want this responsibility. I didn't want to have to decide who lives and who dies. I didn't want it, and yet here it was. In my hand was the judge's gavel. I was now the judge who decided the fate of people. I was thrust into this role by simply picking up the weapon. I hoped I would make a good judge.

I got out of the car and started walking. I was no longer Jeff Davis, shy computer programmer. I was now a judge who could bang his gavel and sentence someone to death. I've always had a good sense to do the right thing. Perhaps now the right thing will get done.

I loosened my shirt and tucked the gun unto my pants. I walked for a while in the parking complex, trying to get used to the feel, but it wasn't working. I was about to take the gun out and just hold it, when I saw movement up ahead.

When I looked, I saw the one thing I was hoping to avoid. It was the black van, and the passenger side door was opening. My father sat there, looking at me. He didn't get out of the vehicle. His face looked like he was in pain, or was livid with anger, or probably both. He managed to control his voice though.

"Well, look who it is," he said to me. His voice sounded a little loose, and I wondered if he had taken some drugs to deaden the pain. There was no sign of Max. That was good. In fact, there was no sign of anyone else around anywhere except me and my father.

"Hello Jade," I said back to him.

"'Jade', huh? Why don't you call me 'father' or 'dad'?"

"Because you're not my father." Something emotional got knocked loose inside of me.

"Sure I am," he said.

"A real father doesn't try to kill his children. Or hurt them." My close brush with death mixed with the emotions of the evening started coming out, and they manifested as anger. I started shouting. "You are not a father to me, you are a bad man!"

"Hey, I offered to let you join us. That should count for something."

"Your organization?! Your organization is illegal! It's immoral! It's evil!"

"We're not that bad."

"Yes, Jade. You are bad. You are a pack of greedy, stealing, murdering thieves! You, Jade, are evil! You always have been."

"What are you talking about?"

"You were abusive to me and to Mom! You hurt her! You hurt me! You abandoned us! That's not what a father does! A father loves his children!"

"What do you know about love?"

"I have tasted love. I have felt love in my heart. From a real father. My heavenly father. He loves me. I have felt it."

Jade rolled his eyes. "Oh, don't tell me my own son went and got religious. Is that why you're acting out? You've got some funny notions in your head about God and now you've got a screw loose. That's your problem. You need to get your head examined, boy."

I took my gun out and pointed it at him. My hand may have been shaking, but I meant it.

"I am not your boy, I am your judge."

Having a gun pointed in his face didn't make this man cower in fear. It made him bold and cocky. "Oh, look who thinks he's all grown up now. The little punk thinks he has grown a spine."

"You're going to jail, Jade."

"Oh now you're going to throw me in jail? You're going to throw me in jail because you think I was a bad father? It doesn't work that way, boy."

"You *were* a bad father! A terrible father!"

"I fed you and clothed you!"

"'Fed and clothed'? Anyone can do that!"

"What else is there?"

"'What else is there?' You were supposed to love me! Spend time with me! Play in the sand box with me."

My father rolled his eyes again and another wave hit me. "You were supposed to hold me on your lap and stroke my stupid hair!"

He sneered. "If that's what you want, go back to your Jesus God."

The wave of emotion I was under, topped with the hatred I was trying to suppress suddenly spiked, and in that one second a burst of raw anger came crashing over the logic and reason I had built my life on. In that moment of blind rage, I held the gun up to my father's face and pulled the trigger.

11:23 PM

When I pulled the trigger, the gun went *click*.

And when that happened, I was yanked back to reality by two things. First, the gun went *click* and not *bang*. No bullet was fired. The man still sat in the van, unhurt except, presumably, for his knee. The gun acted as if it were out of bullets. Then it occurred to me that I had never put bullets in it, nor did I have any idea how to do that.

The second thing was that it just occurred to me that I had just shot my dad, or at least tried to. What kind of evil person shoots his father? It shocked me to realize that I had done just that. Me, the person who prided himself on always doing the right thing, just tried to murder his dad.

The weight of this revelation made me stumble back, then I took off running. My dad may have said something behind me, but I wasn't listening. I ran out of the car park and kept going. Rounding a corner, I saw some bushes, and tossed the gun into them. I didn't want to see that thing ever again. I slowed to a walk and forced myself to think again. Max was still out there, and I had to make sure he didn't catch me.

I stood still. Breathing hard, I looked around. Max was nowhere to be seen. Good. Now I need a plan. I had seen Max on the front side of the building. Now I was on the back side. I would just go in the back, careful he doesn't see me, and make my way to the server room. Good plan. I started walking and looking around me.

When I was almost to the building, I saw the hooded Max coming around the corner of the building. It was dark, so I wasn't sure it was him. I hoped the dark also obscured me as well. As I went through the doors, I took one last glance and saw that he was hurrying. He must have seen me.

I ran through the building to the front part where the elevator and stairs were. I didn't have time for the elevator, so I leapt up the stairs as fast as I could.

At the second level, I looked and saw no sign of him. When I was almost at the third level, our floor, I could see down to the main floor and saw that he was starting up the stairs. He wasn't going fast. Good. That should give me enough time.

Arriving at the top, I ran over to the big glass doors. They were locked of course, so I took out my keys. When I did that, my To-Do list I had made earlier fell out. I ignored it. I had a key fob on my key ring and I held it up to the electronic door lock. I expected it to beep cheerfully and let me in. It didn't. Instead of the green light, it showed red. I tried it again. Still red. Why wasn't it working?

Then I threw my hands up in exasperation because I knew why. I forgot that I had gotten fired. Well, suspended. When that happened, I must have also lost my door unlock privileges.

Max would be here soon, so I had to act. I would try to find somewhere to hide. I imagined Max would come to the door, find it locked, and leave because he couldn't get in. I saw my To-Do list on the floor, so I picked it up, not wanting any evidence to remain, and ran to the stairwell. I braced my hands on the rail to look over, and as I did I saw two things. I saw the hooded Max look up at me and start to walk faster. And on the piece of paper in my hand were written the numbers, "5426." I looked behind me at the door. The electronic lock where I had beeped myself in countless times before also had a keypad on it, that I had long ago ignored since I never used it. I looked at the numbers in my hand. I looked at the keypad. I looked at the numbers in my hand again, the ones I had written down when trying to hear from God. It couldn't be. It wasn't possible.

I had time to either run somewhere and hide, or see if the numbers I had gotten on the bus from God were actually from God. I ran to the door, punched in the numbers, and the device beeped green. I didn't have time to think about what this meant. I opened the door and ran as far inside the offices of Omniscient Technologies as I could.

CHAPTER 19

11:46 PM

I didn't turn on any lights. There was enough light coming from various things in the open area so that I could make my way to the server room. I opened the server room door and went in. The mail server sat bolted onto the rack as if nothing was the matter. I went over to the desk, sat down, and tried logging in with the root password. It didn't work. I tried again. It still didn't work. Chip must have changed it.

I sat and waited for an idea to come to me. I sat there a long time, because nothing did. Well, nothing good anyway. I had some bad ideas. It occurred to me that I could try to get God to tell me the root password. That was a bad idea. I didn't have a phone, and besides, God wasn't answering his email anymore anyway. It occurred to me that it may have been him who gave me the passcode for the front door while I was on the bus, but then again maybe I just subconsciously saw someone punch it in once and happened to remember it. That's possible.

A crazy idea kept bouncing around in my head. I tried to swat it away, but it kept coming back to me. I eventually gave in, just to prove that it wouldn't work.

The idea was to follow the advice of the man on the bus and try to hear from God myself again. It was a crazy idea, but nobody else was around to see me, so I went for it. I tried to remember the steps. Oh yeah, it was relax. Perhaps sitting in a work chair isn't very relaxing, so I looked around for somewhere else to sit. I found an empty spot on the floor against the wall and sat down there. Then I tried to forget about the fact that there were people trying to kill me. I tried to gain some comfort from this small room I was in. It felt safe. If I'm in a safe place, I can relax. I took some deep breaths and tried to calm myself down.

What was the second step? Oh yeah, imagine things, like Andy made me do with the doorbell sound. I closed my eyes and started imagining. But then I remembered I needed the third step too. After some thinking, I remembered the third step was spontaneous thoughts. Right. Spontaneity. Something that just comes to you. And step four was to write it down. Well, if I get anything, I'll write it down.

I closed my eyes and tried to relax. Then I tried to picture something in my mind and let something spontaneous come to me. I remembered being down by the river emailing God. I remembered the feeling it gave me when he told me he loved me. He had sent me a text saying he enjoyed spending time with me in the sandbox. That had touched me deeply when I read that.

I kept imagining. I remembered the picture he sent me of me as a boy and him as a man with white hair. The care and love in his eyes had touched me then. That was a good memory.

I remembered chatting with God, trying to convince him to give me money. That was funny. Just imagine chatting with God. Crazy stuff. I smiled to myself and kept remembering.

I remembered the video God sent of me and my parents and him at our table. That wasn't a pleasant memory, but it brought some healing, and that was good.

As I sat on the floor of the server room, I looked back at all the ways God was communicating with me. I have no idea why he chose me. But he did, and I appreciated it. Then one more thought came to me. At one point I had asked God in a chat why he was doing this for me. He said something like, "Because I love you. I am revealing myself to you in these half dozen ways so that you can see my heart. I am showing you my heart, my child. I love you."

I started counting on my fingers. Email, of course. Chat. There was a picture. There was a video. And there was a voice message. That's only five. I tried to think of any other way God had revealed himself to me, but I only counted five, not six. Did I miss something? Or is he just not done yet?

As I pondered this, my eyes rested on something in the server room that was delivered to us on Tuesday. The manufacturer was hoping we could integrate it into Omniscient. But no. God couldn't mean this. This couldn't be the sixth way he'll communicate with me. It was impossible. It was impossible.

It was a simple black box that had a small power button that dimly glowed white. I stood up and walked out to it. Holding out my hand to press the button, I thought it would never work. It was silly. I should get this thought out of my head.

But still, I pressed the button. And it worked.

12:11 AM

The blinking white button stopped blinking and stayed solid. Then it began humming faintly. Then a white light shot out from it, towards me. I stumbled back and crouched on the floor, wondering if this was a mistake.

The light formed itself into a three-dimensional image that appeared to be a man. He may have been glowing, or maybe it was just holographic residue.

The image wasn't static. He moved gently, and his clothes fluttered as if there were a slight breeze all around him. He seemed pleasant and at peace, even happy. And he was looking straight at me. I couldn't help but stare back. Those eyes seemed so full of peace, like a deep ocean gushing with love and ancient wisdom. It moved my soul, but my head couldn't accept it.

I kept telling myself it was impossible. This must be just the user interface, like a personified menu, to control this device. Or maybe we got connected to a real person in a virtual conversation somewhere.

"Who are you?" I asked.

He smiled at me like a proud father. "I am the one you've been searching for."

I dared to say it. "Are you God?"

"I am."

I sat there, not knowing what to say. A million thoughts ran through my mind, but nothing seemed proper to say at a time like this. So he spoke instead.

He bent down to my level and said, "Jeff, I love you." He placed his hand on his chest. "From my heart, I love you, my son Jeff. I love you so very much."

For some reason those words connected with some emotions deep inside of me and I found myself crying. I looked down. "You shouldn't. I don't deserve it."

"I do love you, Jeff. Why do you think I shouldn't?"

"Because I failed. You... you said I should pursue justice. It was my calling, or something like that. I tried, but I didn't do it. Instead I got fired. I failed at getting Max arrested. I tried to record my dad's confession, but my phone got destroyed. And I even gave them access to our server. I'm no man of justice; I'm a failure. I don't deserve... I don't deserve you."

When he didn't respond right away, I looked up and was surprised to see a tear running down his cheek. I didn't know

God could cry.

"You are not a failure to me, Jeff," he said. "You are my son. How could you ever stop being my precious child? No failure on your part could ever change who you are. You are dear and close to me, and I love you because of who you are, not because of anything you do. You can't earn my love, Jeff. Nothing you can do could ever earn it, and nothing you could ever do could ever take it away."

I stopped crying and looked this apparition in the eyes, wondering if what he was saying to me could be true. The compassion in his eyes made me believe him. I managed a small smile in response to his words.

"Now," he said, standing up, "there is something you must do."

"What?"

"You must show your dad's confession to the police."

"What? How? It's at the bottom of the Red River."

"Jeff, you think you're smart, but I'm smarter." He winked at me. "Do you remember what version of Omniscient was running on your phone?"

"4.1 beta."

"And what new feature does that version have?"

It suddenly dawned on me and I felt like a complete idiot. I said, "It stores video on the server."

God pointed to the server across the room. "Your hard evidence is right there on a hard drive. Bring it to the police right away."

I walked over to the server and took note that it had a removable hard drive. The hard drive was packaged to slot into a hard drive bay in such a way that you could just pull the handle and yank the drive out whenever you wanted. Of course the operating system would instantly stop working, but maybe in this case it wouldn't be so bad, because by pulling this hard drive, the Underground could no longer have access to it. I pulled it. I heard an angry beep and a flashing light, and then nothing else.

When I turned back, God was still smiling at me.

"One more thing," he said.

"What?"

"Don't be afraid to meet the person out there." He gestured to the server room door, then disappeared.

I was left standing in the dark, without my father who loved me, but with a heart full of acceptance and a hand full of evidence. The good guys might still win tonight. I went to open the door, but when I looked outside, I saw the hooded Max in the hallway.

12:23 AM

I jumped back and almost slammed the door shut again, but then I opened it and peeked again. He was still walking around. He had not seen me. I looked back to see if God really meant me to meet this guy, but of course he was gone.

In the face of immediate physical danger, I started rationalizing God's words. What exactly did he say? He said, "Don't be afraid to meet the person out there." Was he telling me to give my position away? No, he was just telling me to keep fear out of my heart. OK, I could do that.

I decided to try sneaking my way out. Since the interior of our floor was composed of cubicles, I could see over them all, and therefore Max could see me. I had to duck to not be seen. When it was safe, I left the server room and quietly closed the door behind me. Peeking over the cubicles I could see Max's position. I crouched and made my way around toward the entrance, but then Max slowly started making his way that way too, so I had to backtrack down the hallway around the corner.

I did that successfully, and waited a minute or two.

Max didn't come back from the entrance. Maybe he left the building. So I walked down the hall again to check. No, he was still there. He was looking around all over as if he could smell me. Then he started walking back toward me. The door to the board room was open, so I jumped in there. I went around to the other side of the big table and crouched down on the floor. My heart was pounding, hoping he wouldn't notice me. I was very scared. It didn't occur to me that this was the exact opposite of what God told me I should do.

By looking under the table, I could just make out the dark shadow of a person entering the room. I could tell he was looking around, but then he left again. A minute later I made my way back to the door of the board room. I saw him again on the other side of the cubicles, so I made my move to the main doors. I half crouched, half ran for the doors. They opened easily from the inside, and soon I was out. I ran down the three flights of stairs as fast as I could. I may have made noise doing this, because at the bottom of the stairs I looked up and heard someone running down too.

I ran for the doors of the Johnston Terminal, threw them open and ran outside. When I got to the stairs going to ground level, I was so panicked that I took them three at a time. I wasn't doing very good at keeping fear out of my heart, and in my fear I got hurt. My first two steps down were fine, but on the third I landed wrong. I crumpled to the ground in pain. My ankle didn't like that landing at all. I managed to not yell very loudly, so I hoped Max didn't hear me.

I looked behind me. Nobody was there yet, so I still had a chance. I crawled over and hid in the darkness beside a half wall, expecting Max to run out behind me at any moment.

A second later the hooded figure came bounding down the stairs. He too stumbled, but he didn't hurt himself. Instead, he stood up and said to himself, "Stupid stairs!". His voice was not low and gravelly like Max's. It was a voice I recognized and knew very well, one I hadn't heard in what seemed like a long time.

I finally started to obey God's command to not fear this guy. "Scott?" I said, barely out loud.

His head whipped around, looking for the sound. When he did that, his face caught some light, and I recognized him. "Scott!" I cried. I climbed up on my good foot and beamed at him.

He came up to me and said, "Ah Jeff, I was supposed to be in hiding. How did you know it was me?"

"Hiding?! You were in hiding?!" I didn't know whether to be overjoyed or mad at my friend. "I thought you were dead!"

"Yeah, it was Detective Wakefield's idea."

"Joseph Wakefield?! He knew you weren't dead?"

"Well I hope so. He arranged it."

"He never told me that."

"Of course not. It was a secret. That's what being in hiding means."

"I should hit you. Do you have any idea what I've been through here?"

"Yeah, I have a pretty good idea. He and I have been exchanging notes."

"So you knew all about Max threatening me in my car, and in their hideout, and everything else?"

"Yup."

"And you didn't do anything to help me?"

"Hey, wait right there, Jeff. I saved your life at least twice by my count."

"What? What are you talking about?"

"It's a long story. I could tell it to you some time."

"Yes! I definitely want to hear the whole thing. Maybe on the way to the police station." I held up the hard drive. "I have video evidence here of Jade confessing to everything."

"You have what now?" Now it was Scott's turn to be surprised at me.

"It turns out Jade is... No, we don't have time. Let's get this to the police." I started walking, but found my left foot caused me pain every time I set it down.

"Are you hurt?" Scott asked me.

"I tripped going down the stairs running from... well, running."

"I'll go get my car and pick you up. Will you be OK staying here for a minute?"

"Yeah, I'll be fine. Thanks for the ride."

Scott took off running for his car, and I sat back down. A minute later I looked over and saw a vehicle coming. But it wasn't Scott's. It was a black van.

12:39 AM

I remained in the shadows as I watched Max, the real Max, get out of the van and walk toward the Johnston Terminal building. I crouched as low as I could and tried not to breathe. To my relief, he didn't see me. He opened the doors and went in. I could only imagine he was looking for me. Maybe they noticed the server was down and concluded I must be in the server room. I guess they're not stupid.

While Max was in there, I contemplated my situation. When he comes out, there would be a good enough chance he will notice me here. I didn't want to move because of my foot, and I didn't want to hide from Scott when he got back, but on the other hand I didn't want to give Max the satisfaction of killing me either.

I got up and started limping. I headed away from the black van and away from the Johnston Terminal. This meant I was going down to the river. I was doing pretty good too. I was halfway there when I noticed Max came out of the building. I froze. He looked around all around him, then started back to the van. I breathed a massive sigh of relief. I had been spared one last time.

But then to my horror I heard my dad's voice ring out over the clear night air, "Max! He went down to the river! He's limping toward the river!"

I had no choice but to limp faster. I hobbled down toward the river as fast as I could. There were fewer lights there, and I thought I might be able to hide in the darkness. I looked around for somewhere dark to hide, and found a dock leading out onto the water. The end of the dock appeared shrouded in blackness, the perfect place.

I never made it into the shadow, because when I was almost there, I heard Max's low voice behind me. "Jeff, we meet again for the last time."

I whipped around to see the man who wanted to kill me, who now had permission to kill me, and armed with a gun ready to kill me.

I faced him, but in my fear I kept backing up.

"And it's nice of you to hide in the shadows, Jeff. There can be no witnesses this way."

I found myself right at the end of the dock. The only hope in my mind was that Scott would get back and save me. I looked around, but there was nobody in sight.

Max said to me, "I'm not going to threaten your life this time, Jeff, I'm just going to kill you. Goodbye." And with that, he held out his gun, aimed, and shot me.

Instinctively I held up my hands to my chest, as if my hands could stop a bullet. I heard a loud gunshot and I felt myself pushed back. For a brief instant I was falling, then I hit the water. It was cold, shockingly cold. I went under.

But I wasn't dead yet. I swam for the surface and broke through. I could still breathe. Good. That meant the bullet must have missed my lungs. If I wanted to stay alive, I would have to think fast. I moved myself through the water around to the side of the dock instead of the end, in case Max would come look for me there.

He did. I saw him looking over the end of the dock. He saw nothing obviously. When he came to look over the side where I was, I took a deep breath and pushed myself under. I hoped he wouldn't be able to see me. When I ran out of air, which was far too soon, I broke the surface to breathe, and to my relief he wasn't there.

It gave me even more relief to hear police sirens in the distance. Scott must have called them, assuming they were coming here.

I saw Max start running along the path near the water's edge. It looked like he was going to escape, and there was nothing I could do to stop him. But then again, maybe there was.

I dragged myself out of the water, and stood trembling on the dock. In my stubbornness to bring these people to justice, I had done many foolish things in the past few days. What I was about to do was by far the most foolish thing of all. I yelled to Max, "Hey Max! You missed! See? I'm still here. Come back and do the job right!"

That made him stop. He turned around and came toward me. I couldn't see his face, but I could imagine how mad he must be right now. I noticed Max got mad a lot, and I was hoping this weakness of his would be his downfall. He should have run for his freedom, but he didn't. I played it up. I said, "What, you can't even hit one single guy just standing there?" The sirens were very close by now, and Max was still walking toward me. He fired another shot at me, but it missed. I heard the bullet scream past my head. Maybe I had pushed him too far. I started running away, but then the police officers arrived. They shone their flashlights at Max and at me, but when they saw Max was armed, they concentrated on him. I heard someone yell, "Put down your weapon!"

Another police flashlight and yelling came from the other side of Max, and now he was effectively surrounded. Since they saw Max armed, and no doubt witnessed that last shot of his, I had no doubt that the police officers would not hesitate to fire back. He must have concluded that too, because after a very short time of deliberation when I feared he might try to shoot his way out of it, he put his weapon down on the ground and lay down.

I put my hand over my heart and when I took it away, I saw blood on my hand. Maybe Max hadn't missed after all.

12:54 AM

I sat there trying to find where I was shot, but I couldn't find any injuries on me at all. I felt fine all over.

Then Scott showed up. "I called the cops as soon as I saw their black van." He held out his hand to help me up.

I accepted it and said, "Thanks. You saved my life."

He grinned. "One last time?"

"What do you mean?" I asked. "When did you save my life before?"

Then he looked at his hand, then at mine. "You have blood on your hand. Hey, are you OK?"

"Yeah, I'm fine." Then I looked at my hand too. That's where the blood was coming from. Then I looked at the hard drive I was still holding. It had several big cracks in it, and a chunk was missing from one side. I shook it and it rattled noisily. "Oh no, Jade's confession was on there"

"Stupid hard drive."

A police officer finally came to see us.

"Detective Wakefield!", said Scott. "What brings you here

this time of the morning?"

"Aren't you supposed to be in hiding?" Joseph replied, looking a little grumpy.

"I don't need to be anymore," he said cheerfully. "The bad guys are going to jail."

"Good," he said, "but without hard evidence, it may not be for long."

"I had hard evidence," I said, holding up the broken hard drive, but Max shot it.

"Did he?" he said.

"Well, he shot me. The hard drive stopped the bullet and got destroyed."

"You got lucky," Joseph said. "Well, you both need to come to the station to answer some questions."

As we made our way up, away from the river, Joseph said, "We'll probably get Max for attempted murder, because we all saw him take that last shot at you. And the shot at your hard drive. You got lucky there too, kid. I'll need that for evidence, by the way. But with no hard evidence on Jade, he'll probably walk."

He called me lucky, but I didn't feel lucky. I didn't want this to be all for nothing. I still held on to hope, and then it hit me. I heard Bono sing out, "I still haven't found what I'm looking for."

I said, "Scott!"

He stopped and turned to me. "Yeah?"

"That's your phone!"

"Yeah?"

"It's still connected to our server?"

"I guess so. I just got an email."

"How's that possible?" I shook the hard drive at him. "The server's hard drive is broken."

He also looked confused for half a second then snapped his fingers. "Oh! The hard drives are RAIDed."

"What does that mean?" I asked.

"It means that all the information is stored on multiple hard drives, so in case one goes down, the other one still works. You know Jeff, for a computer guy I'm surprised you didn't know that."

"I'm a software guy, not a hardware guy," I said. But now the hope in my heart that I was holding onto, was about to come to life. "Can I see your phone?"

"Sure." He handed it over. Then, as the three of us stood around in the dark, I logged Scott out from his Omniscient app, and I logged in as me. Soon I found the video I recorded of my dad confessing, and showed it to the detective.

At the end of the video, he looked at me and became less grumpy. "I think that will do it. You did it, Jeff. You did it. Good job."

And I relaxed. With those words, all the stress of the past few days began leaving me. The adrenaline wore off, and I realized just how tired I was.

As we walked past the empty black van, Scott said, "Detective, It's late. We promise to stop by first thing in the morning. You'll get statements out of us when we're fresh. And you could use some more sleep too, considering that recent bump on the head."

He looked at us, considered it, then he held out his hand to me. "Give me that hard drive, and take off. Come see me in the morning."

I did gladly, and he left.

Scott turned to me and said, "Let's go for coffee."

"Coffee? At this hour?"

"Sure. I want to hear your story."

It was late, but I agreed. "OK, as long as we drive there, because my foot is still sore."

1:19 AM

My friend and I sat on two uncomfortable chairs in an all-night coffee shop, sipping coffee.

Scott told me his story, everything from when he first met Jade to when I found him out this evening. I interrupted him a few times just to say, "Wow."

Then I told him everything that happened to me from my perspective.

"It's too bad about Veronica," he said. "I liked her."

I didn't respond right away. I guess I was still hurting about that, but eventually I said, "It was all an act. She was just trying to recruit us."

"She was cute though."

We both chuckled.

After a few minutes, Scott said, "So I guess after you recorded your dad's confession, he must have called Veronica right away to set up the fake kidnapping and told her to call you as soon as possible."

"I guess so."

U2 started playing again, and Scott checked his email. After reading it, he said to me, "Joseph Wakefield says they can't find any trace of Veronica Stansin, but they just picked up both Chip and George Mannel."

"Wow."

"That's four people behind bars because of you, Jeff. How do you feel about that?"

I shrugged. "It's probably a good thing."

He laughed. "I wasn't asking about the goodness of the thing; I was asking how you felt about it."

I shrugged again. "I feel fine," I said, then added, "I feel... relieved it's over."

"Yeah. Now we can get back to work. If Peter will let us back."

"I think he will."

"Me too."

After another minute, I said, "It's good to have you back, Scott."

"It's good to be back."

EPILOGUE

Tuesday, 8:12 AM

I was running late, so when I went through the doors of Omniscient Technologies, I barely had time to say "Good morning" to Luanna the receptionist.

I paused outside the boardroom. They probably started already, and if I came into the room now, they would all stare at me. I took a deep breath and pushed the door open.

As I walked around to an empty seat, Randal said, "It's good of you to join us today, Jeff."

I kind of waved and kept on walking, then sat down low in a chair.

"In other news," Randal said, "some of you might be interested to know that we have received emails from two other open-source software companies. They must have read about us in the news. They both said that someone claiming to be a hacker called them and demanded Bitcoin in exchange for disclosing a security bug."

"Wow", said Scott.

Garth added, "I have looked into each of these accounts. The Bitcoin address this alleged hacker gave both of these companies is identical to the one he gave us."

"Which means?" asked Scott.

"Which means," said Randal, "this hacker is not a hacker, he is just some guy trying to get money."

"So there never was a security bug?" asked Scott.

"There never was," said Garth. "There still isn't."

Randal continued. "I think Jeff is going to tell the press

this good news, aren't you, Jeff?"

"Yes," I said. "And it's even better than that. We all know that Bitcoin is anonymous, but its ledger is also completely public. When I noticed that some of the Bitcoin we paid the hacker got paid out to someone else, I contacted Detective Joseph Wakefield, and with the help of the FBI, they tracked down that purchase to a furniture store in Iowa."

"Iowa?!" said Scott.

"Yeah," I continued. "They got his address because his sofa was delivered. So they went and arrested him, and there is a chance we might get some or all our money back."

Garth said, "It seems this hacker isn't quite as smart as he could have been."

"That's good news," said Randal. "I didn't know it worked that way. Good job, FBI. But moving on, Ronja has replaced the hard drive that Jeff pulled the other day. And all is well, Ronja?"

Ronja said, "Yes. It took about two and a half hours to synchronize, but the RAID held up perfectly. We were not down for even a minute, except to reset the root password."

"Good," Randal continued. "We should probably rebuild that server in case those guys did anything with it while they were in there."

"Yes, I think so," said Ronja.

"Good. And we have found a few small issues with 4.1 beta, so let's get those done so we can release 4.1 final. And that's it for our meeting, except for one more thing. The Fire Department says they found a faulty sensor that was triggering the alarms, so we shouldn't get any more false alarms. That's it. We are dismissed."

As we got up, Randal said to me, "Oh, Jeff, we have a new customer service rep starting today. Will you please show her around?"

I sighed. Now I have to talk to a girl, again.

GOD'S EMAIL ADDRESS

8:22 AM

Randal and I stood outside the board room.

He said to me, "Oh, here she comes now."

I looked at her and my eyes grew wide.

Randal continued, "You may have met Cheryl Bankowsky before. She used to look after the plants here. Please show her around."

"OK."

Randal left. I reached out to shake this person's hand and said, "Hi Cheryl."

She shook my hand and looked at me with peaceful and strong eyes. "Hi Jeff. How are you?"

"How am I? Wow. Where do I begin?"

"Did you try God's email address?"

"Yes."

"And did it work for you?"

"Yes."

"Good."

"I...," I hesitated, then continued. "I would like to tell you about it."

"It's between you and him. You don't have to share if you don't want to."

"I think I do want to, and I don't know anyone else I can share this with. Everyone else will think I'm crazy."

She smiled, as if we shared a secret.

Then summoning up my courage, I said, "Maybe we could talk about it over lunch today."

She looked at me and said, "I would like that. But first you have to show me around this place."

"Of course," I said. Then my phone chirped with an email message. I took a quick peek to see who it was from. When I saw the From email address, I read the whole thing to myself, right then and there.

> From: god@heaven
>
> To: jeff@omniscient.software
>
> Subject: Well done
>
> Jeff, my son whom I love. I love you, son Jeff. I love you with all my heart.
>
> I'm so proud of you for finishing this assignment I have given you. You did good. You did very good. Well done. Good job, Jeff. I, your dad, am very proud of you.
>
> I was with you the whole time, and I will always be with you.
>
> And now, it's time for your next assignment.

SCOTT'S STORY

Do you want to hear Scott's story too?
Get this FREE short story and find out what happened to him.

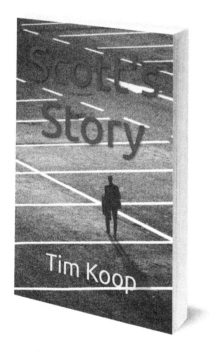

timkoop.com/scott

THE AUTHOR NEEDS HELP

Hi there.

I noticed you read through this whole book.

I hope you enjoyed it. If you did, or if you just want to help a guy in need, it would be awesome if you could do this:

Could you please go to where you got this book from, or some other popular place, and leave a review? Reviews go a long way to to help sell books, and a minute of your time would do a lot.

Thank you very much!

ABOUT THE AUTHOR

Tim Koop lives in Canada. He is married and they have four kids. His background is in computer programming, although it is a matter of speculation if he wrote his first story or first computer program first.

As of the time of this writing, he drives neither a Honda Civic, a Mercedes Benz, a Ferrari, nor even a black 4-door BMW 328i with X-drive and a manual transmission. But maybe one day.

What else can I say about him? Hmm... his favourite foods are peanut butter and ice cream. For ice cream to be properly consumed, it should be eaten with a plastic spoon, because a metal spoon conducts electricity and interrupts the tasting process somehow. I don't know how. (I mean he doesn't know how.) If you don't have a plastic spoon, a metal fork is better than a metal spoon. As far as milk shakes go, I'm on the fence if they should be enjoyed best with a spoon, a straw, or just tipped in like a liquid. I'm leaning toward liquid right now, because the more contact with lips the better. This is also the reason a fork is better on ice cream. Yeah, a straw does have a high coolness factor to it, but if you suck it in, it lands too far into your mouth. Needless to say the more time spent in contact with taste buds the better, and sweetness is tasted up front, so please don't by-pass that. That brings us to flavours of ice cream. I already mentioned peanut butter. A good peanut butter and vanilla go well together, even though chocolate and peanut butter have been good friends since time immemorial. But I digress. (I mean he digresses.)

(5,3,4,5) (7,5,4,1) (12,9,5,4) (1,1,11,4) (19,4,4,2) (19,2,8,2)
(16,12,5,1) (7,1,4,1) (4,1,7,5) (4,1,1,1) (2,3,2,4) (9,2,9,5)
(11,2,2,1) (15,2,2,3) (8,11,13,4) (1,5,1,1)

Made in the USA
Monee, IL
21 August 2022

12145067R10184